# The Deadly
# MONDAINE

## CRAIG N. WILLIS

outskirts
press

Outskirts Press, Inc.
http://www.outskirtspress.com

ISBN: 978-1-9772-0905-4

Library of Congress Control Number: 2019901292

Cover Illustration © 2019 Outskirts Press, Inc.
All rights reserved - used with permission.

Outskirts Press and the "OP" logo are trademarks belonging to Outskirts Press, Inc.

PRINTED IN THE UNITED STATES OF AMERICA

*To Nancy B. Willis, my spouse, my law partner, my best friend, and most recently, my sharp-eyed beta reader.*

Mondaine: a fashionable woman.

*Oxford English Dictionary.*

The mondaine Empress was at once merged in the adoring mother; her whole soul was wrapped up in the boy.

Henry J. Coke; *Tracks of a Rolling Stone.*

# 1

# Tell your Mama

Ines called me on the day I decided to kill Dottie Tyler. Ines Rosales is my spectacularly successful daughter who, in editing the most popular Latina style magazine in the United States, efficiently manages her sixty-five hour work week, but who had not found the time to call me in almost a month.

This particular day had started, like all days for me at Shady Rest Retirement Home, here in Gethsemane, Illinois, with a confrontation with my "medication matrix", the box with a plastic grid of capped compartments, arrayed like the calendar, holding the pills that I was to take each day. It was always a bit of a struggle, at 6 am when I made myself get up, to focus my eyes and mind, to lift the lid on the little box for this day of the week. Today, Monday, there were two small white pills, one green/gold capsule, a reddish brown tablet, and, noticeable to me even in my early morning fog, a bluish purple capsule that had been appearing in my matrix only for the last week.

I methodically swallowed each one until the day's container was empty. I closed the lid and realized that my pill grid, identical to the one used by ninety percent of my fellow residents, was one of the few solid coordinate systems that triangulated for each one of us the diminishing sense of self, memory, family relations, personal hopes, and professional history, all of which seemed to be receding from our individual perceptions, as if we all were standing on the rear platform of a speeding train, watching as our lives inexorably faded from view.

My phone rang.

"Good morning, Mom", Ines' voice sang through the phone.

"Just a minute; I have to check my calendar to see if I have time to talk to you." After a pause, "You're in luck. The Obamas just left, and the conference call with the Pope doesn't start for forty-five minutes. So, let's talk."

"Don't be like that, Mom. I know it's been awhile since I called."

"It has been three weeks. Several new galaxies have formed."

"Mom, you know that I have been crazy busy."

I did know that. Ines was just settling into her new position as editor of Con Estilo magazine and her new office in the headquarters in Dallas. It was unquestionably a big deal.

At that moment, I was smitten with the image,

indelibly printed on my brain, of the first time I laid eyes on Ines. The nurse had handed me this small bundle with black hair and beautiful unblinking brown eyes that regarded me with uncritical, accepting eyes. She was, at one time, so entirely me, but yet so entirely not me. I knew right then that I had just signed a contract to do everything in my power to protect and promote every advantage for this person, whatever the risk or cost. I did not at the time realize that the contract did not include clauses about what I got back in exchange.

"I do appreciate the time demands of your new job." I could picture her, unpacking her boxes in her office, hanging up her Ivy League diploma, her many writing and photography awards, and that framed display of four burgundy buttons that she was never without.

"How's what-his name?"

"His name is Eduardo, Mom, and I haven't seen or talked to him since I moved."

"Aren't you engaged?"

"Not really, and, Mom, it is really none of your business."

"Ines, I am your mother, and I know I don't run your life. But I do expect some basic information in recognition of what I have done to get you where you are today".

"I do really appreciate it, Mom."

"Do you? You have no idea of what I did for you."

"I know all about the Tupperware thing, and I am deeply appreciative." I snorted to myself.

"As I said, you have no idea", as I realized, for the

first time, that as much as I had intended to tell her the whole story, I might never have the opportunity.

"Gotta run, Mom. Let's get together at the end of the summer; late August, early September."

"I'd like that. Ines, I love you."

The phone had gone silent.

The next task was, as always, to select the right attire, particularly hat and gloves, appropriate for breakfast, and the rest of the day. Since it was late May, I chose to accessorize my sleeveless, pale pink sundress, with a white pillbox, tilted to a slight angle, and pink three-quarter opera gloves. Satisfied after a quick peek into the mirror, I took the elevator from my third floor room down to the main floor common dining area.

Breakfast was still being served by the dining room staff to the group of residents sitting at tables set for six. I slid into an empty chair at the table at which were seated Ming Ji Chang ("Mary"), retired chemistry professor at the local community college, and her husband Yu Qi Chang ("Luke"), former owner of the Jade Star restaurant in town, Earl Sampson, United States Navy, retired, and his wife, Eunice, and my floor neighbor next door, but one, Mabel O'Bannon. The Changs are intelligent, warm people who don't have a thing to say unless you drag it out of them. Earl, by distinction, would never shut up. Mabel was one of those people who was, because of the onset of something that looked a whole lot like dementia, was either "in" or "out" of the moment.

"Good morning, all", I said as I sat down. Earl, who

had been holding forth on some folderol, said "Nice hat, Hattie!"

"Thanks, Earl", I said seizing my role in allowing someone else to talk.

Turning to Mabel, I asked, "How are you feeling today, Mabel?" Mabel was in.

"Oh, very well Hattie. My son called last night and he is taking me to see my sister's children this weekend. Swallowing envy, I said "That's great. Where do they live?

"Peoria. I haven't seen them in such a long time."

Before we could go further, our wait staff person came over to see what I, the newcomer, wanted for breakfast.

"Buenas dias, Yasmin." I said. I knew Yasmin Asturias Sarabia for a Latina the minute she stepped on the dining floor from her looks, style and grace. I have cultivated her acquaintance ever since.

"Como esta tu Mama?"("How is your mama?") I asked.

"Very well, thank you, senora."

"And your studies?

"Not so well", she said sheepishly.

"English is important for you. Keep up your good work."

The dining room was thinning out. Earl, having his fill of breakfast and oration, hooked up Eunice and towed her out of the dining room.

About this time, Dottie Tyler rumbled into the room on her motorized wheelchair, and pulled up to the space vacated by the Sampsons.

"Hello Dottie", we all more or less simultaneously intoned. Dottie Tyler lives in the unit between Mabel and me. Dottie (Dorothy) and her husband, Emmett, were the proprietors of Tyler Insurance Consultants LLC in Gethsemane, a casualty insurance firm. My sense of their business was that it had the intellectual content and financial well-being of printing money. Dottie was a big fish in a finger bowl, and took every advantage of it.

"You, girl", she hollered across the room at Yasmin, who stopped what she was doing and came over to take the order.

"I want one poached egg, one piece of white toast, and tea" Dottie shouted, as if talking loudly, not more slowly or more clearly, was the way to communicate with someone whose English was not perfect. Yasmin headed for the kitchen.

"I really don't understand what all of these Mexicans are doing here" Dottie declared to the rest of us at table. The Changs, who had had their own immigration saga, looked appalled.

I took a deep breath and decided to take up the gauntlet.

"Yasmin, not "girl", by the way, is not Mexican, she is from Guatemala."

"All the same to me. They're all wetbacks."

Thinking to myself that it would be one heck of a swim from Guatemala, said, with some heat, "That's offensive, Dottie. I know that Yasmin and her family are fine decent, hard-working people. They are here to improve their lives and to contribute to the country. "

"I bet they are illegal. Donald Trump is right; we should send them back to where they came from and build a wall around the whole place."

We had strayed into dangerous territory. I knew that Yasmin's brother had been killed in a MS13 recruitment raid, and the rest of the family had gotten out of there before the same gang got them. Among her mother, who worked the late shift at the hotel as a chambermaid, her dad, who worked seventy hours a week for a landscaping company, and Yasmin, I was pretty sure that there was not a single green piece of paper to be had. "Dottie, aren't you descended from German immigrants in the 1840's?" I asked, hoping to change the subject.

She ignored me. "It makes me mad, our country being stolen by foreigners. Do you know what I am going to do? I am calling the ICE tomorrow, and have them check out the entire dining room staff."

"That's ridiculous, Dottie. Do not do it."

"I will do it. And I forgot, Mrs. Rosales, you're one of them."

And that was that.

Later that evening, after I had looked in on some of the people I keep an eye on, I took my wheeled walker down the hall, and poked my head into Dottie's apartment. Unlike a large number of residents of Shady Rest, I do not need a wheeled walker to support my frame. I like mine for two reasons: first, it leads people to underestimate one, which was a result that I actively cultivated in my work life, and second, one can discretely carry a whole lot of useful stuff in the saddlebag compartment. I had changed into my black slacks, and grey, long-sleeved blouse, with the black "Barbara Stanwyck" close-fitting hat with a small red feather and a net veil, which I had not pulled over my face. Black gloves completed the outfit.

"Dottie?" I called through her door, which, as usual, was not locked, and stepped into her unit. Her motorized chair was sitting in its accustomed place, next to the door. The TV was in its usual stadium volume mode, and Dottie was sitting, snoozing, in her manual wheel chair, in front of it. I closed the door and pushed my walker over by her. "Dottie".

She started awake, recognized me, and said:" Oh. Hattie."

"Dottie, I need to talk to you. Let's have a drink." I knew that by this time she already had several. I pulled from my saddlebag a bottle of the crummy white wine she drinks by the gallon, went to the kitchen and brought a chair into the area between the living room and the kitchen and sat on it. I pulled two plastic cups out of my bag as she wheeled over, and poured two glasses. I gave her one. She took a belt.

"Dottie, please do not call ICE on the staff. No one wins that game."

"Gotta do it, Hattie. Have to draw the line somewhere", she slurred.

"I'm sorry you feel that way. Let's part on as good terms as possible. Cheers" I held out my glass, toasted by touching glasses. She drained hers as I put mine on the floor beside me. Bon voyage, I thought, as I waited for her to doze off. When she did, I sprang into action. I pulled the washcloth out of my bag and stuffed it in her mouth. Next a roll of bumpy tape that they use when you give blood allowed me to strap her arms to her chair. Finally, I tightly cinched a kitchen-sized garbage bag over her head. I locked the door, just in case, and waited. It didn't take long. When the wiggling stopped, I removed the bag, and into it put the glasses, the bottle, the washcloth, and removed the tape, adding it to the collection.

Her body slumped to the floor in a very convincing fashion. "Classic cardiac arrest" I thought. I replaced my chair in the kitchen.

I wheeled my walker to the door, thought a minute, and then turned off the TV. I quietly unlocked the door, turned back and said, to no one in particular. "Goodnight, Dottie, I have to do my recycling." And I did, into the trash container at the end of the hall.

They didn't find her body for two days. On the third day, at breakfast, the residents were abuzz with the news. "Died in her chair"......"Heart just quit" ..... Never was in good health." No one is really surprised when one of us passes on, but it is sobering for the group none the less. The doctor and the hearse came and went. No police were in evidence.

After breakfast, I caught Yasmin at the dining room door.

"Yasmin, I want you to do me a favor, a very important one.

"If I can, senora."

"Dile a tu Mama que la amas."("Tell your Mama you love her.")

Will you do that?"

"Yes, gramma Hattie, I will" she said, as she headed off to the kitchen.

"Because you really never know what she has done for you", I thought to myself.

## 2

# Dangerous Places

After the ripple on the pond caused by Dottie's demise had passed, daily life at Shady Rest had returned to normal, when the Roy Winston problem presented itself for solution.

It was about two weeks after Halloween, so just within a shout of Thanksgiving. My medication grid did present me, on the critical morning, with a purple capsule, the presence of which I have come to regard as a harbinger of Big Things.

In the spirit of the occasion, I decided to dress for breakfast, even more formally than I usually do. I selected a black suit with straight skirt, jacket with stand-up collar, emerald blouse with affixed neck scarf, and matching emerald opera gloves. For good measure, I slid a large faux ruby ring over my right glove, and topped it with a black, asymmetrical wide-brimmed hat that always reminded me of Katherine Hepburn.

I took my wheeled walker, and headed down the hall towards the elevator, noting that while Dottie Tyler's apartment had been cleaned out by her family, it had not yet been re-assigned by the management, and was vacant. I stopped at the next door, Mabel O'Bannon's place, and lightly knocked, and put my head in the door, which was, as usual, unlocked. I had nagged Mabel to make a habit of locking her door, since Mabel was subject to sessions of amnesia, if not dementia. She was not in, so I went downstairs, via the elevator, to the dining room.

Mabel was seated at a table with Mary and Luke Chang, Bella Carson, and Elroy "Roy" Winston. Roy Winston, a retired Chevrolet dealer, is a widower, his wife, Karla, having passed away about two years ago. Roy was the self-regarded "Ladies Man About Town" of Shady Rest and was a shameless flirt. The empty chair at the table was between his and Mabel's, so I sat there.

"Good morning, Hattie" Bella said "You're dressed fit to kill". I let that remark pass, as Bella continued: "Roy is telling us about his new Corvette." Of course he was. If he wasn't rambling on about cars, he was chasing women, the combination of which made him about as interesting to me as Druid madrigals. It had been amusing to watch him and Peg Bauer, the resident Mae West, put on safari gear, load their hunting rifles and stalk each other around the place. You really could not tell who was the hunter and who the prey. No shots seem to have hit home.

"It has a five speed transmission, and of, course it's a

convertible. I just love the red color, don't you Hattie?" he
asked, looking at me for the first time. The only red vehicle that ever mattered to me was the fire truck that evacu-
ated my family from the burning apartment in Chicago
when I was a kid, so I didn't say anything. I looked at the
Changs who also were saying nothing, probably because
they had no idea what on earth he was talking about.

"Well, gotta get gas for my baby" Roy said, standing
up and bustling out of the dining room. Mabel, who had
not said anything yet, watched Roy head into the hall,
sighed and said "Oh, that Harold." Harold O'Bannon,
proprietor of O'Bannon's Furniture in Gethsemane, was
Mabel's husband, dead for five years. I had the beginnings of a cold sinking feeling in the pit of my stomach.
"Mabel, we need to talk after breakfast" I said in a low
voice. I immediately turned to the Changs and asked
them how they were planning to spend Thanksgiving.
Grateful to be part of the conversation, and on a subject
they knew well, they described their upcoming dinner
with their adult son and daughter. Bella asked them
questions about their families. We passed a few minutes
in pleasant conversation, as the diners began to filter out
of the room.

Finally, after everyone except Mabel and I had left,
and after the dishes and cups were being cleared by the
wait staff, I took her hand in mine and looked her in the
eye. "Mabel, this morning you called Roy 'Harold'. You
do know that Harold has been dead for many years,
right?" I asked.

"Yes" she said, slowly, showing confusion by squinting her eyes.

"So, why did you call him Harold?"

"Well, he's my husband" she said frowning.

"Does Roy come to visit you? At night?"

"He's my husband" she said more loudly, while looking wildly around the room. "It's how it has always been."

The cold sinking feeling got a whole lot worse. "Damn, damn, damn" I thought to myself.

"Mabel, Roy is NOT your husband. He should not be acting as if he is. Howard is dead. We will be locking your door." I walked with her to the elevator and rode with her up to her apartment on the third floor.

As I saw her situated in her room, I said "Mabel, I care for you and will look after you. Do have a good day."

I took the elevator down to the parking level, one floor below the dining room, and sat on the seat of my walker to wait for Roy.

He showed up in less than an hour, bursting through the automatic door separating the parking garage from the elevator core.

"Hattie, I didn't know you had a car."

"I don't. I'm here to talk to you. It's about Mabel. Let's go sit there" I said, pointing to a pair of chairs just inside the fitness center next to the elevators.

"Sit." We sat. "Roy, I know about what you are doing with Mabel O'Bannon. It must stop, now. Do you understand me?"

14

my cane between his shoulder blades and, gripping the right handrail with my right hand, pushed as hard as I could, allowing my body to fall downward as far as my right hand would allow.

He immediately pitched forward, simultaneously reaching for the rail at his right hand. He missed, and as a result, had both a pitch forward, and a roll counter-clockwise. It was a spectacular fall. His neck broke at about the third step. As I carefully, followed down the stairs and looked at him carefully, it was plain that I did not need the icepick in my purse to finish the story.

I picked up my walker at the second floor and went on with my day.

You heard it from me. Stairways are Dangerous Places.

## 3

# Prescription for trouble

Roy's death caused a bit more stir than had Dottie's, but not much. There were a few "scene-of crime" cops, with their cameras, tapes and prints kits. But in the end, it all blew over with no questions asked, as least of me.

We were now in that period of the year where a resident of Shady Rest could actually get a feel of the difference in the days, without looking at a newspaper, a calendar, or the television, for it was just before Thanksgiving, one of those times of year where our memories of who we were drew us magnetically back into to force fields of our former lives, to departed spouses, careers, family. Shady Rest buzzed with that temporary liveliness, and with plans to visit children, nephews and nieces or friends.

I, of course, desperately wanted to visit Ines, but, of course hadn't heard a word from her except for a few hurried words in brief calls about new projects, acquisitions, promotions, and achievement through her vibrant and exciting magazine. We had, to my great anticipation, made plans to actually see each other in either October or November. To my bitter disappointment, those plan were not going to happen.

"Listen to this, Mom," she said during our last phone conversation. " We're putting together a pilot for a "Con Estilo" television show with uniVision. We'll be working on it around the clock until the rollout in early January. You and I will get together when that's over, I promise." Her enthusiasm was as dramatic as was my deep disappointment. "Sure, Ines. Right after the Trump White House hosts the Dia de los Muertos party."

Don't get me wrong here. I am aware that her career is on fire and that I am completely happy for the person that she has developed in herself, but am inexpressibly sad that she does not seem to recognize the small element of me in that person. I also know that it is my greatest desire to tell her, in person, soon, the story of where the funding came from to make her career possible.

As it was, I gratefully accepted the invitation from my son Roberto to spend Thanksgiving with his family in Moline.

In the meantime, to keep my mind occupied, I decided to acquaint myself more completely with the day-to-day operations of the Assisted Living side of Shady Rest. No small part of my interest was generated by the unmistakable increase in the presence on that side of uniformed police. I did not think this had anything to do with Dottie or Roy, but it seemed to me to be prudent to find out.

The Assisted Living portion of the facility is physically separate from the general residential portion, where I live. It is accessed from the central lobby by a single hallway into the two single-floor wings, that house the Assisted Living Units. At the junction of the two wings is a nurse's station, nominally staffed 24-7 by trained medical staff, and a dining room dedicated to the AL residents. The Assisted Living side has no direct access to the parking garage or the fitness center on the lower level, except back through the elevators off the lobby. The living units in AL are laid out in the same basic floor plan as the residential only units, except that there is no kitchenette, with the kitchen having been swapped for a storage area, the only kitchen-like accommodations being a small bar-sized refrigerator and a microwave.

The services received by the AL residents differ significantly from those we on the Residential Living side receive. First of all, AL serves three meals per day, while the main dining room is open for breakfast and dinner only. But the most significant difference between the two different living modes within Shady Rest is the medical attention the respective residents enjoy. Contractually, the residential occupants are responsible for all of their health and personal hygiene needs. Shady Rest does not have any responsibility beyond that of any other residential landlord for the physical well-being of its tenants. The deal changes completely when one makes the "quantum leap" to Assisted Living. One, as an AL just retired from her forty-five years of practicing law. She sat down next to Bella.

In dramatic distinction to Betty's discrete entrance, Margaret "Peg" Bauer catapulted into the room as if she were the drum majorette for a hundred piece marching band, the music of which she alone could hear. "I'm so sorry to be late, but I have been so busy." She happened to be two minutes early and we all knew very well that she had nothing in her 'to do' list that was any different than any of the rest of us. "I'm Peg Bauer" she said to me, sitting down next to me. "Hattie Rosales" I said, ignoring the fact that I knew her and she should know me, since we had played bridge together twice, once as partners.

Bella, who seemed to be the chair of the group, looked at the empty chair between Muriel and I, and said "Dottie has not been getting around very well since the stroke, so I think we should begin."

"First order of business" said Muriel, pulling from the grocery sack behind her chair two chilled, corked bottles of white wine, and a stack of plastic glasses. "The good crystal is in winter storage". She uncorked a bottle and poured us each a glass. "Cheers." It was a very nice, dry Riesling.

I was just beginning to realize what Muriel meant to Shady Rest and what Shady Rest meant to her. She was not just the manager, but, with her husband Herman, the sole owners, having built the facility with Muriel's inheritance from her folks and a chunk of Herman's pension from his years as principal of a local elementary school, a grant from the local economic development authority, and a sweetheart bank loan. Muriel and Herman were involved in all of the issues at SR, and knew, and cared for each of the residents. That care was palpable to us, every day.

"Thanks for the wine, Muriel", began Bella. Now, let's talk about the Halloween party. We've got it scheduled for the Saturday night before Halloween, from 7 to 9. Is there anything we want to change about last year's event?"

"Well for one thing, we need to stop Roy Winston from spiking the apple cider, like he did last year. Things got a little out of hand" Betty, always the voice of reason, said.

"You are no doubt right, Betty, but I do have to say that the wheelchair races were hilarious" giggled Bella.

"It is a wonder no one got hurt" sniffed Betty.

"Yeah, they might wind up in a wheelchair" rejoined Bella, simply not able to resist.

"Let's do this." Muriel posed. "We'll provide container beverages, like bottled water and diet soda, and let people BYO, if that is their wish. Nobody gets blindsided that way."

There was general agreement on that point with a mild protest from Peg: "I think you need to give that nice Roy Winston a break. He was just trying to make it fun for everyone." This point was let drop as everyone else in the room had heard the rumors about Peg and Roy.

Peg was now on a roll. "I think there should be prizes

for the best costume." I learned later that Peg had some sort of theatrical career, and had accumulated a closetful of impressive costumers. She was picturing herself hoisting the trophy.

At that point, Bella executed on of the smoothest maneuvers that I had ever seen. Instead of saying, "That is the silliest, most self-absorbed, impractical idea I have ever heard" she simply said "Good idea, Peg. Why don't you write up the rules, the qualifications for the judges, and the prizes for each category, and get that to me. Of course, the committee members are ineligible to win, but the others will love it." A clean shot to the head. The matter dropped.

After another glass of wine, there followed discussion of whether there should be pumpkin cookies or spice cake, whether candy was denture-friendly, whether dinner should be moved up to allow more time for costuming, and several other fairly trivial details. The event outline seemed clear.

At that point, Bella turned to me and asked "Do you have anything to add Hattie, with a newcomer's perspective?"

"I don't. But I do have something to say. I have enjoyed the meeting a great deal, but because I wasn't here for last year's party and because I have no special party planning skills, I have been wondering just why I have been asked here. The answer just occurred to me." It was plain to me that the Council was composed of Muriel's drinking buddies, except for Peg, who they included so they could keep an eye on her, and prevent her from undermining the operation of the Home. But I wasn't going to say that. What I did say was: "I'm a mystery to you, unlike 99% of the residents, I am not from here, or did not move here to be near someone from here. So, why, you ask, am I here? As you know, I lived my whole life on the South Side of Chicago. It was a tough life. I needed to get away. I like it here, I like you all, and I want to be a part of this place."

"We're glad you're here, Hattie" Muriel said after a pause. "We get it."

The Halloween Party came off without a hitch, and life at Shady Rest went on with its pleasant rhythms.

Until the next January.

At the January meeting of the Residents' Council, with Bella, Betty, Peg and I in attendance, Muriel wasted no time to get to her point. "Herman and I have just signed a contract to sell Shady Rest, effective February 1. We're very excited. We can now travel, see our grandkids a lot more, and, you know, just plain rest a bit. I do want you to know that I will miss the place, and particularly miss all of the residents who are all, my friends." There was weeping and hugging and expressions of best wishes and be sure you keep in touch. No one thought more about it, at least then.

It turned out that the new buyer was Midwest Retirement Enterprises, Inc. a company headquartered in Peoria that owned twenty-five other nursing homes across the state. It became apparent that the company's concept of the basic service contract with the residents was way different than had been the case with Muriel and Herman Hagenbuch. The activities were drastically reduced in number, and a fee was imposed for all those remaining. The gym hours were reduced to eight hours a day, and no supervisory staff was available, either in the gym or at the pool. The shuttle van driver, who had been more or less on call throughout the week, as if he were a private chauffeur, was reduced to eight to five, Monday, Wednesday and Friday, and subject to a four hour reservation policy. Out of town trips became much less frequent.

But the worst change was the elimination of the front desk staff on evenings and weekends. During the Golden Age of Muriel, there was always a person at the front desk, right inside the main door to the outside, whose nominal function was to greet everyone who came in, but whose job it was really to find out if a visitor had legitimate business in the building and to keep track of the comings and goings. In addition, this person, since the desk was right next to the mailboxes and the common library with the shared computer access, and right outside the Director's office, served as an informal contact with the rest of the world, keeping track of event schedules, meetings and being able to call service people, or in an emergency, medical assistance. Under the new regime, this spot was physically occupied only during business hours, Monday through Friday (lunch hour excluded).

And of course, there was the new director, Janet

Jennings. I made a point of dropping into her office short-ly after her arrival, just to scope her out. Janet was un-packing boxes of knick-knacks and office supplies when I poked my head in her door. "Hi, I'm Hattie. Welcome to the 'hood," I said, holding out my hand."

"Oh" she said, startled, and after limply shaking my hand, "Please sit down."

"Well, I can see you're busy, so I won't take a lot of your time." I did have what I wanted: an initial impres-sion. Janet was about two inches shorter than I am, was approaching, but was probably not quite fifty. She has middle length brown hair of an indeterminate cut, with-out any noticeable gray. She was wearing a navy wom-en's business suit, the jacket of which was too tight at the shoulders, too loose at the waist and too short for her frame. The effect was as if she had picked the suit because she thought that it conformed to someone else's notion of how someone in her role should look, not because she liked it or because she knew it looked good on her.

Janet herself is a nervous person in a visibly twitchy kind of way. She will not look you in the eye or even in your direction, unless absolutely necessary. One of the pieces of paper newly hung on her walls was a nurs-ing diploma, suggesting that her corporate masters had taken her from her professional comfort zone, and pro-pelled her into a managerial role for which she was clear-ly unsuited.

"Janet, I am a member of the Residents' Council, which meets regularly with the Director to exchange ideas about Shady Rest. We are looking forward to sitting down with you soon." She looked as if the idea of the residents having some sort of input into the management of the home was as exotic as dairy cattle forming a labor union. "The next meeting of the Council is at 3PM on the second Wednesday of March, in the Card Room. We would take it as a great favor if you would be there." She wrote the date into the blank Day Timer on her desk. "I will see if I can make it" she said dismissively. Taking my cue, I left.

On the day in question, the Residents' Council assembled in the Card Room in the persons of Bella, Betty, Peg and me. Dottie Tyler was still immobile from her stroke, and therefore absent. There was no wine, and a generally uneasy feeling in the air. At about ten minutes after three, Janet dithered into the room, raising in my mind the thought that maybe she had trouble finding the Card Room, since it was over one hundred feet from her office, outside of which none of us had ever seen her.

"Sorry to be late." She sat down with us and pulled a folder from her shoulder bag, opened it and began to read from a typed sheet inside. "Midwest Retirement is excited to own this property, and is anxious to show how much it cares for its residents. We know that you all appreciate that we have made and will make changes consistent with our goal of providing the best possible residential experience within a carefully controlled cost environment. We will be initiating a program of promotions for prospective residents that involve open houses, local media advertising, and new guest tours."

In other words, I thought to myself, you're going to market more and deliver less. Hello, corporate America.

"Now, Janet" began Bella, in her most civil, dispute mediation tone, "Here at Shady Rest, we all have enjoyed a culture of mutual consultation before any changes are made. I understand that the situation is different, but I'm sure you will find it in your interest to take advantage of that culture."

"Here is the real thing, Janet. It is just unacceptable that the building is unsecured at nights and on weekends. It is your obligation to provide that safety to the residents," I said, not being able to keep my mouth shut any more.

Janet looked unhappy and uncomfortable. "The changes that have been made in staffing and programs are a result of careful study and directives from senior management. I have nothing to say about them. I really have to go now, "she continued, without giving a reason for the urgency. She slunk out.

"Well", said Bella, "I think we know where we stand."

"Betty, let me ask you a professional question. Is the owner required by the lease we signed to provide the level of security 24/7 that Muriel and Herman did?"

"In a word, no. The services covered are the occupancy of our respective units, and the meal programs we individually elect. Other services are at the option of the Owner. And while the rent is guaranteed for the period of a year, the Owner has the option to terminate, for any reason, our right of occupancy on thirty days' notice. We are essentially month-to-month tenants" Betty advised in her calm, professional manner.

"Okay, I have an idea about how to make the point about the security situation, but I need you all to help."

After I explained the plan, Bella did not hesitate. "I love it. I am in." "Me too", echoed Peg. Surprising me with the conviction and certainty with which she answered, and making me worry a little about the continued secrecy of the project.

We turned to Betty who looked at each of us in turn and said "This is complete anarchy; a remarkable departure from civilized behavior. Sign me up."

The first step was for me to secure access to Janet's office. "Why stop there?" I asked myself, thinking that general access to all of the locked portions of the facility might come in handy. So, on the next occasion that I visited Janet on the pretext of some Residents' Council business, and sent her off to find a file, I took a quick impression of her office key, which she stupidly had left on a big bundle of building keys in the top drawer of her desk, and had even more stupidly, labelled "Office". With the key I had cut from the impression, it was easy for me, on the Friday night before our February bus trip to the Art Institute of Chicago, to let myself into Janet's office and "borrow" the full set of keys.

When our bus rolled into the bus parking on the Michigan Avenue side of the Institute, I hailed a cab and hustled down to Manny's Locks on South State Street.

The shop looked the same as I remembered it, with brass shavings in drifts like fallen leaves, and the incessant scream of the grinder. Manny, wearing his coveralls and safety glasses, peeked over the counter as the door bell announced my arrival. He blinked a couple of times, as if to focus in on me.

"Hattie. What a great surprise! I haven't seen you in decades. Are you still working?"

"Special projects, Manny. Nice to see you, too. Look, I've got an emergency request for you", I said putting Janet's key ring on the counter.

"Hattie, I'm awfully, busy" Manny whined, looking at the thirty keys of various shapes and sizes.

Without saying anything else, I placed a wrapped bundle of ten one hundred dollars bills next to the key ring.

"My schedule has suddenly opened up. Mr. Franklin and his clones can be very persuasive."

"I'll be back in four hours. Does that work for you?

"See you then" said Manny scooping up the keys and the bills at the same time.

The result was, after our return to Gethsemane, and my covert replacement of Janet's keys, that I had full access to any part of the building.

The next step in our plan to illustrate the folly of not having a staffer on site 24-7 was a shopping trip by Peg and I to Loew's. Then, after a phone call by Betty to the service provider and a satisfactory contract being agreed upon, an early spring Saturday morning found Betty seated at the reception desk in the lobby, looking official, and keeping watch, and me, seated at Janet's desk, admitting the work crew who emptied Janet's office, covered the furniture with a tarp and painted the entire office the most awful color that Peg and I could find, a yellowish pink that reminded you at once of infected tissue, decaying dairy products, and stomach indigestion. It was disgusting in any light, natural or artificial, day or night. The crew worked efficiently and finished by Saturday night. I told them not to worry about moving the furniture back, as we had plenty of help for that, thanked them, signed the invoice with a very good facsimile of Janet's signature, and locked the door behind me.

I waited until about 9:30 on the following Monday morning to wander over to Janet's office. She was sitting on a chair next to her still tarp-covered desk, staring at the yellowish pink (or is it pinkish yellow in this light?) with a mixture of horror and incredulity.

"Oh, Janet, What a lovely color", I said, in a tone suggesting that I was about to call "House Beautiful", while I was actively suppressing the urge to throw up.

"By the way, the Residents' Council would like to revisit the weekend security question with you. Wednesday, 3 o'clock. Card Room. Be there."

But that was just Round 1 of my battle with Janet.

5

# Chutes and Ladders

On the Wednesday night before Thanksgiving, my son Bobby drove up from Moline to pick me up. The ninety-minute drive back to his house was a wonderful opportunity to visit with him, one-on-one. Bobby is a mechanical engineer who works for John Deere. He is, by any definition, a wonderful kid; he was always respectful to me and his father, was a diligent student, and has led a quiet, respectable life. He calls me a lot. He is not, however, Ines.

"Okay, Mom, what is happening in your life?", he asked as well rolled out of the parking lot of Shady Rest. I could hardly tell him that I had just killed two people, so I told him about my bridge group, my trips with the Residents' Council into Chicago, and the mundane scuttlebutt from Gethsemane. He nodded sympathetically, but uncomprehendingly, and proceeded to bring me up to date on his family. He and his wife Cheryl, an Illinois farm girl who he met while they were students at the University of Illinois, have two children, Brianna, who is 11, and Colton, age 8. Cheryl is a licensed property insurance agent and works three-quarters time at a local State Farm agency. The kids have a brain-dulling schedule of clubs, sports, social activities, and schoolwork. They live, frankly, on a different planet than one with which I am familiar.

By the time we pulled into the driveway of his house in Moline, my other son Javier, "Javy" had arrived with his wife, Isabella, with their daughter, Manuela, age 5. Bobby and I came into the house, to hugs, hellos and the infectious excitement of the children.

I find it interesting to note the different paths that my sons' lives have taken. While they both grew up, first in a concentrated Hispanic neighborhood in Chicago, and among a significant similar community in Downers Grove, as inseparable companions, even to the point where I had stopped worrying about them, their lives were very dissimilar. Bobby lives a frankly Anglo life: Anglo town, Anglo wife, kids do not speak Spanish, while Javy is married to a Latina, lives in Phoenix, and as an architect, deals with Hispanic life and culture every day.

Thanksgiving food preparations were underway, and I, of course, volunteered to help in the kitchen, chiefly to be part of the camaraderie of the cooks, which does not occur in a nursing home. My daughters-in law were having none of it.

"Maman" said Isabella, with her accent that brought to mind the beautiful voices of Emilio's sisters, "You may rest, and entertain the children."

So I found myself at the family room game table with Brianna, Colton and Manuela. I thought briefly about giving them each twenty bucks and teaching them to play draw poker. (Milly would have cleaned them out in twenty minutes.)

"Okay, kids, let's play games. I don't want to play electronic games. And I'm not real excited about watching you fool around with smartphones, Ipads or whatever. Let's see what board games are in the cupboard."

Brianna and Manuela spent some time sorting through the games and came back with Chutes and Ladders. In my life, I have played a lot of games, card, dice, board, but the only game I really despise is Chutes and Ladders. Ines loved Chutes and Ladders. She and I played probably a thousand games of Chutes and Ladders. I do not ever recall winning a single game.

For those who have the grave misfortune of never having played the game, or for those who have forced the memory of it from their minds, Chutes and Ladders is a pathway game, where the winner is the first person to get to square 100 by moving the number of squares the player spins on a one-through-six spinner. The outcome of the game is made unpredictable by the presence on the board of a series of Chutes, which cause the player landing on the top of one to "slide" down to the foot of the slide, and Ladders, which gives the person landing on the foot of one a boost to the top of the ladder. Players make no decisions, so there is no strategy, only luck.

"Aw, that's a little kid game" said Colton. "I don't want to play"

"Well, let's make it a little more interesting" I said, reaching into my purse and pulling out a hundred. "Winner gets this picture of Benjamin Franklin." I tucked the bill under the corner of the board by square 100. That seemed to solve the interest issue for Colton, so we started. "Manuela, you count for me, but you have to do it in Spanish." I had not realized how much I missed my Hispanic connections. Manuela was continually exposed to Spanish, but probably experienced the subtle pressure to conform to English. I wanted to do what I could to help her celebrate her heritage. After a few turns, I asked her: "Manuela, what is the name of this game in Spanish? She looked at me blankly. "Okay, what is this?" I asked her, pointing to a ladder. She brightened. "Escalara!" "Bueno, now how about this?" I asked, pointing to a chute, "Think about the playground." She furrowed her brow and thought a moment. "Tobogan!" "Si, or Resbaladilla. So what is the name of the game?"

"Toboganes Y Escaleras" she stated confidently.

And so we climbed and slid our way through the game. Oddly enough, I was in the lead, on square 82, when Cheryl came in from the kitchen with the announcement that Aunt Ines was on the phone. Brianna and Manuela, for whom Ines was a breath-taking idol were off like a shot to talk to her. Even Colton joined the line.

Eventually, the phone was passed to me.

"So what's new in 'Lifestyles of the Rich and Famous'?"

"Happy Thanksgiving, Mom", Ines said, laughing.

"Are going to take any time off, or are you going to eat turkey sandwiches at your desk?"

"About ten of us have reservations at a restaurant, then we will crash for the rest of the day. We'll be back at it on Friday. Scripts are due in the middle of December. With any luck, we'll shoot by the end of the year."

"It is possible to work too hard. And your old mother would like to see you some time."

"I just don't see it happening before, say February, or March."

"I thought we were talking about Christmas. There are a couple of things I want to talk to you about. In person."

"Sorry, Mom. We'll get together as soon as we can."

I don't have all the time in the world, I thought to myself, but said "Keep in touch, Ines, it is important to me."

"Will do. Love, ya, Mom, gotta run."

That all put me in a particularly bad mood. The kitchen crew was not quite done with the evening's work, or ready for dinner, so the Chutes and Ladders game resumed.

"Gramma, it's your turn", said Manuela. I spun. Manuela counted: "uno, dos, tres, cuatro, cinco! Oh, gramma, you get to go down the biggest slide! Whee!"

Of course I do.

As I regarded my new position on square 24, I

suddenly realized that what I had always hated about this stupid game was that it was very much like the lives of the women I had spent my life with, and like how my life would have been without Milly, in that, as people, or players, they had no real choices, but were subject to a bunch of random influences for benefit or burden, all with the overhanging possibility that one of those influences would be the big slide and take you out of the game completely. A morose and cynical prospect at best.

We finished the game as Brianna caught up to and passed Colton who was stuck on square 99 waiting to spin a 1. As Brianna pocketed the bill, Colton looked stunned at what he perceived to be a staggeringly bitter turn of fate. In his mind, he had already spent the money. "Think about it this way, Colton. A lot of experiences in life, like this game, are like being a wild animal tamer in the circus. Algunos dias se muerde el oso; algunos dias el oso te muerde. (Some days you bite the bear; some days the bear bites you.)" He clamored for a re-match. "Not, tonight. I'm all gamed out", I said, heading for the kitchen and a glass of wine.

The rest of the holiday passed pleasantly enough with good food, good family reminiscences and the valuable opportunity to observe the people my grandchildren were in the process of becoming. But I must confess that I had to consciously suppress the bad taste of defeated intention in getting together with Ines, and the realization that it might not ever happen. I know in order for me to have closed the cycle of my life, I had some things to tell Ines.

As Bobby drove me back to Gethsemane on Sunday, I reflected again on what a wonderful kid he is.

He carried my bag up to my apartment, kissed me, and said "Just let me know what you need, Mom. I can be here in the drop of a hat." I knew it, and thanked him, as he left. If only that would do it for me.

# 6
# The Bear bites me

Back at Shady Rest, I took stock of my situation on the Monday morning following Thanksgiving while I took my medications (no purple pills today), and laid out the simple wool herring bone suit that I had chosen to wear to breakfast. I was trying to put my finger on exactly why my mood was so dismal. Sure, I had just killed two people, but each of those decisions had its own satisfactory rationale and result. Ines keeps maddeningly putting off a personal meeting with me at which I could tell her enough of my life experiences to allow that life to remain in focus for me, at least. But that has been going on for years. As I thought again of the image of standing on the back platform of a train caboose watching the past recede into the distance, it struck me that the part of my past that kept pushing itself into my consciousness despite my firm resolution to not expose myself again to the pain of her death, was Milly. "Maybe", I thought, "I need to remember, reflect and grieve." I'll think about it. I selected a brown beret that matched the pumpkin neck scarf I had tied and went down to breakfast.

My mood was immediately enhanced on entering the dining room to find that Bella was holding forth in an animated fashion at a table with Betty and a couple of seventyish kids who I had not met. I sat at the place between Betty and the woman of the new couple.

"Morning, Hattie" Bella trilled "I was just telling the Demorys just how much fun it was during the Eisenhower Administration." The Demorys, a handsome African-American couple had obviously not yet gotten a line on Bella, and were regarding her with expressions of mild disbelief. I looked at Betty, who rolled her eyes toward the ceiling and, as usual kept her counsel. Which is, of course, unremarkable for a lawyer like Betty, who had very little in the way of small talk.

"Oh c'mon Bella", I interjected "The fifties were completely dull. All we were doing was getting pregnant. The clothes were awful. Everything was vanilla, and there was Joe McCarthy" I spouted, not able to resist the bait.

Bella curled the left corner of her mouth in the sign that she was having us on and said "Hattie, I would like you to meet Florence …. and Harrison…. Demory. They moved in last week" Bella said, gesturing towards each. "And" gesturing toward me, and looking at the Demorys, "this is Hattie Rosales, whose name is obviously not a coincidence."

"Nice to meet you. Are you from Gethsemane?" I

asked. "No," answered Florence, in her pleasant voice, "We retired here from St. Louis to be close to our daughter and son-in-law and grandkids." Ah, another family whose generations get closer, not further apart.

I continued the conversation, chiefly so that Bella could eat some of her breakfast, which appeared at this point to have been untouched. Florence and Harrison were college professors, she science, he sociology. They positively radiated that sense of the newly retired that the future is an entirely unlimited possibility, not a period of inexorable decline and disappointment. Good for them, I thought.

About then, Darlene Millsap, the dim-witted part-time office assistant to Janet, bustled into the dining room. "Oh, Hattie. I've been looking for you. Janet needs to see you in her office." Darlene's officious manner implied that her position required an MBA, where the fact was that the only skills anyone has ever seen her exercise were answering the phone and running the copy machine. Bella at one time had observed that no one had ever seen or imagined her doing both at the same time. "Like walking and chewing gum", Bella had said.

"Tell Janet I will be by later this morning" I told Darlene. "Do I need my lawyer?" I joked. Darlene looked briefly confused, said "Of course not" and hurried out.

I finished my breakfast, made my excuses, and headed down the hall to Janet's office. I had briefly considered going back to my room to change into an outfit that would more stridently clash with the wall color of Janet's office, which she hadn't had the chance to change, but decided that it wasn't worth the trouble. I was looking forward to pulling Janet's chain as a means to further improve my mood.

Darlene was sitting at her desk employing her talents with her telephone. I ignored her, and steamed into Janet's office, shouting her name as I came into the room.

Janet jumped noticeably, looked up and said to me, doing the best to re-compose herself. "Sit down, Hattie", she said, deliberately not looking at me and opening a file on her desk.

I sat as Janet took a deep breath, twitching even more than usual, "We have taken all that we can from you, Hattie. We are going to make some changes here."

"We?"

"The management of Shady Rest. We have had enough of your making trouble at every turn. We are terminating your lease. You have thirty days to get out. Here is the formal notice", she said handing me a typed single sheet.

"You can't do that."

"We can, and if you don't, we will report you to the police as the prime suspect in the theft of the prescription medications from Assisted Living."

So there was a police investigation going on. I looked at the notice. It was typed on a plain letter-sized sheet, and was not a form and was not on Shady Rest letterhead. Janet had done this on her own, not as part of an institutional decision.

"I will take this up with my lawyer."

"Go right ahead, but your thirty days starts now", Janet said, closing the file and busying herself with other items on her desk. I left without saying anything else, but headed back to my room and pulled out my copy of my lease. I did remember that at one point, fellow resident and retired attorney, Betty Schwartz had mentioned the presence of the short-notice termination, indicating that the nominal reason was to protect the institution from the onset of an unmanageable condition, like Alzheimer's. Sure enough, the clause was there, plain as day.

Damn. I am now in such a bad mood. I do not want to move. I am tired of being jerked around by a petty bureaucrat. I can't afford, from my own standpoint, and from Ines', to have the police poking around in my business.

Janet, Janet, Janet. You leave me no choice.

You're next.

# 7

# Pathway to the Past

*HATTIE; DECEMBER 2016*

Over the next couple of days, I started to give the matter of Janet's elimination some serious thought. The prospect was no small matter. Janet is much younger than I am. I have to accomplish the task without incriminating myself, or if I can help it, without suggesting that the event was anything except an unhappy accident. I have no access to her private life and only interface with her at Shady Rest. It will have to be here. A kernel of a plan started to form in my mind. It just might work. But it will require a trip to the Armory.

Fortunately, the next Saturday was our scheduled bus trip to the Art Institute of Chicago for the annual Christmas program. Lots of us go, and the bus was full and animated by lively discussions and laughter. Bella, for example, was amusing us with the story of how she and her high school girl friend had driven into Chicago for the first time by themselves in Bella's dad's car, had parked in a reserved spot, had the car towed and spent the next twenty-four hours trying to find out where it was, having to spend the night in the YWCA. " My dad grounded me for the rest of my life (which worked out to be about a week and a half) but we found the best shade of lipstick that no one in Gethsemane had ever seen. It was completely worth it." Only a master story teller, like Bella, could make that simple episode as compelling as she did.

When we got to the Institute and we were let out on the Michigan Avenue side, I quietly advised Bella that I had a side trip to make and that I would return before we headed back to Gethsemane. I hailed a cab and directed the driver to GMO Harris Bank on West Washington St. I don't get to Chicago often, but every time I do, I am struck by two conflicting impressions: how much the City looks different, but in some fundamental way, stays the same. The bank, which was Harris Bank & Trust Company when I worked in the Loop has a couple of new wings, but the original building is still there, and still just as impressive. I tipped the driver, went into the main entrance and took the elevator down to the Safety Deposit Vault. Banking has changed enormously over the years, but depository services have not. I suppose that is because the stuff we put in still has to be in those locked steel boxes that are not very moveable. Also the records of the owners of the boxes, and their visit are still kept on 5" by 8" cards on which you sign each time you access your box. I handed the attendant my key. She looked at my card, and then at me. "You haven't been here for more than twenty years" she said, with some amazement, possibly because she was not a great deal older than twenty herself. "That's about right" I agreed. "You will need a cart to take the box to the viewing room" I added. She called an assistant who took my key, the bank master key and led me into the vault, pushing the cart in front of him. "Let's see. Oh there it is" he said, spotting my box on the bottom row. It is the largest size available. He applied both keys and slid the box out, lifting onto the cart. "That is heavy" he observed. "Full set of family silver", I provided as an explanation. He pushed the cart into the viewing room, slid the box onto the table. "Just give a shout when you are done" he said as he left. I locked the door.

I sat down, took a deep breath, looked at the ceiling and reached with my gloved hand to open the hinged lid. I knew exactly what I would see, but had no idea how I would feel about it.

The Glock 19 was on top of the box, with the silencer still attached. I picked it up slowly and moved it from hand to hand, renewing the familiar feeling of connected competence with the weapon, as if I had handled it yesterday. The next item I removed was the piano wire garrotte, with the two rosewood handles specially carved to fit my hands. This was followed by the seven inch stiletto in its custom tooled forearm sheath. I took a moment to appreciate its balance and its lethal beauty. Remaining in the box were three boxes of ammunition and a spare magazine for the Glock, and banded bundles of cash that probably totaled about seventy-five thousand dollars. The Smith and Wesson 39-2, my favorite "hand-gun as a fashion accessory" with its beautiful wooden stock lay quietly on the bottom of the box. Finally, I came to the item that was the point of today's trip: a leather case with had a snap-shut cover, which contained, when you opened it, a series of sealed vials, along with several packaged syringes.

I was at that point engulfed by not only the recognition of the physical objects as tools of my trade and definition of my professionalism and personality, but more powerfully as passwords to the programs of my memory that I had more or less deliberately locked up the last time I was here. Handling these pieces of the past brought them all back: Henrietta Hruskova, Emilio Rosales, Ludmilla Nesterov; Milly. Oh god, I miss Milly.

I took from the case a vial containing a clear liquid, marked with an "H" and two syringes. I packed these carefully in the shoulder bag I had brought along. I peeled off $5,000 from the stock of cash and put it in the wallet in my purse. Almost as an after-thought, I removed the silencer from the Glock and replaced it into the bank box. I stashed the Glock and a box of ammunition in my shoulder bag. I re-packed the rest of the items and called for the attendant.

"All done?" he asked as he came back in with the cart.

"Yes, thank you. I was able to complete the inventory for my estate planner."

He pushed the box back to its grid, locked it in with

both keys and returned mine to me. "See you soon", he said as he went off. "I don't really think so" I thought to myself. I completed the check-out process with the woman at the desk, who airily enjoined me to "Have a nice day!" I am due for a nice day, I muttered as I made my way back to the ground level. I caught a cab back to the Art Institute. I found our group on its way to Terzo Piano, the restaurant on the top floor of the new wing.

"Hattie, you look like you were dragged backwards through a hedge" Bella chirped. More like backwards through a mirror. "Family business" was all I could muster. "To heck with 'em. Let's have a salad and a glass of wine." So we did. It helped, but on the bus ride back to Gethsemane, the newly stirred memories would not leave me alone. I confronted them, one at a time, while staring out the window over the darkening outskirts of Town, and eventually over the moon-washed stillness of the Illinois countryside.

Henrietta Hruskova. That's where it begins, I told myself, and unlimbered the stiff joints of recollection.

## 8

# Brighton Park

*HENRIETTA; 1941*

Yes, my portion of my story starts, as Henrietta Hruskova, in our family flat on S Francisco Ave , in Brighton Park on the south side of Chicago, the third child, of five, of Jaroslav Hruska, "Jaro" to the world of our neighborhood, and Zofia Peshek Hruskova. We lived on the third floor. My oldest sibling, my sister Brygida, and my older brother, Lucasz, who were five and four years older than I was, and my mom, ran the daily household.

The rhythm of life was predictable, and stultifying, in a way that I did not fully appreciate until an adult. Jaro worked the night shift at Republic Steel, getting hot, dirty and tired on a daily basis, without ever, to my knowledge, doing anything after his shift but coming home, and conking out. Occasionally, he would be awake when we went off to school, and presented as a smiling, although ground down, parental presence.

"What is for you in that school?" He would ask, meaning, "What shred of education have you snatched to lift you beyond the night shift at a steel mill?" He told no stories about his life, or anything else. I knew, somehow, that my mother loved him, deeply, in a way that never changed in their history.

I remember my childhood as remarkably colorless. Grey of concrete streets, brown of building siding, ashen of dimmed hopes, and dreams.

Except for one thing. Zofia was a seamstress of skill, ingenuity and reputation. She took in piecework sewing "to make ends meet". The human body, particularly the female human body, is not a sphere, or a cylinder, or a torus, or any other single geometric shape, but for each single person, is a combination of curves, planes and spirals. Only a gifted tailor can fashion clothes that actually fit that reality. And being a unique threadmaster, she had a pronounced brilliance with alterations of existing garments, tailored and fitted not for the current intended wearer.

And that skill illuminated the otherwise drab neighborhood. We were all Catholics, living in the literal and figurative shadow of St. Pancratius. We were all of some sort of Central European extraction, we were all steel-mill poor, but we were all proud of our heritages, our families, and particularly of the clothes that we all reserved for the most important occasions of our lives, clothes that lived their lives beyond a single wearer. In that world an expert seamstress, a kind neighbor, and a woman with an eye for subtleties of style, manner and personality of the wearer, was, to say the least, a goddess.

"Zofie, Magda has prom in two weeks! Here is Irena's dress from two years ago. Can you fit it for her?"

"Of course, Dorotka, bring her in for a fitting, as soon as you can."

And this is where I became absorbed in our lives as neighbors and service providers. Zofie almost always charged just a quarter for any alteration, except on those rare occasions where some lucky neighbor scored some brand-new fabric to be made into a custom garment, in which case the charge might go up to a dollar. I never thought too much about the money until after Zofie's death as we went through her personal possessions and found, at the bottom of the drawer in which she kept her lingerie, two cigar boxes completely full of quarters. She had plainly regarded them as tangible symbols of the regard with which she was held by her clients, preserved in respect of the sacrifice of the families for which we worked.

And it wasn't just prom, it was First Communion and weddings that kept Zofie busy, and our living/fitting room full of eager people and of colorful dresses and blouses, hanging on the racks in states of partial completion throughout the flat and that broke the general greyness of the neighborhood for us.

The question from the mother with the dress-in-need-of-alteration was always about the same. "Can you do that Zofie?" And the answer was, always, "Yes, we can do that."

"Yes", in Zofie's quiet voice.

At one point, I had thought that Zofie was embarrassed about her accent, and as a result, had damped the volume of her voice to the point that her accent blurred into English. But my kid assessment was totally wrong: she had adjusted the volume of her voice for the only person she really cared about: Jaro, whose hearing had been obliterated by the daily blast furnaces, such that what was left of his hearing was devoted to his beloved wife.

So Zofie spoke quietly, but had a seismic impact on our neighborhood.

And I began, almost as an apprentice, to learn, appreciate, and execute the small details of Zofie's larger skill. I would, on my knees, pin hems, and rip the small stitches that neede to be removed, all under my mother's watchful eye.

Mother was a perfectionist. "Gefjinka,( or "little girl" in Polish, which she called me long after I could have been called "little"), this is not good. You must re-pin that hem" Or "That sleeve does not rest right; Rip it out, We will do it again."

So I learned, pin by pin, and stitch by stitch, how truly tailored garments were made, and how they looked when complete.

I was the tailor's apprentice through my high school graduation.

The mutual expectation of parents, and of children in my community, was that, after you graduated from high school, you left.

"I will miss you more than you will know, Hattie", which name had crept into our lives at some point, and hooked itself to me, Zofie said to me at my graduation party. " Do not forget the difference between Style and Fashion."

Jaro had the energy to muster a "I love you, Henrietta. Run your own life, don't let it run you", before he gave me what was the hug from him that I remember most clearly.

As it happened, I graduated from high school, in 1948 into the upheaval of life occasioned by the massive return from theatres of war the male population of the United States of America. The change in American life was taking place at an unprecedented rate, as if our past was being quickly erased, like a classroom blackboard.

There were a lot of choices for short term careers arcs. Some of my classmates graduated to "food service", some to "Marriage" and the implied role of child- bearer and long-term day care provider.

I graduated to Marshall Field's.

# 9

# Marshall Field's

Everyone in Chicago, in 1948, had some personal experience with Marshall Field's, the Department Store that defined the Loop. It featured the multi-story atrium that housed the Christmas tree that nine of ten Chicagoans would marvel at, every year. But it was not just a show place, like the 1893 World Exposition, but it was an ongoing, everyday Temple to the Goddess of Style, and in particular the style of women's garments and accessories. I was not familiar with New York "department" stores, but I certainly caught the air of sophistication and excitement that oozed out of every one of the individual shops in Marshall Field's, each dedicated to a particular clothing specialty. I could not get enough of it.

So it was natural for me, after having graduated from high school, and being culturally expected to "do something" involving working and living outside my childhood home to look towards Marshall Field's.

# THE DEADLY MONDAINE

I applied for a "Floor Clerk" position in the Women's Department. Women's Clothing was, in 1948, a boom industry, as the women of the country were tired of shortages of silk and nylon, and having little money and no place to spend it. Marshall Field's was only too happy to accommodate their new range of choices and sudden increased means of acquisition. In fact, the store motto, which was drilled into us employees as a mantra was "Give the woman what she wants."

My interview was with the Personnel Director of the Women's Department, a Miss Myrtle Kirby.

"Please come in and take a chair", Miss Kirby said, as she admitted me to the shoebox-sized office somewhere in the upper reaches of the building. She closed the door behind me and sat, stiffly in the desk chair. She was in her late forties or early fifties, and gave the initial impression, from her formal demeanor and severe hair style, of a schoolteacher. But no schoolteacher I had ever known had the manicure, the tastefully applied make-up and the tailored suit that I could not help but stare at.

"How do you think you could help us a Marshall Field's" she opened, brusquely, and closely watched me for my response.

"Thank you for the opportunity, Ma'am. I know a bit about clothing, and would like to help other women make good choices."

That response seemed to be acceptable to Miss Kirby, not from any affirmation I received, but from the fact that I hadn't been throw out summarily.

"What do you make of this suit?" She asked, handing me a suit from the small closet behind her desk. From the size of the garment, which was about a 4, it wasn't hers, but was a test of some sort for me. I took it, felt the jacket.

"Nice fabric" and turned it inside-out. "Cheap lining, badly sewn. The shoulders seams are uneven; and the button holes are completely amateurish." I looked at the skirt. " A chimp could hem this better."

With a small smirk, Miss Kirby rehung the suit in her closet and asked "You sew?"

"My mother alters; I have helped her since I was seven."

She looked at my application. "All right, Miss, er..... Hruskova. You're hired. You start tomorrow in the women's formal wear department, down on fourth floor. Be there at 7:30. Report to Mrs. Jordan."

She took a breath, "Now remember", again glancing at my application, "Henrietta. We need you to be here all of the time, on time. No drinking. No smoking. Mrs. Jordan will fill you in on the details." She stood up and extended her hand, "Welcome to Marshall Field's." She showed me out.

I was there at 7:20 the next morning, at the State Street entrance with the jostling crowd of employees, waiting for the main doors to open, the crowd showing a combination of ennui, determination, and, at least in my case, over the top enthusiasm. The doors opened, and the crowd was ingested whole, like plankton ingested by a whale.

# THE DEADLY MONDAINE

By the time I made my way to the fourth floor, and found my way to Women's Formal wear, Ernestine Jordan was working at whirlwind pace. She had piled on the main counter of the department all of the empty hangers from yesterday's impulses and try-ons and was replacing the merchandise in its place.

"Are you my new help?" she asked with a combination of wonder and relief, "I need you to re-hang all of these garments, and put them back on their places on the racks." Even though I had just set foot in the department, and never seen any of these garments before, this was not as hard as it may have sounded. I can hang clothes, having Zofie's standards ingrained in my DNA, and basically understand that garments that look alike are racked together, in size order. I set to work immediately and got most of it done by the time of store opening.

"Well done, my dear. My prior dimwitted assistant decided, on short notice, to "go west and grow with the country". I am completely unconvinced that she could pick out "west" from straight up or straight down." She took a breath, and said "Hattie, it is Hattie isn't it? I am sorry for the push in the pool, but that is how it is here at MF. Here in Formal Wear, we not only sell our product to women who can afford our dresses, but stand as a tangible model of what women of lesser means can aspire to. The country is changing, and we want, at MF, to sell to such women their first club ball gown, their first child's wedding dress, or just, darn it, a very pricy designer dress. I expect you to learn the inventory, and to participate fully in the Company's employee training program. I like you already. Do good things."

She hustled off to talk to the store buyers, who had just arrived with the next season samples and swatches.

I, of course, was lapping it all up, like a thirsty dog laps water. The employee training programs, which took place on Wednesdays, in lieu of one's lunch hour, were exhilarating experiences, not to be missed. Every week, a different corporate employee would address the staff; sometimes men, sometimes women. The women would teach about grooming, personal confidence, and current trends in the fashions we would be called upon to sell to our customers. The men largely extolled the virtues of selling something to everyone, increasing the "Profit to the Company". Out of all of this I started to get the idea that the company motto "Give the Woman What She wants" meant two entirely different things to the male management and the group that really ran, and made successful, Marshall Field's, that is to say the women who were the buyers of garments, the marketing department, the supervisors of the entirely female sales staff, and those of us on the floor who interacted with all of the diverse and interesting women of Chicagoland who made their way to the store. The men thought that the object was to use marketing, store design, and sales pressure to "sell what we got", while the powerful, intelligent, successful, and largely invisible female management of MF knew that the key to success was to have staff that knew the difference between Fashion and Style, (thank you Zofie, for that early lesson) displayed that difference in their own garments and demeanor, and took it as their mission, on behalf of Marshall Field's, to educate the women customers about what really did look good on them, whether or not it was what "She wants" when she came in the door. After all, if you sell a woman an item that really flatters her, and her friends, say "Where did you get THAT?", and she says "Marshall Field's", that is a win, across the board.

I loved learning all of this, and being part of and getting to know the women staffers who knew clothes and makeup and shoes and coats and, yes, hats. I did find that I had a particular affinity for hat styles, as they related to face shapes and dress styles, and just plain personal expressions of joie de vie. Life is just too short not to wear hats. So the name "Hattie" closed on me from both sides.

The other window that opened to me during the MF employee education was first the rumor, and then the personal observation on the floor, and finally the formal acknowledgement by the male staff, backed up with actual advertisement of the fact, that Marshall Field's employed women who were "Personal Shoppers" for women of means, who could afford not to have to visit individual departments to assemble outfits, but had expert assistance in buying clothes, purchasing wedding gifts and household furnishings, all with a trained and trusted supporting eye. The rumor among the staff was that, not only did the "Personal Shopper" command significantly higher wages than even department heads, they lived in the world of tips and personal benefits like invitations to rich family weddings, graduations, confirmations and christenings.

The role of "Personal Shopper" therefore, was my earnest and sole objective. There was nothing that would stop me from achieving it. I accepted advancements within the store with a clear view of where the path was heading.

So, After having helped Eunice Jordan to restore what she felt to be order in the Women's formalwear department and having helped her train my successor, I leapt at the chance to serve in the vaunted French Room Millinery Salon on the Sixth Floor, with the earnest hope that it was the final stop before Hattie Hruskova could add Marshall Field's Personal Shopper to her CV.

## 10

# Enter "E"

*HATTIE; JULY 1949*

And then Emilio happened.

I had, to my way of thinking, progressed nicely at Marshall Field's, now having the day time shift in French Room Millinery Salon, the 6th floor women's hat department. I had regular customers who sought out my advice on not only hats, but also other issues of personal style. I was on my way, I knew, to realizing my goal of becoming one of the MF Personal Shoppers, those doyennes of the staff who confidently escorted their clients from department to department with easy style and grace. I was positive that I was destined to do that job, and to thrive at it. It was just a matter of time.

It was, I think, a late Friday afternoon in the spring of 1949. I was practicing the retail clerk's art of perfunctorily adjusting the merchandise, in an effort to appear to be totally occupied, and not concerned with my real task, which was appraising each approaching prospective customer for her style and likelihood of interest in my hats. If one pays attention, one can quickly pick up the clues of dress, hair style, make-up choices that can tell you more about a woman's taste than she could tell you in her own words. Since the sixth floor was exclusively occupied by salons dedicated to women's clothing and accessories, there were a great number of women to see. There were not usually very many men, and the few were always following women, carrying bags, shuffling their feet and looking either bored or stricken.

It was a great surprise, then, to see a dark-haired, un-self-consciously handsome, athletic young man striding down the aisleway to the hat department with the fluid yet controlled steps that suggested a professional dancer.

"Well, let's have some fun with this", I thought to myself as he got near enough to me to speak to. "May I direct you to the lingerie department, sir?" I asked sweetly, knowing full well that no man of that era could think of, spell or imagine buying lingerie. I know that times have changed. I have seen Victoria's Secret. (And just what is the secret, I always ask myself.)

The man stopped abruptly, looked at me in a panicked manner, opened his mouth to speak and said "I, …. Ah …..Ah, …." and then just sighed in frustration. I pointed to the Lingerie department, which was closer to the elevator bank. He straightened up, and hurried off down the walkway, in the opposite direction to the one I had indicated. I smiled to myself and thought no more about it.

Until about an hour later when the same fellow was all of a sudden back at the French Room. He was much more composed, but no less good looking.

"Did you find the lingerie?" I asked, trying not to be too arch.

"No" he answered, "But I did find what I was looking for. You" and he illuminated me for the first time with his incandescent smile. "How would you like to go dancing tonight?"

It was my turn to do the stuttering, at least internally. I could not think of a single coherent reason why I should not, and was aware of about a thousand parts of me demanding that I should. As I think about it now, I know that it was over right then.

"Okay. I'm Hattie, Hattie Hruskova", I said, holding out my hand.

"I am Emilio Rosales, and I am delighted to meet you, Hattie", flashing the smile again while gripping my hand in both of his. "Where may I pick you up? Say about seven?"

I extracted my hand and wrote down the address of the apartment I shared with my two roommates. "Real dancing?", I asked.

"Oh yes, senorita. Wear your best dancing shoes." And he strode off, leaving me feeling like I had just been flung from a merry-go-round. The rest of my shift sailed by in a blur. I somehow made it home in time, to clean up, change into a light grey pleated skirt with an off white short-sleeve sweater and spring weight navy jacket. The outfit was finished off with a burgundy scarf and, of course a narrow brim fedora. I shooed my nosy roommates out of the door just in time to answer Emilio's knock.

"Buenas tardes, Senorita Hattie!" he said as he swooped in. "Ready to go?" He was wearing a short-waisted, black zippered jacket over a black shirt with a fashionably thin gray necktie. I was impressed that he was carrying a bag that clearly held his dancing shoes.

I grabbed the shoe bag with my dancing shoes. "Where are we going?'

"Mambo City. Victor Parra is playing."

That was kind of ironic, since Mambo City was on West Randolph, on the next block west from Marshall Field's. In any event, we jumped a City bus and headed back north.

I didn't know exactly what to expect. Ballroom dancing was big, particularly after World War II, and Chicago was crawling with dance venues, many of which I had visited. Most of the places of my acquaintance featured "Big Bands" which played a mixture of swing and the more traditional dances, like fox trot and waltz. The Latin music that I had experienced up to that point either was arranged into standard "American" formats, or occasionally played by guest Latin bands that played between the sets of the feature group.

What the Mambo Room offered was non-stop, high energy, unfiltered Latin dance music played with the soulfulness, irresistible rhythm, and joy that defines the genre, and that I had never felt in a dance hall before. It seemed like everyone in the place danced every number. That night I learned the mambo, polished up my rumba, and learned some cha cha steps way beyond my previous comprehension. It was more fun than I may have had at one time in my whole life. My initial sense that Emilio had the body presence of a professional dancer proved to be totally accurate. He danced with restrained power and grace, and was a careful and thoughtful leader. We closed the place down.

What followed was a string of dances at places like El Mirador, the Cuban Village, and even The Merry Garden Ballroom (home of the world's Dance Marathon record) listening to and dancing with artists like Congo Castro, Quique Orchard and Valeria Longoria.

We got to know each other better. Emilio's parents came to Chicago from Mexico in the 30's. His dad was approaching retirement age at the Stockyards. His mother still worked part time at a Mexican restaurant in Pilsen, where they still lived. Emilio was the assistant manager of a local branch of First Chicago State Bank that served the Mexican neighborhood. He liked the job, as he knew and enjoyed his customers.

Besides dancing, Emilio's other passion was baseball. He had been a high school third baseman, accomplished both with his glove and his bat. He still played weekly on an adult league team. He was, of course, a huge White Sox fan, as were all of us Southsiders. Fandom became part of your DNA. No matter how difficult your individual life experiences were, being at Comiskey Park, or listening to the game on the radio, you felt a commonality with the other fans, and the sense that you did belong to a community larger than yourself. The players on the Sox had also started to display the same diversity as did the South Side itself. That trend started, if I remember right, with the Sox activating Luis Aloma, a Cuban. During my young adult life, there was of course, Nellie Fox, a more or less "usual" demographic type, but he was joined in the lineup by Aloma's fellow Cuban, Minnie Minoso, who specialized in getting hit by pitches, and then the Venezuelans Chico Carrasquel and Luis Aparicio. It was an entertaining team, always bouncing around the standings in the middle of the American league, until, course the pennant year of 1959, when we all had our hearts broken in losing to the Dodgers in the World Series.

Seasoned with dancing and baseball, the soup of our relationship simmered along at a slow comfortable pace. We got engaged at some point, with the intention of getting married after I turned 21, and after we had saved at least some money.

We did the "meet the family" thing. I was delighted and a little surprised that Jaro really liked Emilio. It made me realize that I had never observed Jaro in a male companionship situation. Francisco and Carmela, Emilio's parents, liked me fine, and I them, but my most amusing relationship within Emilio's family was with his older sisters, Isabella and Esmerelda, or "Is y Es", as Emilio fondly referred to them, as if they were really one person, like they behaved a lot of the time. They were, at the time, unmarried, and since they had spent most of their young life together, had an uncommon rapport. In my presence, they would gossip happily in quiet Spanish tones, largely about me, not suspecting that because of my six years of Junior High and High School Spanish and close acquaintance with my close Friend, Esmerelda Mendoza, I could read, understand and speak the language.

I strung them along, even while they were talking about the "skinny gringa" or some such thing. About the third time we were all together and they were asking each other in Spanish which burrowing animal's fur my hair color most resembled, I went over to where they we sitting, looked them both in the eye and said "¿quieres café o té con la cena?" (Would you like coffee or tea with dinner?). They looked sheepishly at each other, broke into their musical laughs and said " La broma esta en nostros, hermana!" (The joke is on us, sister!), and each gave me a hug.

Having passed the family test, we set a date for our wedding: June 14, 1952. As if things could not get better, in the fall of 1950, the HR supervisor of Senior Female Employees called me into her office, seated me at her desk, upon which I could see my personnel file, and said:

" Miss Hruskova, you have been with us for a long period. You have done extremely well in every position you have occupied. We want you to consider becoming a Marshall Field's Personal Shopper.

I thought to myself "Consider? What do I have to do?

Bite nails? Jump out of a plane? Wrestle a bear? Bring it on!" but merely said, with as much calm as I could muster, "Thank you ma'am. I would very much appreciate the opportunity."

And so, on top of the world in all respects, I started my training as a Personal Shopper. At any given time there were eight to ten women on staff who were Personal Shoppers. I was in a "class" of three women who were filling that number of spots that uncharacteristically became available at the same time. Because we were all store veterans, we already were familiar with store inventory, lay-outs, promotional activities and all of the details that the floor clerks live and breathe. The essence of the PS training was to teach us to cultivate and respect the unique relationship that a store patron expected in a Personal Shopper.

How the program worked was that an interested customer would apply, through Customer Service, for the Personal Shopper program. There was a fee, an initial $100 (a lot of money in 1949), and the same amount on an annual basis. That fee bought a newsletter with special announcements of new lines, holiday events, sales, and the like; access to the special Patron's Lounge on the sixth floor, and, of course the services of the Personal Shopping staff. While the patrons were free to use any PS, most of the time, a one-on-one relationship resulted.

The employment circumstances of the Personal Shoppers included the fact that, unlike department clerks and assistants, who were expected to be noticeable to all shoppers by adhering to the dress code (white blouse, dark skirt) and wearing a store name badge, Personal Shoppers were intended to be anonymous, such that when you saw a PS with client, you would assume that you were looking at two women who were shopping together. A PS got to "model" several of the new featured items in the store. For me, this perk was beyond price. We got a salary, better than the clerk position, regular hours (or by appointment at the mutual convenience of PS and client), and a small commission on client purchases. And, while the store did not either condone or prohibit the practice, it was common for a client to tip her PS, to recognize her for holidays and even include her in wedding invitations. The whole arrangement had the feeling for me as if I were a lady-in-waiting in the court of a European queen. Far beyond just providing a living, being a Marshall Field's personal shopper was for me an expression of my personal attitudes and abilities, and one that was largely within my control. This was, I realized at this point, in clear distinction from the jobs that Jaro and his generation, had, whether they liked them or not, and without regard to being fulfilled as a person.

I was soaring like an eagle.

And then we got married.

## 11

# What does the Lady want?

In the years after I started as a PS, and before the date of our wedding, that being essentially the years of 1951 and the first part of 1952, both Emilio and I flourished modestly. He was promoted to manager of his branch. I had right at ten regular clients at the store who were interesting and adventurous liberal spenders. Emilio and I spent lots of time together, with dances, dinners, family events. We came to be regarded as a married couple, even if we did not live together.

Zofie loved planning the wedding, especially with the access to the resources I had at Marshall Field's. I had a traditional white wedding dress with veil and train that Zofie insisted on altering and fitting to meet her particular standards. She designed and fitted individually my bridesmaids' dresses, which were sheath-skirted, cowl-collared, and in forest green, my favorite color. Emilio, after some grumbling, consented to tailcoat tuxes for himself and the groomsmen, courtesy of the formalwear department of MF.

St. Pancratius was packed to the rafters with our friends and extended families. It was amusing to observe the people on the groom's side looking around the sanctuary and imagining them thinking. "This does not look like any Catholic Church I have ever seen! It is dark, colorless, and reminds me of a stone catacomb."

The ceremony went off without a hitch. In a nod to the cross-cultural nature of the crowd, the reception was held in the Parish Hall of St. Ann, Emilio's family church. It became the turn of my family to remark on surroundings not being consistent with their personal experience of a Catholic Church. But with the beer, the plentiful and delicious Mexican and Polish food, great Latin dancing music, and general conviviality, we became, at least for that evening, one big diverse family.

Emilio and I took off for a short honeymoon to Lake Geneva, and returned home to our new apartment at 47th and Wood, in Pilsen, about two blocks from Emilio's parents' house.

Like went on pretty much as it had before, at the Bank, and at Marshall Field's. Social life was a lot easier, since we ended any "dates" in the same place. Hardly a bump in the road.

Until, that is, as was inevitable, in light of being young, married, healthy and Catholic, I got pregnant. When I was about three months in, I went in to see Mrs. Sheffield, the HR director at Marshall Field's to see about the maternity leave policy.

"Well, Mrs. ...... Rosales" she said, having had to look at my file to come up with my "new" name, "the company is very firm about this topic. You must go on leave while pregnant. You will be on leave status, starting tomorrow. You are certainly welcome, and encouraged, to come back after your baby is born."

"What is wrong with the state of being pregnant? I feel fine and can do my normal duties. Marshall Field's sells maternity clothes. Women get pregnant all of the time. Why can't I decide when I stop work?"

"I'm sorry, I do not make the rules, but the Company is very firm on the point. We do not find it seemly for women to work while they are pregnant."

'You mean, the MEN in the company think it unseemly', I said to myself, as I left the room in stunned silence. I cleaned out my employee locker, for what proved to be the last time, said goodbye to some of the colleagues in the store, and went home.

That began the worst period of my life. There was a whole lot less money coming into the household I was at home, in an unfamiliar neighborhood, without anything really to do. I did not like to listen to the radio during the day, we didn't yet have a television. We didn't have a car. I didn't really know anybody nearby, except my in-laws, and as much as I liked them, I certainly was not going to spend huge blocks of time with them. To stave off madness, I set up my sewing machine in the spare bedroom, and repaired every clothing item of mine and of Emilio's that needed mending. I relined coats. I sewed curtains for the baby room, and made an enormous quantity of baby clothes. Zofie would often take the bus over to visit and we would either sew together or just sit and talk.

The final stages of pregnancy, particularly a first pregnancy, pass at a rate that decelerates to the point that it seems that time has stopped, and that there is a chance that the end of the experience will never be reached. Until one day, unanticipated, things start to happen, in rapid succession. Water breaks; throw items into pre-packed suitcase; trip to the hospital; medical professionals, testing, preparing, counseling. Delivery room; exhortations to push, breath, relax; indescribably uncomfortable expulsion; relief.

But the sense that the important mission has been completed is obliterated on that moment when you are handed the child you have been carrying with you for months, and you know in looking into that child's eyes that you now have a fixed and immutable mission in life: to create advantage and opportunity for this child by whatever means you have at your disposal. In my case, where I had been drifting about in a rudderless ship since I had been unceremoniously booted out of Marshall Field's, I now was at the helm of a sleek, full powered yacht, having electronic navigation tools to guide it to a very precise destination.

Hello, Ines. I am your Mom. Let's get to work.

So, I became a full time mother. I suppose I could have gone back to the store, but child care was more or less non-existent, unless you took unfair advantage of your parents and in-laws. But the real reason I didn't go back is that I didn't want to. I dedicated my time to not only the necessities of Ines's daily life, but also her education and enrichment.

It became immediately apparent that, because I no longer brought in a significant salary, our household income was inadequate to cover those additional expenses.

When I mentioned the fact to Emilio, he was less than sympathetic.

"E.", I said when Ines was about a year old, "You know that we need more money to take care of what we want to provide to Ines. Have you thought about looking for a better job, or taking the training to move up at the Bank?"

"Well, no, Hattie, I haven't", he said, after a pause, bristling a bit. "I like my job. I know the people. I know the work. I am happy where I am."

And that was that. I attempted to emulate Zofie by taking in alterations, but cheap, mass-produced clothes had all but eliminated the former interest in maintaining old, but serviceable items. Emilio got modest raises at the Bank, but it was clear that the Bank would rather pay its employees with titles, rather than money.

Navigation through the financial straits got more difficult as we were joined by our sons Roberto, in 1956 and Javier, in 1958. They were, and are, great kids, were blessings to the family, but they did eat their share of food, wear their share of clothes, and participate in their share of kid activities. We had to move to a three bedroom apartment, at an increased rent. I did whatever temporary or part time jobs were available when the kids could be looked after by someone else.

It was not just the money. We had finally purchased a television, and it drew Emilio like a magnet to all of the sports on it. With this fundamentally unsocial absorption in sports on television, the discontinuation of our dance dates, and his enduring commitment to softball and bowling with his men friends I came to the realization that "The Hattie and Emilio Story" was a novel for which new chapters were not being written. I don't want to be misunderstood, Emilio was never a bad man, he never drank too much, he never abused me or the kids. But he had stopped being interested in our relationship. As a consequence, he became less interesting to me.

As a result, sometime about in the Spring of 1961, I remember thinking that at one time I was dedicated to an organization whose mantra was "Give the lady what she wants". Where was I to get what I wanted?

## 12

# Tupperware

The answer to my question came from an unlikely source. At one point, I think it was in March of 1961, Denisa Torres, one of the other mothers from Ines' school asked me if I wanted to go to a Tupperware Party.

"What in the world is Tupperware?" I asked, thinking, but not saying, "And why would you give a party for it?"

"Oh, it's that plastic stuff that you can seal leftovers in. The hostess has the party at her house, and has a bunch of women over to look it over, and maybe buy some. It is actually kind of a fun evening. And you will never meet anyone like the hostess, Milly."

As I look back on it, that understatement marked the turning point of my life. Not really knowing what to expect, I did decide to dress up a bit, selecting a short sleeve pink shift with matching pillbox hat. Not wishing to look "too too", I skipped the gloves. Denisa picked me up for the ride south.

Ludmilla "Milly" Netsurov lived in a small single family house on Vincennes Ave. South of 121$^{st}$ St Place, not too far from where I grew up. Milly was a widow, her husband, Vladimir, having died in 1959 in a trucking accident at the mill where he worked. She had two kids, Hugo and Katarina, who were just older and just younger than Ines.

When we arrived, the house was already energized by the convivial interactions among the women guests, who were talking to each other in laughing, hugging groups, after having helped themselves to the refreshments which were small hors d'oeuvres, carrot and celery sticks and white wine. Every woman was dressed to a degree beyond that which would be usual at, say, a PTA meeting, all out of apparent respect for each other, our host and the occasion. Mine was not the only hat in the room. I felt my spirits lift, just as soon as I came in the door. I should have worn the gloves.

Milly's appearance was deceptively ordinary. She was about my height, solid in a way that was not obese, but in a way that very much reminded me of Nina Khrushcheva who we all saw in the news all of the time. As a person of Slavic stock myself, I recognized her body type as representative of lots of my female relatives. It made me feel at home. She had a round face with prominent cheekbones. When she smiled, which she did often, not only did the corners of her mouth curve up, but the corners of her eyes curved down, giving the impression that she was grinning at you with her entire visage. So the deception was that the more you regarded this completely ordinary woman, the more complex you perceived her to be.

That night, she was wearing a simple straight-cut skirt, with matching short jacket that she had removed and a short sleeve light grey collarless blouse set off by a single strand silver necklace. Straight-forward, no nonsense stuff, which I would come to know as Milly's trademark.

"Welcome, friends. Go ahead and refresh your drinks, if you want. After a bit, we'll get to the business of the evening, but first, as always, I want for all of us to get to know each other better" Milly announced, and then started around the room, asking each of us to either introduce herself, or in the case of about half of the guests, say a little more about herself than she had on previous occasions.

When she got to me and I had told a little about me, she said "Rosales....?" "Born Hruskova" I answered the unspoken question. "I thought so. Welcome, Hattie. Nice hat, by the way."

After she had heard from all of us, she went over to the dining room table, where she had laid out the Tupperware samples. "Here are the brand-new items" she said, indicating and describing each. She went over all of those and the standard items, with animation and confidence. The dramatic point of the sales presentation was when Milly partially filled one of the Tupperware containers with liquid, snapped the lid into place and turned the sealed container upside-down. The contents did not leak. "Preserves freshness" Milly said, with emphasis. By the end of the evening, most of us had purchased or ordered something from the Tupperware line.

The group started to filter out, all around, I supposed, kids' bedtimes in the nine o'clock range. Emilio was taking care of the kids, and Denisa was in no hurry to leave, so I stayed on, enjoying the company until there about six of us left, at which point Milly asked "Who wants to play some poker?" The ones of us who were left did. I was pretty comfortable with card games, mostly because I could remember and keep count of what had been played.

Milly sold us 5 and 10 cent chips to use in the quarter-limit 5 card draw game that followed. It didn't take me long to realize that the chips were being inexorably drawn, as if by a gravitational force, into Milly's stack. By the end of the evening, I had lost the $5 of chips that I started with. I did not have bad cards, I did not do anything foolish, but, nonetheless, I did lose convincingly.

"You'll have better luck next time, Hattie" Milly said to me as Denisa and I said goodbye to her on her doorstep." "There won't be a next time, at least for poker," I thought to myself.

So when the next Tupperware Party by Milly rolled around about a month after the first, you could not keep me away from the most satisfying female camaraderie I had experienced since leaving Marshall Field's some eight years ago. After the evening which had both the same format, and same satisfactory feel, I did hang around for the poker, but feigned insolvency, and offered to get drinks, refresh ice and snack trays while the others played. I was intensely interested to see what Milly was doing to be such a winner. It had briefly occurred to me that she was cheating somehow. On careful scrutiny, that idea just didn't work. The cards were not marked. Milly was not peeking. What gradually dawned on me was that what made Milly a great poker player was the care with which she observed everything about her fellow players: posture, gestures, vocal intonations, breathing rate until she was able to "read" their intentions, and know why they had formed them, as if she could project her vision onto the retinas of the players, and actually see their cards. I also realized that this mastery of practical psychology was also the reason she was good at sales: she could sense how to connect her product with the desires of the buyer. Suddenly, the phrase "Give the lady what she wants" flashed into my head for the first time in years.

I became a regular at the Tupperware parties, and got to know Milly better and better, not only at the parties, but doing other activities together, like shopping, taking kids to the zoo, and other excursions that are just more fun with two adults. She got to know my kids as people; I got to know hers.

## 13

# M&H Inc.

But it was not just social connections that drove our relationship forward. I began to get glimpses of the sophisticated thinking that resulted in what can only be called the philosophy of Milly's life.

For example, on one afternoon after the two of us had returned to my apartment after some sort of outing in her clunker of a 1953 Chevy, we had gotten to talking about, of all things, religion. I was raised Catholic, had gone to Catechism classes, had been confirmed and had never really thought about the relative importance of that belief structure to my own personal life direction. More particularly, I had started to think about what religion meant to me at this point of my life.

After listening to me describe this minor crisis of belief, and after a bit of reflection where she looked off at the horizon and then looked back at me with the gaze that read poker hands, and said "Think about it this way" which phrase, I came to learn was the introduction to a well-reasoned thought process that I would never, but for Milly, have engaged in myself, and took a long time to really appreciate.

"Think about it this way. Have you ever seen God?"

"No" I said, not knowing where this was going.

"Do you know anyone who has seen God?"

"No" I had to answer.

"Then how do you know about God?"

"Well, people educated about the character of God instruct us about what God wants us to do."

"Have these people ever seen, heard, talked to or gotten letters from God?"

"Well, no."

"So does it make sense to form one's own beliefs based on the beliefs of others who are just acting on hearsay information?"

"Well maybe not, but people need some sort of moral compass."

"Agreed. But why not set that compass based on a personal set of values, and on a serious internal appraisal of keenly perceived moral imperatives, rather than going blindly through the cafeteria line of organized religion, and having a lot of pre-processed garbage slopped on your tray?"

Without a coherent response, and knowing that it would take days to sort this out in my own mind, I just said "Goodnight, Milly," as I got out of the car and went up to our apartment.

As Milly and I grew closer, it was natural for me to help her out more with the Tupperware parties, in planning the events, making sure that an ever wider circle of customers had the opportunity to attend, and actually ordering the supplies that would be offered for sale.

The sales kept climbing until the point, about a year after I first met Milly, that is to say in the spring of 1962, that Milly said "Hattie, I would like for us to be partners in this business. You have contributed a lot with both your hard work and your sense of style."

"You don't need to do that Milly. I do what I do because I like it, and I like you."

"But you can't eat 'like'" Milly observed. "We can both do well in this."

And so, M&H, Inc. was born. We formally incorporated it, agreed on the profit division and worked hard at it. I would be lying to say that the small income it provided was not welcome in the Rosales household.

So we worked along until late October of that year when Ines had her epiphany. To that point, Ines, despite my constant prompting, had no real interest in anything, seeming to be content to sidle anonymously through life as an unremarked and unremarkable kid.

But then in fourth grade, something, and I never discovered just what, struck her like sudden F5 tornado, and converted Ines into an ambitious dynamo. Her grades shot up. She cared about her appearance. She started keeping a journal. She was interested in the sewing projects I was doing. And she had formed some educational plans.

"Mom, Miss Terrell says that she thinks that I should apply for the Journalism Camp next summer at Northwestern. I only need $300 for the entry fee, and a basic camera for the photography session."

"We'll see what we can do, Ines. When do you have to know?" I asked not knowing where in the blazes I was going to find $300.

"Applications are due March 1, 1963."

I was put in mind of the fact that Ines, to this point, had asked for nothing, and also of the fact of the silent pledge that I had made to her when the nurse first put her into my arms, to do all in my power to assist her in fulfilling her promise, whatever it was.

But what exactly had lit Ines's pilot light?

## 14

# The Red Barette

It really was all Miss Terrell's fault.

All of the elementary school teachers we had up to now were youngish women, about the same age as our mothers, who were kind, no-nonsense adults who treated up like a large beloved herd of sheep, rather than a group of individuals.

I found that sort of relationship very comfortable, like with Mrs. Giambi last year in third grade, who was in the habit of regularly asking "Isn't that right, boys and girls?" To which she expected the choral response "Yes, Mrs. Giambi", which answer we made whether what she had just said made any sense at all or was just plain wrong.

I also liked being a member of the "boys and girls" with the expectations and responsibilities the same for each of us in behavior, learning and cultural awareness. It was easy to do well in that kind of system.

But then we landed with Miss Terrell, who looked like she was just out of high school. On the first day of fourth grade, she made each one of us stand up at our desks, say our names, and tell something about our families and what we liked to do. There was a lot of slouching, mumbling and blushing, none of which seemed to bother Miss Terrell. She listened carefully to each of us, taking care to pronounce all of our names correctly, and asked questions to fill in her background files, like "Do you have brothers and sisters, Umberto?" or "Do you have a pet, Marisela?" When it was my turn, and I stood to describe my Dad, Emilio, my dopey little brothers, Roberto and Javier, and my Mother, Hattie, I heard my enemy, Mercedes Munoz, snort just loudly enough for me to hear her from two rows away.

Mercedes makes me sick. She is, even at ten years old, beautiful and self-confident, everything I was not. She was wearing a twin set, with a navy skirt. I was modeling a sleeveless, shapeless jumper of a neutral brown. Her beautiful black hair was perfectly cut and as always looking like it never needed a comb or brush. My hair was held haphazardly in place by a barrette. I have three barrettes to my name, the brownish one I was wearing today, the line of white daisies, and the red bow that I saved for special occasions. My barrettes always made me feel slightly lopsided, while Mercedes had even figured out how to make the gold cross that we all wore look like a fashion statement, not just like another ear tag in a herd of cattle. Her body is in correct proportion to her height, not all knobs and angles, like mine. Her parents, Ernesto and Rosa ran the combined grocery store and Mexican restaurant about a block from our apartment, which served as the cultural and commercial center of our neighborhood. Her folks were friendly, knew everybody and were kind to the point of carrying on credit our neighbors who were having a tough time. Mercedes was completely the opposite; she was just mean. When she found an uncomfortable fact about someone, she would just keeping picking at it, like a sore.

In my case, it was my Mom. My Mom is an Anglo, a mix of a bunch of different Central European countries. Her name is Henrietta, but everyone calls her Hattie. I look like my Dad, but my skin tone is noticeably (to people like Mercedes, and to me) lighter than the kids who have two Hispanic parents.

"Eh, blanquita. You and your Mama havin' tea with the Queen?" Mercedes would say, always in the hearing of lots of other kids. Her message was that I was the racial equivalent of a saddle shoe, and a beaten up one, at that.

When I tell Mom about these incidents, she just says: "I've been there, Ines. You just have to forget about it, and be the person who you are, in the best way you can. The important people in your life do and will love you for who you are. Your job right now is to figure out who that is." I never find this very convincing or reassuring, but since she works about three jobs and is busy with my Dad and my brothers, that's about all I can get out of her.

Miss Terrell kept up with her concern with each of us, and our individual progress in reading, math and penmanship. She would have frequent one-on-one conferences with us.

"Ines Rosales, you can do better in every subject. I don't think that you are lazy, but I do think that you haven't looked for the reason to do well. Let me just say this: You do it for you. That is all you need to know", Miss Terrell told me in our September conference. I took her comments seriously, and tried to now look at schoolwork as a proving ground for me. My grades went up.

In our October conference, I brought up the subject of Mercedes. "Ines, don't you think I know all about poor Mercedes?" Miss Terrell asked. This was the first time I had ever associated the concept of "poor" either in terms of resources or pitiability, with Mercedes. "Her problem is that she is just not smart enough to find anything to think about or do, other than picking on others." She continued, "Do you know what I think, Ines? I think you could be a writer. Writing is hard. You have to drill two very difficult holes. First, you have to drill through your shell to find what you perceive, what you believe and what you know is true. Then you have to drill through the reader's shell and pour in those perceptions, beliefs and truths, just as you found them." She paused while this sunk in, and said "You should start with a journal and write in it every day. It is the beginning of your story."

About in that time, Mercedes showed up at school with a beautiful new coat, burgundy, three-quarters length, with a fake fur collar, and four large color-coordinated buttons. It did look like something from a fashion magazine. And didn't Mercedes know it? She only reluctantly took it off, and was the first person into the cloak room to put it on for recess or to go home. The coat became her weapon of choice in her character war on me. At recess, she yelled, when I was just within earshot: "Hey Ines, where does a jojota get a hand-me-down coat? Goodwill? Salvation Army? Dumpster?" At that moment, a part of my brain meshed into state of calmness and understanding. I walked over to her, looked down into her face and said: "Mercedes, you are mean and you talk nonsense. Just stay out of my life," and walked away.

Two days later, right after afternoon recess, Miss Terrell stood in the front of the room and said "Class, this is a serious matter. Someone has vandalized Mercedes' coat. We cannot have that sort of thing happening around here. Whoever did this will be severely punished. Mercedes is so upset she had to go to the nurse's office, and her parents are on the way to take her home. Let us not see anything like this again." She looked in my direction, noticing, I thought, my red barrette. I looked down at my desk with my hands in the pockets of my jumper, fiddling with my mother's sewing scissors, and four large coat buttons.

As I left the cloak room at the end of the day, Miss Terrell, who was waiting for me said, quietly, "Now, THAT is a story."

## 15

# E-Z Loan Company

HATTIE; NOVEMBER 1962

I told Milly about my quandary as we sat on the park bench in Beverly Park, about half way between our houses, where we had become accustomed to discussing serious topics.

"So you need some money" Milly said, looking off in the direction opposite me, and then looking back directly at me. "Are you ready for a new challenge that can prove very financially worthwhile?"

"Sure."

"All right. I am going to arrange a meeting for you with a colleague of mine. I will go with you. If that works out, it can be most rewarding for you. It will take a couple of days to make it happen."

That is how Milly and I came to be driving her car south along Western Avenue on a weekday in the second week of November.

"We will be meeting with Sid. Sid is, at first meeting,

kind of a strange guy. Do not say anything to him unless he asks you something directly. Let me do all of the talking. I will explain later."

We continued down Western Avenue until we turned left onto 121th St Place and then right to the parking behind the strip of commercial buildings fronting on Western Avenue. We parked and walked around to the front of the building, to the door next to the sign "E-Z Loan Company".

"We're getting a loan?" I asked, incredulously. "No talking. Explanations later." Milly said as she knocked on the door.

"Come" the rough-voiced response grated through the door. We went in.

The room looked like no loan company I had ever seen, or imagined. There were no calendars on the wall, no pens on chains on tall tables full of application forms, no rate charts with exhortations to "Lock in Today". There was only a single desk, with two straight back desk chairs on the door side of the desk and a similar one on the other side in which the gravelly voiced proprietor sat. Sid, I remembered that Milly called him. Sid had a severely short haircut, dark glasses, and a dark sport coat over a white shirt open at the neck. He did not get up when we came in. He held his hands out of sight, presumably on his lap.

"Hello, Sid" Milly said, with a bit of a forced good nature. "This is Hattie, the one I was telling you about." We sat in the desk chairs, me on the left side, Sid's right and Milly on the right.

From the position of his head (since you couldn't actually see his eyes) Sid was looking steadily at Milly.

"Can she do the job?" Sid grated as he looked only at Milly.

"Yes, she can" said Milly, without hesitation.

Then Sid turned his face to me, looked at me for long enough to take my photo, if he were a camera, folded his hands on the desk in front of him, turned back to Milly and said: "Train her up and let me know when she is ready for a closing."

"Thanks, Sid" Milly said, and, as the interview was at an end, gestured towards the door and led me out.

I waited until we got to the car before I blurted "Now what in the world was that about."

"Let's go back to the park and I will tell you."

The reason that Milly liked Beverly Park was that it was across the street from her favorite Ukrainian bakery, Nonna Yana, which was right off Western on 103$^{rd}$ St. We parked in front of the bakery and went into the show room displaying glass cases filled with cakes, cookies and pastries, and exuding an atmosphere composed of the smells of honey, sugar, butter and baking spices that was so rich that each inhalation probably added five ounces to your body weight. There was a customer table at which sat a couple of elderly gentlemen in wool coats, happily stuffing their faces with poppy seed cake. On the wall was a price list showing the available items, in English and in

Cyrillic. Behind the counter with the cash register was a fiftyish woman wearing a white apron with her hair tied in a kerchief. She greeted Milly as we came in.

"Hi, Irena, nice to see you. This is my friend, Hattie Rosales."

Irena looked at me. "You don't look like a Rosales."

"And you don't look like a Nonna. I'm Hruskova by birth."

"Touché. Yana was my grandmother. But it is my show now," she said turning to Milly and asking, "What will you have?"

"What just came out of the oven?"

"Well, the chocolate bubka is probably cool enough to eat."

"Sounds good to me. Want one, Hattie?"

The bubka looked to me to be about the same volume as two enchiladas, so I said "I don't think I can eat a whole one, Can we share?"

"Great idea. We'll get a bubka and take it over to the park." Milly settled the bill and we walked across the street and sat on the bench overlooking the tennis courts at the southeast corner of the park. No one was playing tennis, because it was November, but I was struck by the sense of order and purpose that the green surface and white lines of the court gave. I finished my part of the bubka, dusted my fingers and turned to Milly impatiently. She methodically finished eating, took a deep breath, looked off to the horizon to her left, turned back to me and said:

"Okay, Hattie, here's the deal. What happens is that Sid will call you to come to his office when he is ready, and he gives you a file, usually with a picture of an individual, and some facts about where this individual lives and works and perhaps some other details. You take the file, study it, and then you kill that person. After you do, Sid will call you back in and give you a bunch of money.

I could have fallen right off the bench. "Are you out of your ever-living mind? The more I know you the less I understand anything about you! You want me to kill people for money? And you do this yourself? That can't be right, let alone legal!"

She looked at me with her small smile that made Mona Lisa look like Jimmy Durante, which smile I came to learn would often precede her signature line. "Think about it this way. I do not know, and do not want to know, the people that we and Sid work for, but it is clear that they have some rather rigorous standards of behavior for their employees, colleagues and competitors, and that they occasionally will feel that certain breaches of those standards, require that the offender die. You see, we do not decide that the subjects are to be eliminated, as that has already been decided. By the time we get those files, those people are dead men walking. If we don't kill them, somebody else will. We are like the Fates. You do know the Fates?"

"The who?" I said, bewildered.

"The Fates were the three sisters in Ancient Greek Mythology who spun, measured and cut the threads of life, as so determined the time of death of every individual. They were not viewed with fear, but as agents of predetermined destiny. That's what we are: agents of destiny. And the money is nice."

I was still trying to get all of this into my head. "Do they tell you how do you do it?"

"That is one of the great parts of the job, you get to plan the adventure, and the means of its completion."

"Isn't it dangerous?"

"Of course it's dangerous. Nobody likes to be killed. Most people will go to extraordinary, even violent, lengths to avoid it. The art is to perform the job without the subject having any idea of what is to happen."

There was a period of silence as I sat blinking and thinking.

After a bit, Milly said "Look Hattie. I like this job because it allows me to use my wits in a way that no other job available to me can, it gives me an autonomy that I am guessing is hard to find for any woman in this day and age, and it gives me an income that allows me to pay the mortgage and feed and clothe the kids. If I didn't do this, I would sit around the house, eat bubka all day long, weigh five hundred pounds and be totally unhappy. I do this because I want to, not because I have to."

As I gazed over the tennis courts, I imagined seeing on the nearest court, the figures of two tennis-clad women, confidently serving with authority, carefully placing powerful backhand, or clever lobs, and reveling in their collective skill.

"Okay, Milly. I'll do it. How do I start?"

"I'll pick you up tomorrow after the kids are off to school. Say nine? Wear something that you can comfortably move around in. And bring gloves. We're going shooting."

"Guns? I hate guns."

"Stick with me on this one. Tomorrow at nine."

## 16

# Life Insurance

Promptly at nine the next morning, Milly knocked on my door, asked "Ready?" and ushered me out in a business-like manner to her car. Milly was dressed in her everyday preferred outfit of a light colored, floral-patterned housedress, with short puffy sleeves, under a gray cloth short coat. She was carrying a large well-worn brown leather shoulder bag that I had not seen before. I had chosen a gray long sleeve blouse, with gray her-ringbone slacks. Since I was unclear as to what sort of headgear would be appropriate for a firing range, I did not wear a hat, but simply tied my hair back. My black pea coat finished it off.

As we drove into the west suburbs, Milly began her lecture.

"Before you start to learn the physical skills that you will need, there are two sets of rules that are important to know, and stick to."

"The first set is what I call 'Sid's Rules' and they are important to keep Sid and the people that we, and Sid, work for comfortable with us, and willing to use our services on a regular basis. The risk of breaking any of Sid's Rules is the possibility that your picture winds up in a file that Sid gives to someone else. Here they are:

- Do not ever call or visit E-Z Loans or Sid unless Sid calls you first.
- Do not ever write to, or acknowledge the existence or any connection with E-Z Loans.
- If you even run into Sid away from Western Avenue (and God help you if you do), you do not know him.
- Do not attempt to learn, or even think about the people behind E-Z loans.
- In performing a closing, do not get caught.
- If somehow you get caught, you are on your own
- Do not work for anyone else, or with anyone else, except me.
- Leave no witnesses.
- Never negotiate the commission for the closing.

Do they make sense? They do to me. Don't write them down but remember them.

The other set is my personal set of practical guidelines for carefully succeeding in this job, both physically and mentally. They're based on my practical experience. As I think about it, you can call them Milly's Rules:

- Research and plan the details of each closing with meticulous care.
- Always prepare a "plan B", equally detailed, usually involving a different closing method.
- Always wear gloves. Always.
- Never leave at the site of a closing weapons or physical evidence of any kind: gum, tissues, anything that could be conceivably connected with you.
- Never think about the reason for the closing.
- Never look a subject in the eye, or make any effort to personify him.
- Always take your gun.

And there are some special situation rules that we'll get to when they apply, like "When confronted with two subjects, eliminate the most dangerous one first. That is usually the one with the gun.'

Get all that? Don't worry, we'll go over it a lot."

By that time we had arrived at Mike's Guns and Ammo, a combination gun and ammunition sales outlet, gunsmith operation and firing range, all housed in a long one story building on Austin Boulevard in Cicero. Mike proved to be a sixty-something middle height fellow wearing half glasses on a chain that hung over a denim shirt and trousers that appeared uniformly stained with what must be gun oil. He had, and I was to learn, always had a cigarette in the corner of his mouth. "How does he not just burst into flames", I thought. He knew Milly.

"Need a lane?" Mike guessed. "Yes", Milly replied.
"An hour will do."
"Standard silhouette?"
"That's fine."
"Take lane one." ?
"Thanks, Mike."

We went into the range, which consisted of eight lanes of about four feet in width, each culminating with a target 75 feet away. Lane one ended with a paper target showing the dark outline of a human form, marked with lines, indicating critical areas. We were the only people on the range, so we didn't put on ear protection.

As we went in the door, I blurted out "Milly, I have to say this again. I HATE guns."

Milly looked at me with that wisp of a smile. "Think about it this way. You hate life insurance, don't you? You hate paying those darn regular premiums for something you never get the benefit of, because it deals with your death, not your life. Your gun is real life insurance, because it really can keep you alive. Let me demonstrate" she said as she put down her shoulder bag, put on a pair of gloves, and produced a conspicuous Luger. She snapped in an ammunition clip, and stepped to the firing line.

"That's a Nazi gun!" I shrieked, thinking of all of the war movie images in which lugers showed up in the hands of bad guys.

"Well, it is a gun" allowed Milly, "but it is just a tool, without a political or even moral philosophy. It does what I want to do, and I like it. Watch."

She put the gun in her left hand, and stood with her feet parallel to the firing line. Sighting over her left shoulder and fired, dotting the target right about in the center of the area representing the heart. She then switched the pistol into her right hand, turned one hundred eighty degrees, aimed and fired over her right shoulder. You could have covered both holes with a dime.

"See, Life Insurance, get it?" she asked me. "Aetna, I'm glad I met ya'" she facetiously told the gun.

"I'm beginning to understand the argument."

"Okay, it's your turn. Put on your gloves. Since we always wear them, I want you to get used to shooting while wearing them." I put my gloves on. Milly handed me the gun, after pointing out the trigger, the safety, and stepped back. "Fire away".

The whole thing felt awkward: the weight of the gun, the grip on the stock, how to orient one's feet. I pulled the trigger with the gun pointed in the general direction of the target. I am pretty sure that the paper did not even feel the breeze of the shot as it went past.

"I see that we need to go back to basics. See that vertical piece at the end of the barrel? And the notch on the part of the gun closest to you? That is the sight. The idea is to have the vertical piece appear in the notch while both are over the target. That zeros you in left and right. Up and down is trickier. You have to get used to where the base of the vertical needs to be. Try again." This time I gave the target a severe pain in its right elbow.

"I think you are jerking your hand right before you shoot. Try just squeezing the trigger, just gently enough to fire. And be sure you are using on the sight the eye that is on the same side as the hand in which you are holding the gun. Don't close the other one, but focus on the use of that one eye."

This time I got a collarbone.

"Better. Bye the way, how many shots do you have left?" I had no idea.

"With semi-automatics like this, you need to keep track of remaining bullets. We started with eight."

"Okay, you shot twice, and I did three, so there are three left."

"Good, shoot the last three with your left hand." I did that with less success but increasing accuracy with each shot.

"Now I will show you how to load the clip." And we did that.

And so we went to the range about twice a week. I got more comfortable with firing, and with either hand. After about three weeks, Milly said "Now, Hattie let's have you pick out a gun model that fits you."

Mike had several demos on hand of models that he sold. We had decided on a semi-automatic, which limited the range of choices somewhat. I didn't like shooting a .45 which felt like holding a cannon when it went off. In the end, I chose a Smith & Wesson 39-2, for the stated reason that it was about a quarter of a pound lighter than the Luger, but for the real reason (which I never told

Milly) that I liked its looks with the walnut panels on the stock, and that it went well with several of my outfits. At Milly's suggestion, and with the skill of Mike, I got a silencer for special applications. I did not like the gun, but didn't dislike it either, and got better and better at shooting it. I absorbed Milly's philosophy that guns were to be used only when necessary, and not for any emotional or self-lauditory purposes. We were not, as Milly would say, cowboys.

In addition to the firing range, we also visited Tony's Gym where we got general physical training, like lifting light weights, and skipping rope, but also for me, at Milly's recommendation as a satisfied former student, Tony's special brand of training, gleaned from his years as a Navy SEAL, in the use of hand to hand weapons, like knives and garrotes. Tony was about my height, with about 30% more muscle mass, and of Italian extraction. He had a special respect and affinity for Milly that seemed to carry over to me. Through the use of mannequins and dummies, and training films, I learned where the vulnerable points were and how best to exploit those vulnerabilities.

Somewhere in the process of this unconventional training, I was struck by the fact that I was absorbing all of these new basics with the same degree of attention as I had to the training at Marshall Field's. Time flew.

In March of 1963, on the way back to Pilsen from Tony's, Milly announced "You're ready. I will have Sid give you a closing.

## 17

# First Closing

I got the call at home.
"This is Sid, see me tomorrow 10 AM."

I of course called Milly.

"I will go with you this first time. Sid won't mind. I will pick you up at nine."

I was nervous about this meeting, but not to the point of being disabled from thinking, or of planning what I would wear. I chose a perhaps over-the-top femme fatale, all red suit, with complementary red fedora (thin brim, no feather). I carried a red clutch.

When Milly arrived and took a look at me, she just shook her head and said "Hattie, I think we all do this job in our own way, with our own style. I love your style, never lose it."

We drove, in silence, down Western Avenue to E-Z Loans, parked in the back, walked around to the front, and knocked.

"Come" intoned the human voice through the gravel. We went in.

Sid looked pretty much the same, except that he was not wearing dark glasses, and he was looking directly, intensely, at me, even though Milly was with me.

"Miss Rosales", Sid started making it clear that he did not give a damn about my proper title, or anything else about me as a person. "We do business for the first time."

He reached into the drawer of the desk, pulled out a file, and propelled it across the desk to me. Sensing that this was expected of me, I opened the file which had on top an 8 by 10 photograph of a 70ish man, bald, with round, wire-rimmed glasses.

"This man has stolen our money. Repeatedly. In an underhand way. You have a week to eliminate him. Are there questions?"

I actually had approximately two thousand questions, but said, after looking over at Milly, "No."

"Do it. Good Luck. We will know when it is done."

Milly and I left. "Hattie, let's go to my place and look at that file."

We sat at her dining room table, as she read through it. " This guy lives in Skokie, is unmarried and is otherwise unremarkable, except that he worked for Sid's bosses. Let's do our first recon." So we drove north, found the address, and start the Milly-prescribed detailed planning.

Milly had emphasized this phase of a closing; personally observing every detail of the intended closing site.

This is where Milly's learning about determining whether anyone else lived in the subject's house, whether he
had a dog or dogs, came into focus. This was another
point where Milly's knowledge came into play: in order
to stake out a subject properly, one could not be conspicuous in any way.

I came to learn the Milly Philosophy of Disguise.
"Disguise, or the art of being unobserved as out of the
ordinary, consists, first, of appearing to be part of the
scenery or background, and second, having a disguise
that diverts a casual observer's attention to the details
of the disguise, and away from the features of the wearer" Milly said, "And that is what I like about your hats,
Hattie; I always find myself looking at them, not you. So
that, for example, if you were in a police line-up, without
your hat, I might have a hard time picking you out, even
having seen you."

So on this job, which involved spending time in a residential area of a suburban community, we assumed the
personae of domestics. We always wore work clothes,
and, from time to time would get out of the car and conspicuously arrange the buckets and mops that we had
brought along with the idea that anyone seeing us on a
quiet street would just assume us to be the cleaning ladies hired by someone in the neighborhood.

After a couple of days of fairly intense scrutiny, we
concluded that our subject, in addition to living alone,
and not having a pet, did not go out of his house very
often, and had no visitors that we ever saw.

It remained for us to come up with a credible, non-threatening method of getting access to him in his house.

The answer came to us as we watched the UPS rumble to a stop at a house about a block away.

"Flowers. Our guy is going to get a delivery of flowers."

So Milly helped me track down an FTD floral delivery truck, follow it around until the driver took a break for lunch and borrowed the truck. We had already come up with an FTD uniform of a white shirt, with the name "Herb" stitched in cursive over the pocket and sporting the logo of the guy with wings on his feet and his hat, dark slacks, and one of those six-cornered caps with a bill.

With Milly's help, I put on the uniform, tucked my hair into my hat put on my gloves, checked to be sure there some floral arrangement in the truck that I could deliver, and prepared to drive to Skokie.

Milly stopped me briefly as I stepped up into the truck.

"You know the plan. Follow it. Remember the rules. I won't wish you 'good luck', because in our business it is unwise to rely on luck. Do well." She hugged me.

And so I headed off on my first independent professional assignment since the French Room Millinery Salon at Marshall Field's. On the way, I could not help but think about the story I had constructed about the subject. I figured that he was some kind of accountant, who handled cash for Sid's employers, and had figured out some way of skimming off, to his own benefit, small but significant and regular amounts. He had worked for these guys for lots of years and was probably ready to retire. His life circumstances did not suggest that he was rolling in the dough. He probably was not a real bad guy.

I rolled the truck to a stop in front of his house, taking care to see whether there were any casual observers either in the form of service people on the street or residents out gardening or washing their windows. None. I did not even detect any breaks in the neighbors' blinds that would indicate someone peeking out.

I went to the back of the truck and carefully got out the spray of two dozen red roses into which I had carefully placed the Smith & Wesson, with the suppressor attached. I went up the front walk and rang the bell. No one answered the first ring, but after I rang again, I heard slow footfalls approach the door. It opened.

"Wha'd'ya want? The subject asked, roughly. He was looking at me through the face in the 8X10 photo. He was a little shorter than I had imagined, was wearing a shapeless cardigan over wrinkled brown slacks. He was holding the newspaper he had been reading.

"Flower delivery" I said in the kind of bright voice that I felt was suitable for an FTD person.

"I never get flowers" the subject observed with a combination of sadness and disbelief.

I was about to say something like "Oh, I'm sure that you do" or something like that, but I heard Milly's voice say "Do not engage with your subject. Do your job."

I took a controlled breath, made sure of my grip on the trigger, pointed the barrel towards him, took a step inside, away from the still-open door, said "Here, these are for you", pushed the bundle towards him and fired. A few roses, stems severed by the bullet, fell to the floor.

I made the mistake that Milly had been to great pains to warn me against: I looked the subject in the eye as I shot him. I read there, in the short time before he toppled backwards into his entryway, first surprise, then anger, and then the extremely disconcerting notion that he was looking at me in order to freeze my being into his memory, so that he could stalk me throughout eternity, for revenge.

I dropped the rest of the roses on the mess that his chest had become, after having retrieved my gun. I left as quickly but as inconspicuously as I was able, and drove the truck as well as I could amid the growing feeling of disgust that was crashing over me like storm clouds off the lake, easterly along Touhy Avenue, and up to Touhy Park. I parked the truck and ducked into the women's rest room, where I peeled off the FTD shirt and cap, stuffed them into my shoulder bag for later incineration, took a breath, and immediately was volcanically ill. I splashed some water on my face, put on my jacket from the bag, and walked the block to the Touhy station of the Red Line.

I don't remember much about the ride back to my apartment, except that whenever I looked out of the window at the scenery, all I could see were my subject's eyes, clicking that last snapshot of me before death.

I got home about 2PM before the kids got home from school. Milly's Chevy was parked across the street from our place. I had just taken off my jacket when the doorbell rang.

"How did it go?" Milly asked anxiously, as she burst into the room. She looked at me and stopped.

"Hattie, you look terrible. Are you okay?"

"Well, I don't know, Milly, I guess I am not cut out for this work."

"You completed the closing, right?" she asked, her voice rising slightly in pitch.

"Oh, no problem there. I just was unprepared for...... well, how it feels."

She looked me closely in the eye, put her arm on my shoulder and led me to the big armchair in the living room. She sat opposite on the couch.

"You broke the rule, didn't you? You allowed yourself to personify the subject. You didn't look him in the eye, did you?" When I didn't say anything, she said "You did! Don't do that ever again! You see the reason I told you that."

"Well, I won't do it again, because there won't be a next time. I feel so dirty and insignificant."

She looked off in the distance. I should have seen it coming. I did when the little smile appeared.

"Think about it this way. In ancient Egypt, the people revered the beetles called scarabs. Those beetles gathered manure from larger animals, rolled it into perfectly spherical balls, and pushed those balls into their own nests for food and for breeding grounds. Rather than thinking of the scarabs as dirty bugs, the Egyptians revered them as analogous to their Sun God who tirelessly and artfully rolled the sphere of the Sun across the heavens. Pharaoh Amenhotep III used the form of the scarab to commemorate important events and achievements. So, we are like scarabs in that, while we may do something regarded as dirty, if we do so carefully and tirelessly, we can be regarded as fulfilling a divine mission."

It was like being slapped in the face to be woken up. I no longer was feeling abjectly sorry for myself. I blinked a few times, trying to process this latest revelation.

"Milly, you are making all this stuff up! First we are talking about Greek goddesses weaving and cutting threads of life, and now we are Pharaoh-approved, poop ball pushing beetles!"

"Really the only point I am making here is that how you regard yourself should not only be based on what you do in life, but how you do it and if you do it with respect for the job, and for yourself. Also, I remind you that the subjects that Sid picks out for us are not just random people, but individuals who, in one way or another, have subscribed to the code, the penalty for breaking which is their elimination. They have assumed the risk of their errors."

"And one more thing" Milly said, "Do me a favor. Don't be turning in your two-week notice until after we see Sid. Let me know when he calls, and I will give you a ride down."

"Fair enough."

Sid's call came at nine the next morning. "Be here at 11 this morning." I called Milly, hustled myself into a dark suit, with white blouse and a string of faux pearls, and an Audrey Hepburn style half hat in gray.

We presented ourselves at E-Z loans at 11 sharp, to be greeted by Sid's now-familiar-to-me "Come". He was dressed as was his custom in dark jacket and white open-necked shirt. I realized that I had never seen him standing, so had no idea as to his taste in trousers. He was not wearing his dark glasses. For the first time in my experience, he looked primarily at me, rather than primarily at Milly. He reached his hands from his lap over to one of the middle drawers on the right side of the desk, opened the drawer, pulled out a business-sized manila envelope which he slid across the desk in my direction.

"Good job, Miss Rosales. The roses were a real nice touch. We liked that."

Milly reached across and picked up the envelope and put it in her purse.

"Sid, we want to ask you if it is okay with you if, when you give one of us a closing, that both of us do the background work and planning. We kind of view ourselves as partners. We will, of course, respect your wish as to which one does the closing."

"I'll check and let you know with the next closing. It will be soon."

"Thanks, Sid" Milly said, gesturing towards the door

with her head. We left.

Back in the car, she handed me the envelope and said "Sorry about the little grab act back there, but I forgot to tell you about another one of Sid's rules. He does not want to know how much money we are getting. He is very firm about it. So it would be rude to count it in his presence. But you can count it now."

I opened the envelope, which had a very pleasant thickness. It was filled with hundred dollar bills, ten, twenty, thirty of them. $3,000. I let that number sink into my consciousness. I just earned $3,000 in a day, compared to the $5,500 Emilio earned in a year. I now had enough money to send Ines to journalism camp, with a camera. Maybe this job was worth considering for the long run, after all.

"Money's pretty good, isn't it?" Milly asked. "I think it is fair for the risk involved and the care of planning required. Let's go to Nonna Yana's for lunch, and then we'll talk business."

I was surprised at the noon-time activity at what I had regarded as a bakery of confectionery-type items, but all of the customer tables were full, and the line at the counter was about three deep. Irena was filling all of the orders and ringing the old manual keyed cash register, with an air of enjoyment in the prosperity of the moment.

"Oh hi, Milly, and it's Hattie, right? What can I get you?"

We each got a paper tray of three pryizhy. Milly also got a garlic pickle.

"I love pickles", Milly purred happily, which I found amusing in that I had not yet observed any foodstuff, particularly a Ukrainian foodstuff that Milly did not love. We took our food across the street to the bench by the tennis courts. Even if it was February, it was a warm day for the season, and two women were playing on the far court. They were both a bit older than we were, one blonde, one redhead. They were both wearing tennis skirts, each with a long sleeved light sweater appropriate to the season. The blonde had a white skirt with lemon yellow sweater, while the redhead modeled a navy blue skirt and tan sweater. They each wore white anklets with those no-nonsense tennis shoes that made that satisfying noise as they gripped, pushed off, stopped and started on the court surface.

The two played energetically and confidently, making powerful shots and returns and occasional tricky lobs. Each player was good at the game, liked being good at it, and reveled in the joy of the game and the skill of both herself and her opponent.

They finished about the same time we were discarding our paper trash. They packed their rackets into their special tennis bags, changed out of their court shoes, and walked to their cars, laughing pleasantly.

"They make a pretty good partnership" I observed, watching them drive off.

"So do we, but we have to be smart about it" Milly said. "The first thing to avoid is the Al Capone mistake. You remember that the only way he got sent up the river was for income tax evasion. So we will pay tax on what Sid pays us. We don't have to say where the money comes from. We already have M & H Inc. set up. We will treat Sid's money as if we earned it selling Tupperware. I suggest, then, that we deposit your $3,000 into the M&H account, and then write you a check from M&H as if it is a distribution of Tupperware profits. I suggest that you then take that check and deposit it in an account in your name only, probably at a bank other than Emilio's. You need to remember that you should save something like 10 to 15% of everything you get from Sid for taxes at the end of the year. Personally, I put that portion into a savings account, just to be sure it is there. Any questions about that?"

"Gosh, Milly, you've really given this a lot of thought."

"Well, we take enough risks without the IRS coming after us."

Milly took a breath. "One more banking recommendation for you. You will want a safety deposit box so that you don't have your gun or other such paraphernalia lying around your house where the kids can find it."

I took Milly's advice and opening checking and savings accounts at Harris Bank and Trust, the bank I used while I worked at Marshall Field's before we were married. I opened a safety deposit box, and placed in it any items that I would not want to explain to the family.

I, of course, immediately got Ines enrolled in the journalism camp, and took her shopping for a used camera. I remember clearly coming out of the camera store, Ines holding the new-to-her camera with a reverence as if she had unearthed a jeweled crown from an ancient royal tomb.

"Mom, thank you for this. I really do appreciate it" and she hugged me in a way that she never had, and come to think of it has not since. She had apparently realized that the circumstances of her life were now falling into line with her newly-formed life intentions.

"Ines, I am glad to help. You are going places, and good for you. You don't have to take me with you. But I do ask that you tell me about it as you go." We cried.

I also recall driving her up to Northwestern for the camp in June, and watching her disappear into the dormitory door with her suitcase and camera, and feeling as if she had gone through an invisible portal, to a place markedly different on that side than this.

That camp was the beginning of a series of fashion and journalism, courses, camps, internships and jobs that led, not exactly linearly, but inexorably to the place she now occupies on the top of the Latina fashion magazine echelon.

Bobby and Javier benefited from the M&H success as well with sports camps, travelling club teams, and out-of-town academic opportunities. They are all great kids, receiving the benefits of their fortunate circumstances without expectation or demand for more.

The activity level of M&H, Tupperware division, ramped up to present a credible receptacle for the income we were receiving from the Sid division. We had outgrown Milly's dining room/kitchen, so had started renting parish halls, school auditoriums and gymnasiums, and other semi-public spaces, where we could host, instead of our original, say 20 guests, we could easily do 75, sometimes 100.

At Milly's insistence, we kept the format of the Parties the same as they had been originally, in that they always started with brief guest self-introductions, had a refreshment period featuring appetizers, savory and sweet, and wine. There followed our brief description of the new items, as well as the old favorites, in the product line. Milly always performed, with the same panache as used in a magic trick, the demonstration of filling one of the Tupperware containers with a liquid, burping the lid into place, and turning it upside down to show the absence of leaks.

"Preserves freshness!" Milly would always say, simply but dramatically. We sold a lot more Tupperware than we had previously. Occasionally, we would buy out the entire inventory remaining after a party, in order to boost sales, and donate the items to a convent, a hospital or some non-profit.

Since we were both hauling a lot of stuff around, and doing a lot of driving in our background work for closings, we had to upgrade our transportation. Milly traded in her 1953 Chevy for a navy blue 1956 Chevy 210 four door sedan. Its classic conservative style made it all but invisible, and useful whether we were pretending to be insurance agents, bankers, or social service workers.

I, who had never had a car of my own, and only rarely got to use Emilio's car, a 1960 black and white Buick Invicta, which he somehow thought fit his "station" at the bank, bought a late 50's Chevrolet panel truck, which held a lot of stuff, and was a terrific disguise, particularly when we were performing the "two domestics, with mops and buckets" bit.

Sid and his bosses, having thought about us, and our track record, were fine with the idea that we worked together and if Sid called either one of us, both of us would show up and participate materially in the details of the closing. Sid called every month or two, and as a result, no matter how hard we worked at the Tupperware gig, we were grossing eight or nine times more from Sid than from our plastic domestic wares. It was an agreeable problem to have. We had paid all of our debts, and our children were well-educated, happy, interesting people. We were well-respected and competent in both of the professional spheres. In 1971, in light of our successes, and because of the increasingly difficult nature of our neighborhoods on the South Side, Milly and I relocated to the relative suburban calm of Downers Grove. We found houses a block and a half apart. It took a bit of cajoling to get Emilio to agree to the move, but was able, at last to convince him that the new location was in keeping with his "position" with the Bank, which, if truth were to be told, had not changed for fifteen years. All of the kids, except Roberto and Javier, had graduated from High School by that time. Ines had started her joint journalism and fashion design program of studies at Northwestern, to be followed by a graduate degree from Columbia.

It was the Golden Age for M & H.

I was aware, even at the time, that the turning point of all of this success, for me, had not been any particular event or decision, but the moment that Milly came up with that then-ridiculous story about the scarabs, which, as far-fetched as it sounded at the time, contained an essential truth. It was only natural for me when, during the Christmas shopping season following my first closing, I spotted at the jewelry counter at Marshall Field's two gold scarabs, identical except that one had red faux stones for eyes, and the other green, and bought both. I gave the red-eyed one to Milly for Christmas, and kept the green-eyed one. We didn't wear them often, and almost never at the same time, but they meant a lot to both of us. I could tell, because when Milly opened hers, she flashed the smile of wisdom, which meant, this time "I see you thought about it the right way."

Golden scarabs for a Golden Age.

But nothing is forever.

## 18

# I bite the Bear.

I kept to myself on the Sunday after returning to Shady Rest from the Christmas program at the Art Institute, catching up on my laundry, sorting mail, cleaning out my email, but mainly pondering my current situation. In the past year, I had killed two people, basically because I had determined that they deserved killing. Milly would decidedly not approve. Why did I kill them? Because I am angry at Ines' remoteness? Because I miss my former life? Because of the influence of my purple pills? Because I mourn Milly? Because I am losing it? I really couldn't say, but here I am, about to get thrown out of my home, and having resolved to kill yet again.

The following Monday morning found me in need of the cheering up, and general life context that only Bella Carson in her cheerfully irrepressible manner could provide. I was happy to see her in the dining room, holding forth over breakfast, and at a table that had an empty seat, into which I slid. Also at the table were the retired navy officer Earl Sampson, the human foghorn, and his wife, Eunice, whose voice I realized I had yet to hear say anything except "yes" "no" and "one egg poached", and also the Demorys, the relatively new couple who were retired university professors.

Bella, characteristically, was telling a story and ignoring her breakfast, dramatically adding flourishes of her fork and raising and lowering her voice for dramatic effect. The story seemed to be about the time she and one of her high school chums had gotten access to the teachers' lounge at her high school, had distributed about a carton of "loaded" cigarettes, filled at the ends with those about three quarter inch white slivers impregnated with gunpowder such that the cigarette blew up with a pop that was startling to everyone present, while cascading tobacco in the smoker's lap. They then apparently framed Bella's former boyfriend, Ralph, by leaving a bunch of partial packages of the "loads" outside his locker. Ralph had apparently jilted Bella as a date for the Winter Formal, asking instead Lucretia, (I confess I did not exactly get the significance of the name), Bella's hated rival. Of course, Ralph was suspended from school, and missed the Winter Formal altogether. Cosmic justice for Ralph! Delicious Vindication for Bella! A wonderful story. Even though, in the years I had gotten to know, and really like her, I had formed the opinion that Bella's stories were just that, stories.

Earl, taking his cue from the explosive aspect of

Bella's story, interrupted, even before the denouement, and started off of on a loud, and tedious story of gunnery practice in a cruiser in the North Atlantic, where, instead of the dummy barge set afloat for target practice, the ship was shooting at a fleet of whales! Ha, Ha. Choke down nausea.

Eunice, who had clearly heard this claptrap maybe seventy-five times before, shot Earl the dart of a glance in which resided " You moronic egomaniac. Your life, and the life you imposed on me has been completely meaningless, and, frankly, stupid. I don't know how I got here, but, ya'know what, I will outlive you, you two-bit blowhard. It is really too bad they don't serve gin for breakfast."

I would have to take Eunice to lunch.

And what I got from this seemingly mundane, breakfast table 'compare and contrast' story was what I am sure that Milly knew, and knew at the bottom of her being: it was not just acts and deeds in the ordinary course of life that defined us, but the Stories that we laid down, embroidered, etched and painted in oils about who we, and why we do what we do, are what matter. Bella continually defined herself, and her life, through her Stories. Maybe my problem was that I had no one to tell mine to, despite the fact that I desperately wanted to do so.

I had eaten my muesli, with fruit, without, tasting anything, but getting oriented, plainly, in what I had to do next.

At right before nine o'clock, before Darlene had the

wit to show up for work, I ventured into Janet's office.

"JANET" I yelled, as I walked into her office, to see her start, in a satisfying way in her chair.

"Hattie, what do you want? You have twenty three days left here" she snorted, desperately.

"You have way fewer than that" I thought to myself.

"I wanted to see if there was any way we could make peace, and go on as usual."

"No way." She twitched all over. "You are a trouble-maker and I can't wait to see how well this place will run without you."

What I really wanted from this meeting was not rec-onciliation, bur reconnaissance. I wanted to be sure that the resident files were kept in her ante-room, and that her Keurig coffee pot was in the room with her desk and that the locks on her suite of room had inside deadbolts.

"Well, I don't really harbor any ill-will towards you" (which was a total, abject and unapologetic lie), " but I do have to note that you have made your choice. Goodbye." I left.

My basic plan for Janet had been, all along, to come up with some chemical intervention that would dope her out just enough for me to administer the contents of my vial, which was the purest heroin, in such a lethal dose that she would be dead before the syringe was empty. The art to the whole business was to make the injection where a clumsy CSI person would miss it: under a fin-ger- or toenail, in an earlobe next to an earring piercing, in the backside, really close to the anus. I was not looking forward to any of this.

I had the knockout punch, but needed the set-up jab. My idea here was that among the medications that the staff managed and administered to the Assisted Living patients, there would should be something that one could covertly give to a subject in either food or beverage that would induce a state of lethargy such that one could go on to the last step. Like about three whiskeys. I thought about that idea for a minute, but could not imagine either Janet or I being comfortable as drinking buddies.

I knew from my trips around the facility that each Assisted Living resident had a box for his/her medication that resembled a tool box, with a handle on top, and a fold down hasp locked with a ridiculously flimsy little lock. The boxes were labelled with the residents' names, and delivered to the doorsteps of each individual unit, for the nurses to make sure each person got the right doses each day. After the nurse finished, the boxes went back into the hall, for pick-up and returned to the meds room, which I had not been inside, but in which I assume that the staff sorted the pills from the pharmacy packages into the boxes per the prescriptions.

I have to admit that I really don't know a lot about the bucketloads of medications that all of us seem to take. I have refused on principle to learn the names of my own meds even my sentimental favorite purple pills. But I do get the general idea of the kind of drug I was looking for: a fairly strong painkiller with an effect like the contents of my vial, maybe one of those opioids that I had started to see articles in the paper about. I need to snoop around in the Assisted Living Meds Room. Thanks to my pal Manny I had a key. I just needed to find a time to use it.

My pretext to be over in the Assisted Living wing was my former floormate, Mabel O'Bannon, whose family had finally realized had gotten too far around the twist to stay in Independent Living. I dropped in on her after the dinner hour in the AL dining room. Mabel seemed glad to see me, and seemed to be triangulating details fairly clearly.

"Hattie, is it true that you are leaving?" she asked just as I sat down on the settee opposite her easy chair. No need for high-speed internet to get information in a small facility in a small town. Everybody knows a lot about everybody else, and talks about it.

"Well, I do have some issues to resolve with Janet. But it will get worked out. How do you like Assisted Living?" I asked, anxious to change the subject.

"Oh, I do. I like being on the first floor, for one thing."

I asked her if she needed for me to do anything for her.

"No, my kids take pretty good care of me." Which was not strictly true, but I was glad she felt safe and looked after.

We visited about simple gossip until about 7:30, when I made my excuses, and indicated that I would be back later that week.

My hope was that, since the staff shifts change at 8:00, I just might catch the old shift leaving early, before the next one came in. I was in luck. I saw the desk nurse disappear through the exit door, leaving the desk temporarily unattended. I pushed my walker by the desk and around the corner to where the Meds Room was. The door was locked, until, that is, Manny's key eased me in. I turned on the light, locked the inside deadbolt, took the climber's headlamp from my walker, put it on, and then turned out the overhead light.

I looked carefully around the small room to absorb the details. The only features were a set of interior cabinets, some of which were locked, a counter space below the upper cabinets, and, in the center of the room, the open metal shelving on which the medication toolboxes, which had been retrieved for the night, rested, name labels facing out. I was going to have to look into at least some of the boxes, I was sure. I did not know all of the people in Assisted Living, but many of the names were familiar. Where to start? It was then that I noticed a fact that jolted my attention: there were an odd number of boxes. I counted them: twenty-three. Now that was fascinating because there are only twenty AL units, one of which I knew was empty. So there are four boxes that do not match a unit and its resident. I went through the names, one at a time, until the light went on. On the bottom shelf there were four boxes, one of which was labelled "Goodnow, Phyllis". Phyllis, the poor woman had succumbed to ovarian cancer about three weeks ago. But her meds live on. How very interesting. Let's start here. The lock on Phyllis' box was laughably weak, and in any event the wonderful Manny had duplicated a key of the right size and shape that popped it open, like a bottlecap flipping off of a 1960's Coke bottle.

I expected the interior of the box would look like my own medications grid, or the one I had observed while visiting Mabel: a calendar of compartments, with individual pills in individual compartments. Easy for the staff, easy for the patient. But what was in Phyllis' box, from which the top tray (the grid) had been removed, was a series or original pharmacy packages; those orange tinted cylinders, with child-proof caps, that did contain very detailed information about the contents, the number of pills, the dosage and, most importantly the names of the drugs. As I looked, one by one, at the packages. My first thought was "God help me; I do not want to die like Phyllis Goodnow" because of the sheer volume of chemicals that went into her last moments.

But then I found a container labelled " OxyCodone HCl, 60mg". It was about half full of round white pills that had "OC" impressed on one side and "60" on the other.

"Okay, Janet. I am a dumb person, but the light is starting to go on."

If one could keep a dead person's drugs, including the addictive opioids, for even a month, you could sell them, on the street? to a dealer? Or maybe even cream off a few to ease the stress of life?

Thinking about this for a bit, I put the entire "Oxy" package into the storage compartment of my walker. I relocked Phyllis' box, and replaced it on the shelf, in its original place. I surveyed the Meds Room to be sure that there were no conspicuous signs of intrusion, switched off my headlamp and stored it in my walker, wheeled my walker to the door, and listened. When my eyes had re-acclimatized to the dark, and after a period where I heard no sounds, I quietly turned the deadbolt, opened the door a crack, and looked into the hall. Nothing. I quickly pushed my walker through the door into the hall, pushed the door quietly closed (let someone else figure why it was unlocked) and moved down the hall to the Nurse's station at the AL desk.

As I expected, the desk nurse was drowsily, texting some equally worthless human being, and only barely looked up, as I stopped to speak to her.

"Mabel O'Bannon is doing well, for the record." I smiled and leaned on the counter. "She is much happier here than on the Independent side."

She looked at me blankly, but with that frame of mind that she would never recall that I had even been there.

The next part of the plan required me to get Darlene out of the picture for most of a morning. I thought about this as if I had to divert a particularly dumb and single-minded golden retriever for that period. All I had to do was throw the tennis ball far enough away.

And so it was that Darlene found on her desk the next Wednesday morning a memo, typed on SR stationery:

"I need you to do three things this morning before I get in. First, go to Staples and buy two boxes of legal size manila file folders. Then please mail the package you find with this memo to the Springfield office of the Nursing Home Regulator of the Illinois Department of Public Health. It is addressed. I need it to be certified, return receipt requested. While you are at the Post Office, pick up the forms for insured deliveries.

Third, go to Target and pick up three stands of colored lights for the dining room Christmas decorations.

Janet."

The full can of tennis balls. Particularly because the Post Office would be backed up with Christmas traffic, and that the zip code on the package had a deliberately transposed set of digits, and that Staples and Target were on opposite sides of town, with the PO downtown.

I was puttering around the mailboxes within sight of Darlene's desk. She came in, read the note before she took off her coat, picked up the note and package, and hustled back out the door. See you later, Darlene.

I had gotten up early, to be sure of my preparations. After some consideration, I picked out a more or less monochrome outfit: black bell-bottom trousers, mock turtle neck black sweater under a black blazer. The black beret was the right touch. Before heading out of the door, I pinned onto the left lapel of my jacket the green-eyed scarab pin. I imagined it to have blinked several times at the light, since it had be years since it had been out of my jewelry box.

I hated to miss breakfast but I had to be sure that I timed my actions so that I would be early enough to leave the note for Darlene, and then early enough to catch Janet right after she got into her office.

Darlene had departed at about five minutes after 8. Janet didn't make her grand entrance until about 8:25. I was sitting in the lobby outside her office "working" on the public access computer. I gave her enough time to hang up her coat, heat up the water in the coffee maker, and pour her first cup, before sitting down at the desk.

I had it pretty close. She was taking a swallow of coffee, when I quietly opened the door, stuck my head in, and yelled "Janet!" as loudly as I could. Janet was even jumpier than usual, and sloshed a bit of coffee on the desk before recovering enough to bark "Hattie, what do you want?"

"My lawyer wants to know how much of a damage deposit I made. And, oh yes, she wants me to get a signed copy of my lease."

Janet made a sour face, but stood up and headed for the file room next door. "Stay here", she grumbled and went out of my sight. Show time. I pulled from my purse the packet containing the two Oxys from Phyllis' meds that I had carefully pulverized last night and emptied the contents into Janet's cup. It was just a few minutes before Janet came back with a photocopy, which she thrust at me. "Here. Damage deposit is on page two. If there is nothing else, beat it."

I stood up, retrieving my walker, moved toward the door, but paused before I got there.

"I am a bit sorry about how this has worked out" I

said, vaguely hoping to have a rapprochement.

"I'm not. Goodbye and good riddance."

Suit yourself.

I went out, closed the door, and affixed to the outside the sign prepared on Darlene's printer:

"In conference. Do Not Disturb! Janet.

The plan now was to wait for about a half hour, which should be about long enough for Phyllis' meds to slow Janet to a crawl, at which time I would come back and finish the job.

No one saw me until I turned the corner into the hall down to Assisted Living. I took a slow stroll down that way, visited with the residents and staff I encountered along the way. I took my time and made my way back to the mailboxes in the lobby by Janet's office. When I was sure no one was looking I quietly opened Janet's door and looked in.

Oh, my, gosh. I quickly pushed the walker in and locked the door.

Janet was face-down on her desk, doing an Academy-Award-worthy impression of dead. No time for the niceties here. I have to move. Step one was to get Janet's finger prints onto the Oxy pill bottle, which was then stowed in her top left desk drawer. I emptied the remnants of the coffee into the sink and stowed the cup into the storage compartment of my walker. I thought about it briefly and turned off the coffee maker. I darted into the file room and retrieved from my file, which I knew that Janet would have too lazy to refile after copying my lease, the "thirty day letter".

I carefully looked out the door and when I could neither see not hear anyone, left. I locked the door from the outside and rushed (to the degree that any eighty-year old can rush) back to my room on the third floor. There were still a few people in the dining room, to whom I waved as I passed.

Back in my room, at about ten of ten, I quickly broke up the pieces of Janet's coffee cup with a hammer, put the pieces, and the hammer into four plastic bags in my walker along with my full set of SR keys, and called a cab.

I went directly to the Farmers and Merchants Savings Bank in downtown Gethsemane, where I had already gotten a large safety deposit box, for the Glock and the ammunition. I added the key ring. I then took a leisurely walk through downtown and disposed of, in discrete installments, the pieces of Janet's coffee cup, the hammer, and the heroin vial. I recycled the syringes in the public restroom receptacle designated for that purpose in the Library.

Exhale.

Suddenly, ravenously hungry, in light of the skipped breakfast, I made my way to 120 Twelfth, the best lunch restaurant in Gethsemane and ordered a glass of sauvignon blanc, along with the soup and salad special, which proved to be a carrot/parsnip soup with a small Caesar. I enjoyed it enormously and only regretted that I hadn't invited Bella to spin tales that would overwrite the narrative of the day that kept insisting itself on my brain. I took a cab back to Shady Rest at about three in the afternoon.

The scene at the facility was dramatically different than when I had left in the late morning. There were three Gethsemane Police Squad Cars under the canopy over the front entrance, leaving only one lane for the cab or any other traffic.

I paid the cabbie, and was met at the door by a uniformed officer who wanted to see my ID and know what I was doing there.

I showed my resident card, and key, and was admitted through the lobby that looked like a movie crime scene. There was yellow tape across the entry to Janet's office and a cluster of tan-shirted cops surrounded Darlene, who was weeping inconsolably into her hands. The "loot" from her morning shopping trip sat on her desk, in bags, unopened.

I asked the nearest Tan what was happening and he confided in me, in subdued tones "Drug Overdose".

Story over, I thought to myself, with admittedly smug self-satisfaction.

But it was only beginning.

## 19

# Blood Root

L aTasha Cranton, the newly appointed Chief of Police for Gethsemane, Illinois, was pacing around her office, reading a fistful of stapled papers, muttering to herself as she made notes on the pages, and acting as if she was about to explode through the walls. Chief Cranton is African-American, about five foot eight and of average build. She moved, as was usual for her, with a subtle, controlled grace that suggests that if she wished to accelerate to a higher level of action, she could do so in a heartbeat, like some sort of super-hero. She is in her fifties, one would guess from the distinguished wisps of gray at her temples radiating into the tight bun in which she wears her hair. She was not wearing the GPD uniform today, but had on a burnt orange long-sleeved blouse over autumn brown tailored slacks. She was sporting no jewelry except simple gold stud earrings and a thin wristwatch.

The office itself is large, with a single window that

looks out of the second floor of City Hall over the park across the street. The window features a blind, but no curtains as yet. The desk, placed in front of the window looking into the room towards the door to the hall, was piled with boxes of pencils, files, note pads and calendars destined for, but not yet sorted into, the desk drawers. There were two guest chairs by the desk, stacked with groups of wall hangings. The bookshelves along the wall to the left of the desk were filled with boxes of books, unopened. There was a small conference table at the hall side wall, with four chairs, on which was a new coffee maker, in its store box, and some coffee supplies, which would, at some point, be put into the cabinets above the counter in the corner of the room opposite the door.

There were only two pieces hanging on the wall of the office, both in the alcove to the right of the desk, visible primarily to the occupant of the desk chair.

The first was a Chicago Police Department Award in recognition of Meritorious Service awarded to Lieutenant LaTasha Cranton and signed by Mayor Rahm Emanuel, and the Chief of the Bureau of Detectives as well as the Commander of the South District. It also prominently displayed the motto:

"We Serve and Protect."

The other, much smaller item is a framed poem, printed over the picture of the blooming woodland flower:

# THE DEADLY MONDAINE

## Blood Root

Your leaves impose a Rohrschach test
    on schizophrenic Spring.
Is it to be green vernal truth, whose track is traced in bloom,
        or but another rash of Mideast revolt to accrue anew,
        as bodies, in the name of God, are carelessly strewn?
Does your yellow-centered flower, with eight even spokes of
white, show us that the wheel of life resumes its yearly turn,
        or does your Whiteness, and your name, mock us
          when we smoothly preach that Black Lives Matter?
Whose blood?
    What root?

    The papers in her hand comprised the first draft of a proposal to the Gethsemane City Council for a Citizen's Police Review Commission, which she was to present at the Council meeting on the following Tuesday. She had been hired a month ago by Gethsemane to replace a long-serving, and beloved Chief of Police. The Council, to their credit, led by the two African-American Councilors, saw the vacancy as an opportunity to address the ugly issues of racism in police practices that had blown into national consciousness, with Michael Brown's hateful murder in Ferguson, Missouri.

    She had been, for over twenty years, a homicide detective in the South Detective District of Chicago. Over the years, cases she worked on became more drug- and gang-related, and frankly bloodier, to the point that she had felt that she was not using her particular aptitudes in gathering and coordinating difficult evidence with the sometimes obscure motivations of murderers. It was time for a change. Her son had long since left home for his own career path. She had been divorced for what? Fifteen years? In any event long enough not to think too much about that. She had reached through diligent work the rank of Lieutenant, but had started to feel that invisible barrier to upward career progress that some people called the glass ceiling, which effect she felt most keenly as a woman, and a Black woman.

But the real push for a change came from the stark distinction between her sense of nobility of the calling of being a public safety officer, and the more and more apparent reality that police, as a group, treated African American citizens very differently than white citizens, often resulting in injury or death. She could not get out of her head the list of names that scrolled like the stock market quotations on Bloomsberg News: Michael Brown, Freddie Gray, Sylville Smith, Philando Castile, Gregory Gunn, Alton Sterling, Terence Crutcher, and the name that ate at her guts: Laquan McDonald, who was killed by a man wearing the same badge as she had proudly worn.

So when she saw the ad for the job in Gethsemane, she applied. And got it.

This presentation was the first official duty of the new position and she was determined to nail it to the wall.

Her thoughts were interrupted by a sharp knock on

her door, followed immediately by the appearance in her office of Deputy Chief Frank Covington. Frank is a retirement age white man, sporting enough of a paunch to create impressions of donut admiration, dressed in rumpled gray slacks held up by red suspenders. His dress shirt, with sleeves rolled to the elbow, and tie were open at the neck.

"Boss, we've got a problem."

LaTasha, angrily threw her manuscript onto her desk, and snapped " I am not "Boss". This is not some damn' plantation. And why is it that I think that "our" problem has something to do with the white officers thinking that I am out to get them?"

Taken off guard, Frank blinked a couple of times and said, looking over at the conference table, said "Is it okay if we sit down over here?" He pushed the coffeemaker box over to the side of the table and sat down. Latasha warily sat on the edge of the chair next to his.

"First of all, I meant no disrespect in calling you boss. It is just an old habit from my relation with the last Chief. What would you like me to call you?" He waited with his hands folded in his lap for an answer.

The furrows in LaTasha's brow loosened slightly. "I'm sorry, Frank, I am feeling the pressure of my presentation. My friends and close colleagues call me Tasha. I would be happy for you to call me that."

Frank smiled. "Happy to do that, Tasha. Now let me say directly that I know that a key part of your job description is to help this department root out overt and covert racist attitudes and practices in its daily work enforcing the law. I support the mission totally because it makes us all better cops. And I know enough of your record" here he pointed at the Citation on the wall, "and of you from our brief time together to be completely convinced that you are the right person for the job. I will do whatever you need me to do to get the job done."

"But here is "our" problem, and I think you will agree that it affects the whole department. There have been three deaths out at Shady Rest Nursing Home in the last six months, the last of which was an apparent drug overdose by the Director, who appears to have been involved in some kind of opioid sales racket. And, on top of that, last night, a local businessman had half his head blown off in one of the new McMansions on the edge of town.

So, the problem here is that none of us have had homicide training. Except for bar fights and road rage-type incidents, the last murder we had in town was when the cardiologist's wife discovered his affair and felt that he was a good candidate for open heart surgery with a kitchen knife. She was still holding the knife when we got there. No need for CSI or yellow tape or anything.

The point is that we have some heavy stuff happening, and you are our only trained professional, even if you are the Chief. I think that you should cast your expert eyes on these situations."

"Frank, you are right" LaTasha admitted with a sigh, "give me what files you have. Have you called the Crime Scenes people at the State about the shotgun killing?"

"They will be here tomorrow afternoon."

"I will meet them at the site. I'll take a patrol officer with me. What I need you to do for me is to make the contacts on this list" she walked over and pulled it off her desk "and find out how well their Citizen-Police oversight boards are working, and what we can learn from their successes and failures. I will then visit Shady Rest and see what in the blazes is going on there. I'll let you know where we need more troops."

"Sounds like a plan. I recommend Officer Schumacher to second chair for you. Heather is a local, knows everybody, takes good notes and has a good mind. I'll send her up with the files.

"Thanks, Frank. We'll compare notes at the staff meeting."

## 20

# I meet the Chief

*HATTIE; DECEMBER 2016*

I went down to breakfast on the Friday after Janet's demise to find Shady Rest a transformed place. There were uniformed police everywhere; the dining room was completely full of people, actively gossiping among the twinkling colored holiday lights and poinsettias that had been deployed in seasonal array. There was an electricity in air that never seemed to be found here in a nursing home full of post-retirement Midwesterners.

I found an empty seat at a table at which Bella, Betty and the Changs had just sat down. Mary Chang was talking about getting used to American holiday celebrations.

"We first thought, from the dramatically frenetic level of activity around Christmas time that Americans were deeply and demonstrably religious and that American Christmas holidays had a profound spiritual content. We now understand that the meaning of all this" here she pointed to the holiday elements in the dining room, "and all the rest of the trappings of the season have a largely secular, commercial meaning. We know that there are celebrations of the holiday within individual religious communities. But we now realize that most of it is just generic, a recognition of the winter solstice, stitched together from many different cultures. It is much easier for us to relate to."

"The muddling of secular and religious used to be a lot worse at Christmastime" said Bella, after we had ordered our food. "In my public elementary school, we always had a Christmas program, as insensitive as that sounds in light of the fact that there were Jewish students."

"Did I ever tell you the story of how I accidentally transformed our school's Christmas program?" Betty and I exchanged looks which said "Buckle your seat belts. Here it comes."

"The Christmas Program, and I don't think we were snooty enough to call it a Pageant, was traditional and more or less the same every year. Almost every kid in the school had a part, most dressed in some kind of seasonal costume: elves, reindeer, snowmen, carolers, Dickensian shopkeepers, the whole nine yards. All of us kids entered the stage by classes; youngest first. There were songs, some religious, some not. Mrs. Mueller sat at the grand piano on stage, dressed, I think, as Mrs. Fezziwig, and played all of the music. The cast all remained on stage, getting larger and larger until the grand finale, when the last kid, dressed as a little Christmas tree came out to stand by the large Christmas tree, at which point the entire cast and the entire audience sang "O Tannenbaum" and then adjourned to the lobby for cookies and punch.

When I was in second grade, I was chosen to be the Little Christmas Tree. This was a great part since you really didn't have to do anything, and you were the star of the show in the end. The problem was that the Little Tree costume, while cute as all get out, was difficult to put on, and almost impossible to see out of. I had only worn it during the dress rehearsal, but thought I had it down.

On the night of performance, everything was going extremely well. Mrs. Mueller and the choir had all the songs perfectly timed and performed. In the wings I had gotten the Tree on, adjusted the minimal eye slots so that I could just see enough. I waited for the cue. Mrs. Allburger, the director, put her hands on my shoulders, pointed me in the right direction, and whispered "Okay, now Bella. You know what to do." A star is born. I proceeded slowly, with what I felt to be Tree-ish dignity, across the stage to the introductory strains of "O, Tannenbaum." I don't know how it happened, whether some blockheaded kid had left a prop in the path that they had been instructed to leave clear for me, or I just tripped. In any event, I fell forward on my face right about center stage. There were some oohs as if the Olympic figure skater had just fallen doing a triple axel, but Mrs. Mueller kept on playing. And so would I. I got up, adjusted the tree around me, and, even though I had completely lost visual reference with the outside world, walked confidently towards where I knew the big tree was. And directly off the front of the stage, into the laps of the parents in the front row. There were more ooh and aahs, and the beginning of laughter, after it was apparent that I wasn't hurt.

Mrs. Mueller, thinking quickly struck up the song. "Falling in love again; Never wanted to. What was I to do, I can't help it." She played it once through; then started again, this time singing along in a remarkably good voice, with a German accent, channeling her inner Marlene Dietrich.

The laughter became an uproar. On the third time through, the audience sang the whole song, along with some of the older kids who knew it. Everybody loved the fact that it had become a celebration of community, and that we were all human, and could laugh at ourselves.

It was so popular that there was serious consideration of using it in the Christmas show every year, until the School Board director who was a personal injury defense lawyer, put an end to that."

What a great story. Who cares if it is true?

We had all finished our food and were waiting for Bella to catch up, when a fortyish man with a close cropped haircut, wearing a black suit and narrow tie that may have been fashionable for about twenty minutes at some time in the past, came into the dining room and spoke.

"Excuse me, ladies and gentlemen, I am Claude Dumont, assistant vice president of Midwest Retirement Enterprises, Inc. I have been named as Interim Director of this facility until we replace Janet Jenkins, who as I am sure you know passed away suddenly last Wednesday. The Gethsemane police will be here today to continue their investigations and to speak to some of you personally about your knowledge of the unfortunate events. They ask that you not leave the facility without letting them know where you are going. They will be using the card room for their interviews and will call you individually as they require your presence. Shady Rest regrets your inconvenience." He left.

"I wonder who he gets to starch his underwear" Bella mused into the vacuum his presence had created in the room. The residents quietly left to go back to their rooms. I did so as well, knowing that I needed to organize my information, wardrobe, and story for a presumed police interview.

I decided to go for the "cheerful, slightly dotty, grandma" look with a high-collared blouse with long frilly sleeves, closed with a cameo brooch, a long black straight skirt, along with a black, flat "schoolmarm" hat, and, of course, short white cloth gloves.

I sat down on my couch and pulled out my Friday issue of the Gethsemane Guardian, the local daily newspaper. The Guardian is the crummy, chain-owned survivor of a respected journal whose local owners sold out to Mega Media, that now sported bad journalism, stupid features and foolish opinions, but which no one could be without since it had the local obituaries. The news was always at least a day late, so that Friday was the earliest one could expect to read about a Wednesday event, such as Janet's adventure. I found the article on the bottom of page one.

"Shady Rest Director Dies of Massive Overdose" led the headline to the story.

"Janet Jenkins, Director of Shady Rest Retirement Home, died Wednesday of what police are reporting as an overdose of opioids. While few actual details are available at this time, Deputy Police Chief Frank Covington did state in a brief press conference Thursday: "Formal forensic examinations have not been completed, but evidence found at the scene suggest that the lethal drug was Oxycodone, that the deceased was a regular user, and that it is possible that it had been stolen from patient supplies, and that there was a regular pattern of such thefts as part of a scheme to sell the drugs to the general public. We will update you with further details as they become available."

Oh, Janet, you bad girl. Milly would have a fit, since she adamantly refused to allow us to ever factor into our plans any possibility of luck favoring our enterprises ("If we rely on luck, we might as well just play Russian Roulette and be done with it" she would say), but it seems that I hit it lucky in that Janet was already an opioid user, and she was trafficking in the stuff. Hoisted on her own petard.

How the events of Wednesday seemed to have rolled out, from the newspaper report (It was amusing to think about how difficult it would have been for the reporter to get a coherent phrase from Darlene) and from the much more detailed and accurate scuttlebutt from the residents was that Darlene got back in the late morning, after I had taken off downtown, found the note on Janet's door and didn't think too much about it, and went off to lunch. It was not until she returned, found the sign still in place, realized that Janet was never in conference over the noon hour, that she used her key to let herself into the office. And became immediately unglued, running through the first floor shouting "She's dead! She's dead!" without filling in the "who, where and how" details until an astute RN from assisted living sat her down, got enough of the facts, viewed the scene, and called 911.

But, as dramatic as Janet's demise had been, the most compelling story of the day pushed Janet to the bottom of page one. The banner article at the top of page one exploded into your face:

"New Resident Slain in Shotgun Murder in Northfield Glen" screamed the headline.

"J. Hartley Mortensen, local businessman, was found dead Wednesday of an apparent shotgun blast to the head administered in the second floor study of his home in the newly subdivided Northfield Glen. Chief of Police LaTasha Cranton has indicated that the crime scene is secure and will wait to disclose further details pending investigation by the State Bureau of Criminal Investigation Scene of Crimes experts.

Mortensen, 52 years old, has resided in Gethsemane since the completion of his home in May of 2015. His businesses, all of which are centered in the computer business center at the home, involve international import and export of various consumer goods.

He is survived by his sister, Genevieve Mortensen-Pratt, his business partner, Stewart Karlin, one child, Britany Mortenson, age 19 , and his former spouse, Caroline Singleton of Oak Grove.

Funeral services are pending. Detailed obituary will follow in the Guardian as available."

Well. At least the cops will have something besides Janet on their minds. Lucky again?

At that point, my phone rang.

"Hello?"

"Good morning, Ms. Rosales", said a bright young voice, "This is Sergeant Schumacher of the Gethsemane Police. Would you be so kind as to come down to the Card Room?"

"I'll be right down". I gathered my walker, assumed my frailest demeanor, and went to the elevator and down to first floor.

The door to the Card Room was partially ajar, so I easily pushed in to find the scene altered to suit the crime investigation process. Instead of the familiar grouping of round tables, those tables had been pushed to the side and replaced with a single rectangular table placed just opposite to the door. There was another small table in front of the sink and cupboards, at which sat the owner of the bright voice, with her pad and a tape recorder.

My friend, Betty Swartz, has in her room, a charcoal drawing, by Midwestern artist Silvia Schuster, of the figure of an African American woman, her head turned to look at about a forty-five degree angle to the observer, which image is at one time both a compelling personal presence, but also the representation of a larger reality: an icon of timeless wisdom and beauty.

And that image described the woman who sat at the main desk, and spoke as I came in.

"Good afternoon, Ms. Rosales, please have a chair", she said indicating the chair facing her, "I am LaTasha Cranton of the Gethsemane Police, and this gesturing to her right, is Sergeant Schumacher".

So the Chief herself.

"We have some questions to ask you about Janet Jennings. Sergeant Schumacher will be recording your responses" nodding to the Sergeant who pressed the record button on the recording device, "But first we wish to give you these warnings, at which part the Sergeant read off the Miranda warnings."

This was a blit of a surprise, since I had never been in a situation in which these warnings were given to me, but it gave me a moment to observe Chief Cranton.

I guessed her to be about Ines' age, dressed in a carefully pressed tan uniform blouse and black skirt. She wore her hair tied back from her face, and minimal jewelry: stud earrings and a thin wristwatch, both gold. She sat erect, but not rigid in her chair and regarded me carefully. It was about at this point that I got the sense that she had the same sort of combination of vision and intuition that Milly had and used to clean us all out in poker.

One could not hide a lot from the Chief.

But I was going to try.

After the warnings, Chief Cranton opened the file on her desk, briefly glanced at it and returned her eyes to me.

"Now, Ms. Rosales, how long have you lived at Shady Rest?"

Let's see, about ten years, I think; I came in 2006 or 2007."

"Where did you live before that?"

"Most recently, Downers Grove, but I grew up in Brighton Park on the South Side of Chicago, and lived in Pilsen after I was married."

"Small world; that was my patch when I was a homicide detective for the South District of Chicago Police Department."

Oh great. Maybe this luck thing wasn't breaking my way after all.

"What did you do there?"

"My partner and I were regional Tupperware distributors."

Chief Cranton paused, and considered me carefully.

"So why Gethsemane?"

"I had to get away. The big city was no place for a person my age. My husband had passed away. My kids live all over. I like it here."

"You of course knew Janet Jennings. Any troubles with her?"

Dangerous territory. "Well, not really. I would talk

to her about deficiencies in residents' services in my capacity as president of the Residents' Council. It always worked out."

"Is it true that Janet was going to evict you?"

The local rumor mill at work.

"No, no. Janet would sometimes facetiously threaten to "pitch me out on my ear", but it was all just a joke."

"What medications do you take?"

"I can't name them, but I can describe what they look like, and what color they are. I can get you a list."

"Do that. Are any of them painkillers of any sort?"

"Thank goodness, no. I am lucky not to have any painful problems.

"When did you see Janet last?"

Another tough question. But I had anticipated it, and had an answer ready.

"She passed on Wednesday. I was in to see her on Monday morning to get a copy of my lease. I had lost mine."

"Why did you need a copy of your lease."

"I couldn't remember how much of a damage deposit I put down.

"Were you thinking of leaving?"

"No, but I am eighty-four, and may want to move closer to my kids."

"Let me change subjects here, Ms. Rosales. Did you know Roy Winston and Dottie Tyler?"

"Of course, they lived on my floor. I saw them all of the time in the dining room and in the halls and elevator."

Did you get along with both of them?"

"Sure. Roy was a bit of a cut-up and Dottie could be a tad grumpy, but we're all "of an age" and entitled to be a bit prickly from time to time. I was shocked and saddened by their deaths. You never know who's next."

Everything had gone smoothly, in my view, to this point. Chief Cranton had not taken her eyes off of me, and had been, I knew, observing closely my voice intonations and body language. For my part I had made a concerted effort to speak slowly, calmly and casually, without any sort of hand or facial gesture. The line of inquiry abruptly changed.

"Why do you always wear gloves, Ms. Rosales?" came the shot from the blue.

"I have a skin condition" was the best I could manage.

"I do, too" said the Chief with some fervor. "My skin itches every time I encounter a set of odd co-incidences surrounding a death. And what it leads me to do is to look around carefully for the ends of threads that I know are there. I find them, and pull the threads back to the perpetrator."

Darn, I don't want to have to kill a cop, I whined to myself.

"To show you my point", Chief Cranton continued "Let me show you some photographs."

The first one was a grainy blow up of a cell phone picture of Dottie Tyler's body on the floor of her apartment, as taken by one of the first responders.

"What I want you to look at here is not the body, but

the position of the chair. Notice that it is away from the end table, the television or any other place where you would expect Ms. Tyler to be. Doesn't that raise the possibility that she was, at the time of her death, talking to another person?"

It does, I had to agree internally, kicking myself for not picking up on that.

"If so, who?"

She continued "Next, let me show you a still from the security camera covering the second floor on the day Roy Winston died. I do have to tell you that the "security" system here is a complete joke, since there is no way to tell what time of that day this is taken."

The photo she showed me was a blurred shot down the hall showing an object resting outside the door to the stairway.

"Is that a walker? Is that your walker, Ms. Rosales?"

"I don't think so. They all more or less look alike. We all do leave our walkers by the stairways a lot of the time."

"Let's look at the last one". This one was an excellent 8x10 glossy of Janet, face-down on her desk.

"Preliminary autopsy reports show that Ms. Jennings ingested upwards of 100 mg. of opioids with at least two cups of coffee. So, where is her cup?" I had thought of at least that point.

"What I am telling you, Ms. Rosales, is that I sense an unseen hand here. It is my job, and I am good at my job, to find the threads that lead to that hand. Do you have anything to say about that?"

"I don't, and I don't see what it has to do with me" I ventured.

"We'll see about that" she said. At that point Sergeant Schumacher interjected: "Chief, you wanted me to let you know when it was 2:30 so that we could meet the Scene of Crime people out at Northfield Glen."

The Chief looked at her watch. "Okay, Sergeant, you know the way. I will follow you in my car." She turned to me. "Ms. Rosales, I'm not done with you. Would you ride along with me?"

I didn't think I had a choice, and, besides, I wouldn't miss this for the world.

"Yes, Chief, I will."

And that is how I found myself in the passenger seat of Chief Cranton's squad car, driving north out of town behind Sergeant Schmacher's vehicle.

As she drove from the Shady Rest parking lot into the more rural suburban area north of Gethsemane, the Chief had a few things to say.

"Look here, Ms. Rosales. I mean what I say about sensing an unseen hand here. But I have way too many other things to do to spend my time scratching around for clues to potentially send up an eighty-something year old. I have no real evidence and frankly no idea about where I would get any. So let's make a deal. I don't do any thread-pulling, and on the remote chance that you have any involvement with anybody who has anything to do with the unfortunate incidents at Shady Rest, that you see to it that it doesn't happen again. Do you buy that?"

Not wishing to get into this too far, I just nodded and agreed "Okay."

As I had never ridden on this particular road before, I enjoyed observing the landscape become less small town and more agricultural, as the density of the houses decreased and the predominance of winter-fallow farmland increased.

Ahead of us, Sergeant Schumacher slowed and, at a sign identifying "Northfield Glen", turned right into a densely tree-lined, bumpy dirt lane, which we followed for almost a mile when it made a sharp turn to the left, and became, where it had been dirt, a well-graded gravel drive, leading up the hill to the unbelievable house at the top.

It was what I would guess was the replica of a French chateau. It had three stories, topped by a steeply pitched roof from which projected multiple chimneys, and the ornamental gables through which the third floor windows peered snootily. There were rounded turrets at each corner of the rectangular footprint of the structure, each topped by the upside-down ice cream cone roofs. The exterior was some sort of stone. The windows were marked with substantial lattices.

I had never seen, in person, anything like it, and doubted that very many Midwesterners had either.

There were two Gethsemane patrol cars and four various vehicles bearing Illinois BCI plates and placards already parked in the circular drive in front of the house.

Chief Cranton pulled to a stop behind Schumacher's squad car, bent down to look up at the house through the windshield and said "Lawd a'mighty, Miz Scarlett, look at dat res'denz."

Totally surprised, I blinked a couple of times and told her "I didn't think you had a sense of humor."

She gave me a half smile, and, in her regular voice, said "Believe me, Ms. Rosales. If you are in the homicide business, you have to have a sense of humor."

Don't I know it, Sister, I thought to myself.

As she reached for the door handle to get out, she turned to me and said "I'm sorry to drag you out here, but I won't be that long."

"Look, Chief, I have no intention of sitting out here in the car and freezing. I'm coming with you. You know how sensitive everyone is to Elder Abuse."

"This is a crime scene, Ms. Rosales. We can't disturb evidence, and I don't want any of part of the scene to be distressing to you."

"You forgot; I'm wearing gloves", I said holding up my hands to demonstrate. "Seriously, I promise not to touch anything and to stay out of the way. And I assure you, nothing in there will bother me in the slightest" I said, with conviction.

She looked at me sideways, thought a moment, and said "Okay, Ms. Rosales; it's your call. Just be a fly on the wall."

I grabbed my cane, and followed her up the three

steps to the front door which was guarded by a uniformed officer.

"Hello, Chief, they're upstairs on the second floor, down the hall to the left" said the officer, who had that newly-minted, buzz-cut, just-out-of-the-Academy look. He glanced at me, and then back at the Chief without speaking his question.

"She's with me. She'll be fine" was all that the chief said.

The front door opened on a huge two story atrium that seemed to stretch for about a quarter of the width of the house. Doors off the atrium to the immediate left, and immediate right opened into what appeared to be a formal drawing room, and a formal dining room respectively. Past those doors, along the side of the atrium were two massive curved stair cases that arced up to the second floor. There were doors under the left stairs that I presumed were to a guest coat closet. On the right side, past the stairs was the main floor doorway to the elevator. While the Chief took the left stairs, I got in the elevator and pushed two.

The door opened with a clear view down the second floor hall, towards the left of an observer standing at the front door, looking between the stairways. The room to my immediate right, visible through glass doors was a sizeable library with tall bookshelves done in some kind of light fine-grained wood that I had never seen before.

I began to think to myself "What's on the third floor, the horse race track? The half-scale model of Grand

Coulee Dam? The ballroom at Versailles?"

It was the room just past the library where the action of the moment was. The Chief had already gotten there when I arrived and was introducing herself to the unfamiliar members of the Crime Scenes crew, and greeting the ones she knew as old friends. She was clearly comfortable in the situation, and was busily asking questions and taking notes. It gave me some time to take a good look at the surroundings.

The door to the room where the incident occurred had been forced open, with shattered pieces of wood still in the carpet of the hall. Straight across the hall, at the front of the house, was obviously the computer nerve center of the property with a quantity of servers, keyboards, printers, work stations, and screens that looked, to my mind, substantial enough to manage the flight dynamics of a couple of 777's. The small beeping noises, the blinking lights, the hum of fans, and the constant scroll of white characters across black screens said that it was all running fine.

I recrossed the hall and entered the murder room, past the splintered door jamb and forcibly uprooted strike plate of the lock. The room was obviously a study, paneled in dark wood. Opposite the door and facing it away from the two windows looking out on the back of the house was a large wooden desk, which, from the level of scrutiny it was receiving from the CS people, ground zero for the killing. To the left of the door and to the right of the user of the desk was a large fireplace in the left side wall. There was a chesterfield sofa facing the fireplace. To the right of the room, left of the desk occupant, was a round conference table with two chairs. On the left wall, nearer to the door than the fireplace was a low cabinet with a vase of artificial flowers, over which hung a still life.

"All right", I thought to myself "this is supposed to be the site of a shotgun slaying. Where did the blast go?" There were a few pock marks on the desk, but not very many. I had been standing inside the door, looking past the desk to the windows, which I noticed were fitted with bolted interior metal lattice work, probably for security.

Then I turned to my left, and saw on the wall to the hall the answer to my question. The piece of art that had formerly hung in that spot was obliterated by the blast of the shot.

So the killing shot came from the window side of the desk, behind the seated victim.

I sidled over to the evidence board that the CS team had set up over by the conference table. Sure enough there was an 8x10 photo of the corpse face down on the desk, with about the right third of his skull missing.

I waited for a bit of a lull in the general level of activity, walked over to the group of investigators which included Chief Cranton, and asked "So, where is it?"

They looked at me as if I had spoken to them in Swahili, looked at each other and the Chief, who asked "Where is what?"

"The hidden stairway. The secret door. The second

access to the room. The door was locked. The widows are barred. Unless you have the theory that the victim locked himself in and then shot himself in the back of the head with a shotgun, there has to be another way in."

To be fair, Chief Cranton had been involved to this point with the details of the crime scene, and had not had an opportunity to think about the big picture.

One of the State CS crew, a woman with close-cropped hair, walked over to the right side of the fireplace, pressed a button on the underside of the mantle and stepped back to reveal an open door to a spiral staircase contained within the chimney chase.

"Where does it go?" I asked. " Down to a hidden vestibule on the same level as the back door."

"I know it is early here, but I guess that only a very few people know about this stair, and the ones that do will have a perfect alibi for the time of death" I ventured.

"What else, Miss Marple?" the Chief said, with a definite touch of sarcasm. All the crew was looking at me.

"Hattie works fine, if it's all the same to you."

"You are a surprising person in a lot of ways, Hattie. Make it Tasha for me" she said, shaking my hand. "What else?" she asked, this time without the edge.

The reference to Miss Marple brought me back in time to a spring afternoon in Beverly Park. Milly and I had just received our appreciation package from Sid for a particularly delicate job, and were celebrating, as usual with some heavily caloric and highly delicious baked goods from Nonna Yana's while we absently watched the tennis players.

After most of the box was empty, Milly, more or less out of the blue, dusted her hands and said "Hattie, just for fun, I put aside my regular night time reading and got a couple of those Agatha Christie Miss Marple stories from the library." This was a surprise, since I knew that Milly's taste in reading ran to philosophers whose names I couldn't pronounce, and whose thinking was, to me, clear as mud.

"What did you think?"

"I think they are lightweight stuff and not very interesting for a variety of reasons. Miss Marple seems to arrive at the "Who", by intuiting the "Why" in each story, and by her knowing that Major Dufferton's first cousin once removed had an affair with the vicar's wife, but then dumped her for the actress, propelling the poor woman into despondency and alcoholism. The major had egg on his face, everyone hated the cousin, who was killed by being brained with the cue ball at the Manor. Everybody has a motive. Nobody has an alibi. It is all so insubstantial." Milly went on.

"You know that my interest in such matters is not the "Who" part, but the "How" part, in particular, "How to Obscure the Who". The Christie villains are all such amateurs. They always get caught.

And the last thing that bothers me is that you and I know how we would go about a closing in Chafing Staghorn or whatever the name is of little burg where Miss Marple lives. Remember Milly's rule? Eliminate first the most dangerous person. If we had a closing there, no matter who our subject was, the village would remark that it was such a coincidence that Miss Marple had chosen to go for a walk on the mill pond with a purse full of bricks. Or have an almost impossible accident with a knitting needle. It drives me crazy."

"Well, nobody is making you read them, are they?"

"No, and I won't ever again."

I was chuckling to myself at the memory when Tasha's voice, asking again, "What else?" brought me back to the present.

"Okay" I said, turning my attention to the Tech who was prying buckshot out of the front wall, "What size shot?"

"Nine" he answered directly.

"Bird shot" I commented. "No shells, of course, but do you have a guess at the gauge?"

"Probably twenty" he said.

"And not much scatter at the wall, so a fairly long barrel." To Tasha, I said "Doesn't that sound like a strange choice for a murder weapon in a confined room? A long barreled bird gun?"

"Did you by any chance find anything exotic affixed to the victim's clothes?" I asked.

Tasha looked at me curiously, and picked up a small plastic bag and passed it to me. It contained a silk poppy like the veteran's day mementos, but in black, not orange.

Oh. My. God. I hadn't seen one of these for years, but the message was the same as when Milly created the first one. I knew now that my initial guesses about what had happened here were right and that the perpetrators were deadly and ruthless adversaries. I thought carefully about how to tell Tasha and her associates what to look for, and look out for, without telling them how I know.

"Think about it this way" I began, almost inadvertently. "Assume that in this world there are killers for whom the death of their victim is not enough. They may wish to leave a calling card, without incriminating themselves. And for their own reasons, they may want, shall we say, a souvenir, a trophy."

"Were there powder burns on the victim's head?"

The techs nodded an affirmative.

"Does the shotgun now make sense?" The slow light of realization was dawning on the crew.

"Somebody has the ear. That is the guilty party. All you have to do is find it."

I collected my cane, and headed for the door and the elevator.

"Tasha, I'm tired. I'll go down to the car and wait."

"I will be right along, Hattie. I just need to see what the team needs tomorrow."

I walked slowly along the hall. In the room opposite the murder room, the computers were all still whirring, clicking, blinking as the streams of data flowed through them. Someone had been emotionally motivated enough to probably drug our guy, and then have a hired gun cut his ear off, and blow the evidence of that off with a shotgun. But motivated not to disturb the data to the basic

174

commercial enterprise. Hmm.

I rode the elevator down to the atrium where Tasha caught up with me.

"Let's get you back to Shady Rest."

Driving down the driveway, we were silent for a bit. Tasha broke it. "Thank you for your comments back there. A fresh point of view is always helpful, particularly in an investigation that is anchored in facts. I hope you won't mind, but I would like to pick your brain about this case."

We had gotten to the bumpy part of the driveway.

"Do I get a gun?" I asked.

Tasha almost exploded. "A gun! Why would I give you a gun? I hate guns! I have never, since I was a beat cop, carried a gun. No, you do not get a gun."

I did not think it was the right time for the "Life Insurance" lecture that Milly had given me.

"How about a uniform? But I must say that the GethsIemane Police uniform are completely déclassé. I could have my daughter, Ines, have one of her designers make you a killer uniform. Of course the blouse would cost $1,500, but you couldn't pin a badge on it, for fear of ruining it. Then, how about just a badge?"

We were at the end of the drive, on the boundary with the public road.

Tasha stopped the car, looked at me and said "I have no idea about where you get any of the stuff you produce. You completely intrigue me."

"What a great way to start a friendship" I said, and

Tasha pointed the car into town and to the Shady Rest.

It had gotten to that time of night when you stopped seeing what was outside the car clearly, and could see your own silhouette reflected back at you. A lot of reflections had been bounced my way recently.

"I will do what I can, Tasha, but I have a favor to ask. My partner, Milly, Ludmilla Netsurov, was killed by what the police labelled "random" gunfire in Beverly Park on 103rd St. on September 27, 1995. In your district. I would like to see the police file.

"That's a long time ago. But I will see what I can do. Write down the name and the date for me."

When she left me off at Shady Rest, I said "Thanks, Tasha. I have put off coming to grips with this for far too long. I appreciate your help."

I went upstairs to my apartment, but could not get ready for bed, or read, or watch television. The image of the Black Poppy was rolling in my brain, and I had to revisit the past.

## 21

# Bad Habits

Both divisions of M & H had hit their peaks in performance in the summer of 1985. We hosted Tupperware parties about every two or three weeks, and literally filled every Elks hall, civic center, or private home that we hired to house the events. We were selling everything the company sent us and, as a result, kept getting lots of Regional Sales Awards (which were nice but of absolutely no monetary value) even if we had to buy the stuff ourselves. Milly's original formula of personally engaging with each attendee, and the courtesy of better-than-average refreshments, had been refined, and adjusted for the tastes and attitudes of the new target customers, who were, we realized to our surprise, about our own kids age. They still loved us. While a lot of things change, one fact does not: for almost every meal there is a residuum in the form of leftovers, and Tupperware still stores it better than anything else.

On the Sid side, we were doing fewer, but more sensitive, and frankly, more lucrative closings. Our employers, who we still did not know, and did not want to know, obviously regarded us as a valuable resource, not to be expended frivolously.

So, it was a bit of a surprise when I got a call at home to hear Sid's slightly anxious voice:

"I need you two down here, now. In an hour."

"Okay, Sid, we'll cancel our opera practice." I had, after a long period of having the daylights scared out of me by Sid, finally been able to pull his nose, a little. "We'll be down."

I called Milly right away. Nobody home. So I walked the block and a half to find her out in her yard, watering her perennials.

"So that was you on the phone? Sorry, I'm in my Zen mode" she said. "What's up?"

"Sid just called. Something big is up."

"Well, let me put on my Dior gown."

I waited while Milly changed and thought about how far we had come. Life isn't easy, but it can be good.

On the way to E-Z loans we made small talk, about the kids, about the Tupperware business, about the neighborhood.

At a lull in the conversation, Milly took a breath and said "I think I finally have the notion of what Sid's people revere and expect from us. It is not too far from what your friends at Marshall Field's responded when they challenged themselves to "Give the Woman What She Wants."

"Sid's people don't just want our subjects dead. They want them to die in an exotically dramatic fashion, of course, without incriminating them. But that's not all. They like to have their souvenirs of the closing that they can mount on their den walls, like hunting trophies. And finally, and this is the point I realized last, is that they would like to leave their calling card on the victim, as a cautionary message to anyone who would try to cross them. So that is why I bought these." And here she produced a package of about twenty-five four-petalled black silk poppies. "The plan here is to leave these in the buttonholes of our subjects. It'll be like a trademark."

I was fine with all that, as I marveled, not for the first or last times at the depth of thought that Milly gave to any issue to which she applied her talents.

The rest of the ride to E-Z Loans was uneventful, in the way that any often-repeated act tends to inspire boredom, rather than attention. That blasé feeling was immediately dispelled, after the gravelly "Come" from Sid at the door of the office, when we entered and got a look at our now-familiar colleague. He was sitting, as usual at the desk, but instead of leaning back in his chair, with his hands folded in his lap, he was perched almost on the edge of his seat, with both hands flat on the desk, the fingers of his left hand drumming a rapid impatient pace. He had not shaved for several days.

"We've got a big problem" he said, even before we had settled into the chairs.

"Well, tell us about it, Sid" said Milly carefully, in an

attempt to calm the turbulent waters.

Getting the point, he said "Sorry to be jumpy. We really do appreciate the help you have given us in cleaning up all of the uncomfortable situations that you handle, so don't think that anyone is upset with you." He took a breath, and relaxed visibly, leaning back against the back of his chair. "Here's the thing. We have very good information that the people that do your job in our biggest rival organization have a contract on one of our guys. One of our Big Guys. We need you to take these hit guys out. Fast."

He reached into the center drawer of the desk and pulled out two folders. He gave one to each one of us. Milly and I simultaneously opened our respective files.

I was looking at a large black and white photograph of a man walking down the street taken from about ten feet away. The man was neatly dressed, wearing a nicely tailored dark suit, with white shirt and plain patterned tie. He was looking at an angle of about thirty degrees to the left of the camera. He had a serious expression on his face and seemed from the motion implied by his manner to be in a hurry. He was slender, but not insubstantial. The gun in his shoulder holster was evident on close examination.

I peeked over at the photo in the front of Milly's folder. It, too, was a street scene shot, this one from front on, at about twenty feet. This guy was, compared to the other figures in the frame, huge. He appeared to be extruded into his crew neck shirt and tight-fitting sport jacket.

His sour expression, obviously broken nose, and shaved head added to the knife scar that began under his left ear and ended just to the left of his mouth to paint the picture of one unpleasant character.

"Do these guys work together all the time?" Milly asked. "As far as we know" said Sid "But they're not partners, like you two. It's more like Mr. Slick is the brains and Big Ugly is the body guard and gopher."

"Do they know about us?"

"We don't think so. But you gotta be careful, they are ruthless, efficient killers. What we do know about them is in the file. We want 'em gone in two weeks."

"We got 'em right where we want 'em" Milly asserted with what I knew to be false confidence. This was going to be a closing of a different kind. We gathered the files and headed for the door.

"Sid this is an unusual request, but this is a different deal. Can we call you if we have questions?" Milly inquired.

Sid thought about that for a minute, not really caring for the notion, but finally said "Okay, here's the number to reach me" and he wrote it on a scrap of paper and handed it to her.

Standing up, I said, "We're off. We've got some work to do." We left.

We went to Milly's house and spent the afternoon reading and re-reading the files. By this time we had named the Boss "Lex Luthor", and the big guy "The Joker", mostly because he clearly wasn't.

After we had read and thought as much as we could stand, we strategized.

"I think we start with the Joker" Milly offered. "We do have a home address for him. Let's follow him until he leads us to Lex."

So early the next morning we were arrayed in the "domestics" disguises in the panel truck outside the Joker's apartment. He appeared at about 7:45, got in his car and went north, finally pulling into the parking lot of a Gold Coast condominium building just off Michigan Avenue. After a bit, a black Cadillac Eldorado, with the Joker driving and Lex riding shotgun, left the lot and turned north. We let them go, but went in to the condo building to figure out, from the mailboxes, where exactly Lex lived. The mailboxes told the tale.

We continued in surveillance mode for the next three days, sometimes starting at the Joker's house, sometimes waiting at Lex's place for the Joker to arrive. To be completely cautious, we changed vehicles each day, using Milly's car, my panel truck and Emilio's Buick, borrowed on some business pretext. We presented as painters, social workers, and government building inspectors.

On each of the three days, we followed our target pair after the Joker had picked up Lex, and served as the chauffeur of the El Dorado. On day one, the pair pulled up in front of a plumbing supply establishment on Winchester Avenue in Ravenswood. The Joker parked at the curb, and waited in the car while Lex went in. Lex was inside for about forty-five minutes, at which point he strolled out of the building, got in the car, said something to the Joker, who squealed away, and headed back to the south, driving directly to Lex's condo, without taking any evasive action. At least we had not been spotted.

On day 2, the pair headed downtown, into the loop. The Joker drove the Caddy into a multi-story ramp on Monroe, just east of LaSalle. Milly was driving and let me out to wait for either or both of them to come down to street level. I was wearing my painter's coveralls, and painter's cap into which my hair was tucked up. I carried a five gallon bucket in which was a gallon can of paint (empty) and a four inch brush. I was dawdling, looking at a sheet of paper as if I was trying to figure out where my job was when both the Joker and Lex came down the parking ramp elevator to the street level and walked west along the south side of Monroe. I hustled after them as discretely as I could and watched them enter an office building, where I was just in time to see them get in the elevator, note that they were the only ones in the car and watch the floor indicator stop at "4". I consulted the building directory to note that the only tenants of the fourth floor were a law firm, and insurance agency and an outfit called "Fortune Enterprises, Inc." I met up with Milly and reported. "Let's see where they go next" Milly said, as we opened the back of the panel truck where we had parked it at the exit of the parking ramp where our subjects had parked, and placed orange cones around the painting paraphernalia we had placed on the ground and putzed around with it in what we felt was a convincing manner.

In about an hour, we saw the two coming back to their vehicle. We quickly pitched the stuff back in the truck, and we ready when the El Dorado came back down the ramp. We followed back to Lex's. The Joker picked up his car, and headed south, apparently toward his apartment.

"Now what was that all about?" I asked Milly. "I have no idea. Maybe we will find out tomorrow."

So day three found us in Emilio's Buick, on which we had placed magnetic "City of Chicago Building Department" signs, waiting just outside Lex's parking garage until the Joker would show up. He was earlier than usual, rolling into the ramp at about 9AM. In about fifteen minutes, the black Caddy, with the Joker at the wheel, left, heading north, using a familiar path, ending at the plumbing supply business, Gardner Wholesale Plumbing Supplies. They parked in front of the entrance on Winchester.

Unlike two days ago, both men got out of the car and approached the building. The Joker took a position at the door, arms folded, looking out at the street traffic, pedestrian and vehicular. Lex went in. He came back out again in fifteen minutes, obviously in a hurry. He nodded at the Joker, both jumped in the car and they squealed off at a high rate of speed. We lost them after about five blocks.

The next morning we met at Milly's and were having coffee at her dining room table in what was, for practical purposes, a council of war.

"What do we know about these guys?" Milly began "We know where they each live, what they each drive, and that, whatever they do, they seem to do it together. I have not seen any place where they are together that would be accessible to us, except Lex's parking garage, which I definitely do not like as a closing site, since we can't be sure that we have other witnesses. Also, there are probably security cameras."

"So, we may have to take them out separately" I said, following her drift. "The Joker would be easy, but Lex is the problem. The minute the Joker does not show up would set off alarm bells and Lex would go into disappearance mode."

"We do need to catch them together in a place to our advantage" Milly said while paging through the morning edition of the Tribune. Milly was an obsessive reader of not only the Tribune, but also the New York Times and the Washington Post. She paid particular attention to the editorials, and would frequently write responses.

"Wait a minute, look at this" she said excitedly as she finished the article in the local section that she had been reading. "Here" she said, folding the paper back, and handing it to me pointing out the article in question.

"Triple slaying in Ravenswood" read the headline. "Chicago police report the gunshot slaying of three Chicago residents at Gardner Wholesale Plumbing Supply on Winchester Avenue yesterday morning at about ten AM. Dead are Samuel Gardner, age 43, the proprietor of the business, Trudy LeClaire, age 55, secretary to the firm, and Jessica Gardner, age 10, daughter of Samuel, who had been present as part of "Take Your

Daughter to Work Day". Each had been shot once in the head. Police say that no motive is known. Investigations continue."

"They shot a kid!" I yelled. Milly replied, "You mean, Lex shot a kid, and an innocent bystander who was no threat to him. I am so angry." She paced around the room repeating, "Never kill in anger. Never kill in anger. Never kill in anger. I am so close to chucking that fundamental belief that I could track him down and kill him right now with my bare hands, no matter who was watching."

"I agree, but we need to calm down, and do our regular careful, deliberate process" I cautioned.

She sat down. "You are, of course, right, Hattie" she said, taking a few deep breaths. "The Fates are one thing. Nemesis is something completely different."

I had no idea what she was talking about, but nodded in agreement. She picked the paper back up and paged through the rest, scanning the headlines and articles.

She stopped suddenly. "Listen to this, Hattie, as she read: Archdiocese of Chicago to host "Go for the Green" a fundraising golf tournament for local Catholic schools on the weekend of July 25-26. Entries accepted until July 15." She continued, "This is our shot. Here's my idea."

I liked it and told her so.

"We've got to tell Sid and get his help." "Agreed."

Milly searched for and found the scrap of paper with Sid's number and handed it to me. I dialed. The phone rang about twelve times until Sid picked up and answered with customary gruffness, "What?"

"Sid, it's Hattie. We have a plan for our big job, but we need to run it by you. Now."

He thought about it. "Okay give me two hours." Sid hung up.

We dressed up a bit, and headed in towards E-Z Loans. For one of the only times we made the trip, there was no talk of Nonna Yana's.

We didn't have a lot to say until we were seated at Sid's desk. Sid was just as on edge about the situation as we were. He was not wearing his usual sport coat, but was wearing a crew neck shirt and blue jeans. He leaned forward in his seat, hands on his lap. He still had not shaved

"Well?"

Milly started. "We've got a bead on the subjects and will perform the closing as instructed. But here's our problem: We haven't found, until now, an idea that could flush these guys both out into a place where we can get them at the same time. We now have a plan. Look at this golf tournament that will be sponsored by the Archdiocese as a fundraiser. We think if our guy who is the target of the hit by these goons will enter the tournament, and let it be known to them that he did, they could not miss the chance to do their job on the course. Under no circumstances should our guy actually show up, but, let me tell you, if those two show up on the course, we've got 'em; both at one go." She took a breath. "Golf courses are Dangerous Places. There are no cops, there are a lot of places to hide, and nobody expects to be attacked on a golf course. If Hattie and I were assigned to a closing, and we found out that the subject would be on a golf course at a certain date, we would jump at the chance to do it there. They'll think that they are the hunters, but they will be the prey." She passed to him the newspaper article with the details.

Sid looked back and forth between us. "Let me get this straight. You want our man to enter this tournament, with no intention of going, and then make sure these two bozos get wind of the entry"

"Right. And on the off chance that this helps with the publicity issue, Hattie and I tracked our two killers to what we think is their superior's office on the fourth floor of the Sherman Building on Monroe Street in the Loop. The cover name of the office is "Fortune Enterprises, Inc."

Sid took out a pen and slowly wrote down the name and address of the office. I realized that I had never seen Sid utilize a writing instrument, and had half believed him to be illiterate.

"You might imagine that I need to get this approved. I will let you know. If this is not a go, be ready for Plan B. We are running out of time."

It took two days. Late in the afternoon, Sid called Milly, said the plan was approved and that our guy had already entered and received a personal thanks from the Bishop for the entry, and the generous donation that went with it. The publicity faucets had been opened to the max.

"Okay, Hattie, we are approved. We have work to

do. Let's make this our finest hour" Milly said when she told me. This was business, serious business, but we both knew it was going to be particularly satisfying.

The first day of the tournament, Saturday, found Milly and I dressed in summer nun's habits that were grey with the white head covering through which only the face of the wearer showed. Both of us had added fake eyeglasses, Milly with round wire rims that sat on her round face in a way that made you think of a cartoon stuffed owl, and me with pointy framed black glasses straight out of the fifties.

"You look ridiculous" Milly said, between bursts of laughter, as we bounced along the fairways of Edgebrook Golf Course on the bright July morning, perfect for golf, in a golf cart driven by Milly. We had on board two coolers and a box for our equipment.

"And you don't?" I asked having equal difficulty in suppressing uncontrolled laughter.

"Well, at least we are unrecognizable. I suggest that we don't look at each other. Let's see if we can find the Joker and Lex."

"I have a pretty good general idea of where they will be" I said. "Right at the turn point from the eleventh to the twelfth hole, at the back corner of the course. There is a shelter with a restroom and picnic bench. Very remote from the clubhouse." I had wrangled my way into a beginner's class for prospective members about two weeks ago, which had given me an excellent idea about the layout and even a course map, which we had used to hide our car and find a place to liberate a golf cart.

"Let's head that way." We putted along, stopping at each group at a tee or a green to ask if they would like a beverage. We had given out quite a few sodas and a lot of beer from the two coolers.

As we got to the turn point, we were in luck.

"There's the Joker" Milly said, motioning with a nod to the familiar figure, dressed in unfamiliar golf shirt and slacks, in his 'standing guard' pose outside the restroom building, behind which Lex was no doubt holding forth.

"Okay, let's check it out, said Milly, as she gunned the cart in the Joker's direction. He looked at us with interest as we drove up.

"May we give you a beverage, sir? We really appreciate your supporting our schools." The joker bit back a tart response, as his brow unfurrowed a bit, seeing that, as nuns, we were no threat to him or his boss. "No thanks, sisters. We have work to do. " Which was just what you would expect from him, a stupid thing to say. Who does work on a golf course, except the golf pro, or assassins?

We could see Lex just around the building talking on one of those huge walkie-talkie things that had just become popular.

"Well you let us know if you change your mind." We drove back to the fairway to see if there were any golfers in the near vicinity. There weren't.

"You know the plan" said Milly. Only one change for you I recommend: Life Insurance." I got it. The original plan was that I was to come up behind the Joker and pith him like a biology lab frog with my stiletto. We had both just concluded he was too tall.

"Fine. Let's go."

Milly turned around and approached our friend from the opposite direction. She slowed to let me off, out of the Jokers sight, and then drove in a big arc aiming at the back of the building. The Joker saw her coming and watched her progress curiously. That gave me a chance to come up behind him within about fifteen yards. He was still turned away from me when the silenced Glock scored a perfect hit on the silhouette of his back. He dropped to the ground in place. I hurried around to the corner of the building where Lex was still on the mobile phone, oblivious of us, believing his backside to be protected by the late and not yet lamented Joker.

"Where the hell is he? I know he is on the course somewhere! Don't tell me you can't find him!" Lex shouted into his mobile. About that time he must have seen Milly, who had gotten off the golf cart and had just enough time to carefully aim the over-under double arrow crossbow. He was completely dumbfounded by the sight of a hefty nun with such a weapon pointed at him. In the split second before Milly let both bolts go, I imagined that I could hear him think: "It's a nun. And a nun with a crossbow. And I thought I had it bad in Cate……". Both bolts struck home, the first hitting him in the abdomen, the second hitting the bullseye of the heart. Down and out. "That's for Jessica Gardner" Milly said, with feeling. Turning to me, she said, "Give me your knife, Hattie." I unstrapped it from my forearm and gave it to her. She removed Lex's right ear, and put it in the ice-filled Tupperware container that I produced from my pocket. She added the ear, snapped the lid in place, turned it upside down and said, with the same tone and emphasis that she always used at Tupperware parties "Preserves Freshness." I almost lost it.

I took the knife and the Tupperware back to where the Joker had fallen and added to the collection the tip of the Joker's nose. When I got back around the building, Milly was attempting to retrieve the arrows. She had gotten the abdomen shot out, but was wrestling with the center hit. "Damn thing is stuck in his spine."

"Leave it, Milly, we've got to get out of here."

"Okay, but I hate leaving evidence, it's a violation of one of Milly's Rules; but we need to do one more thing" she said as she pulled from her pocket two of the black poppies and threaded one in Lex's shirt buttonhole. She picked up the one arrow and the fallen walkie-talkie and drove the cart back around the building where I affixed the other black poppy to the Joker. We then roared off as fast as the car could go to the drop point of our car, tossing Lex's mobile into the pond on the next hole.

"Mission accomplished. Dramatic method used, employer souvenirs secured, and our signature calling card" Milly said with some satisfaction. "But we have developed some Bad Habits. We have to get rid of them."

"I couldn't agree more" I concurred as we reach the path in the woods at the edge of the course leading to the cut in the fence by our car. We ditched the cart, after removing all evidence we could, got through the fence and went home.

We had expected to hear from Sid very soon, and were a little nervous when Sunday and Monday went by without any call. By that time the papers were full of the spectacular details of what the press was calling the "most ruthless and audacious gangland killing in a town where killing has become an art form."

But on Tuesday morning, Sid called. "Would 11 o'clock be convenient for you?" This was the first time that I remember Sid asking that as a question rather than giving it as a directive. "Sure, Sid we will be there." I called Milly right away, and dressed in my sleeveless yellow sheath, with matching opera gloves accented by white pill box hat. When I picked her up, I found that Milly had also dressed with extra flair. She was wearing a short-sleeve lilac dress with matching jacket. When I commented that I really liked it and had never seen it before, Milly replied with mock indignance "Hattie, you may not believe this, but I actually can dress myself without your help."

I just grinned and said "Milly, I would never disbelieve anything about you."

When we knocked on the door of E-Z Loans, we were shocked to hear Sid say "Come in, please."

The change in Sid since the last time we had seen him was truly remarkable. He was freshly shaven. He had on what appeared to be a brand-new navy blue sport coat, with brass buttons, adorned with an orange paisley pocket square over a crisply ironed white shirt. He was leaning back in his chair with his hands on his lap, an attitude we had not seen him adapt for a long time.

"Well, look at us" said Sid almost smiling. "I have known you two a long time now, and you have never ceased to amaze me in one way or another. I don't think I have to tell you how happy our guys are with the golf course job. They think you have given notice that any attempt to mess with their safety will be dealt with harshly. Well done."

This was the point where Sid would usually reach into the desk and retrieve the envelope containing our employers' estimation of the value of our work. But this time he reached down to the floor and picked up a box a little bigger than a shoe box. "We hope that this says enough about how your work has been and will be appreciated.

"Thanks, Sid, we do the best we can, and are glad that our efforts are appreciated."

"No worry, there. From here on you get the big jobs. We will give you a little break, but we'll be in touch. He shook our hands as we left.

"I knew we were good, but not just how good" Milly said. "You do know where the next stop is."

I certainly did. Nonna Yana's was in full lunch mode when we came through the door. "Where on earth have you two been?" Irena asked with her characteristic burst of enthusiasm she showed her customers.

"We've been working hard, but no matter, what is good today?" Milly inquired greedily. It seems that the pierogis were particularly recommended. I got two, while Milly decided to limit herself to a half dozen, along with a pickle, and a piece of poppy seed cake. We took our lunch across the street, along with Sid's box. We sat, as always by the tennis court which were completely full of players, dressed in summer tennis attire, and playing earnestly for the appointed period, at the end of which a new group was lined up outside the fence, anxious for their turn.

After Milly had finished her lunch (which actually was a surprisingly short time) she peeked in the box. "I think we ought to look at this at home."

So we drove back to Milly's house, and brought the box into her dining room and spread the contents on the table. It was cash, of course, but we had no idea how much. We counted, and rechecked the count. We were looking at $100,000 in crisp new bills.

We looked at each other. "That is one boatload of Tupperware "Milly said "We have some work to do to put our accounting back into reasonable balance."

"It's a nice problem to have. I am not complaining."

And so we had officially arrived at the top of our game. But from the top, the only way is down.

## 22

# Three murder files.

Christmas had come and gone, as always, in a blur. I had gladly accepted the opportunity to be with Roberto's family in Moline, biting back my disappointment that another holiday season had gone by without so much as a hint of the presence of Ines, whose image had lately been pressing itself into my consciousness. Javy and family were not able to head north, due to a commitment to Isabella's family. Of course I understand, but I am struck, hard, by the irony of the fact that the more you really need your kids, the less able you are, physically, to get to see them. This is not really a complaint. I think about a great number of my fellow Shady Rest residents, and know that a lot of them, through no particular action, except time, have none, or few connections to anyone, let alone family, to connect to. They are like those pathetic photographs of the single polar bear, standing, surprised, on an ice floe, as it suddenly breaks away from the main sheet and floats into the open sea. Alone. Milly had introduced me to the Rime of the Ancient Mariner, which she liked a lot, but which I thought, at the time, was stupid. I do now remember the line "Alone, alone, all, all alone, alone on a wide, wide sea....". That, to my mind, perfectly describes the combination of fear, and realization of the inevitable, that is the ageing process.

I went down to breakfast on the Wednesday after Christmas, having dressed in one of my old favorite hound's tooth suits, with off-white blouse, accented by matching harvest brown scarf and gloves. I completed the ensemble with my brown Borsalino, worn, as always at what I regarded as a rakish attitude.

The dining room was uncommonly empty, whether the residents who travelled for the holidays had not returned, were in their rooms fighting off jet lag, or the effects of massive turkey, ham or roast beef dinners, or were just taking time to settle back into the dull rhythms of life in a retirement residence, after having a sudden and complete immersion in what life, before Shady Rest, had been. It's like a hangover, only worse.

I spotted Harrison and Florence Demory , sitting by themselves, and pushed my walker over.

"May I sit with you this morning?"

"Of course" they both said, almost in unison. Harrison got up and held out a chair for me, confirming my original impression of him as a gentleman in every sense of the word. They were both dressed to a degree that was clearly above the Shady Rest median: she wore a tailored,

long sleeve wool dress in a dark burgundy, complement-
ed with gold bracelet, necklace and small hoop earrings.
He wore a navy blue blazer, light blue shirt and orange
bow tie with a subtle pattern. I have to confess that I have
always been a sucker for a man who could pull off a bow
tie. I know that even at the peak of the ebb and flow of the
popularity cycle of bow ties, not very many men could
make the look work for them. Harrison Demory clearly
was one of those few.

"I am sorry that I haven't gotten to know you since
we met a couple of weeks ago. If I remember our meeting, Bella was in the middle of one of her Narratives. How
are you finding Gethsemane?" I asked the question that
way deliberately, to divert the conversation away from
the topic of how they felt about moving into a retirement
community. I know what the answer to that question is,
and that is basically acceptance of the inevitable, with a
variable degree of bitterness. What I wanted to give them
the opportunity to comment on what how they felt about
being African-American, and moving from a majority
Black metropolitan area like St. Louis to a basically white
majority Midwestern small town.

Unlike is the case for a lot of couples, neither one was
the spokesperson for the marriage, each having his or her
voice and opinion.

Florence answered first. "The size of the place was a
bit of a shock at first. We were both professors at Wash U
and were used to the cultural and social activities of not
only the university, but of the City in general. But now

we are closer to the grandchildren, and, on balance, we like the place."

Harrison continued "Our daughter is the Assistant Superintendent of Schools here in Gethsemane, and has a wide range of friends, including many members of the local Black community. We have met a lot of folks that we enjoy a lot, so it hasn't been too hard a change. I have to say that I was getting sick of mowing the lawn, putting up the storm windows and wrestling the snow blower" he said. "But I do feel a bit uprooted from information about the sports teams that I have followed."

"You must be a Cardinals fan. I know what you mean. I'm from the south side of Chicago and almost had a stroke when I realized that the local paper did not have White Sox box scores."

"I do have to say, though," Florence went on "there's an uncomfortable feeling about the place that we can't quite put our finger on, but is here in the background all of the time. It's as if the white population regards us as different, as 'others', not quite entitled to be regarded as equals. We don't see outright bigots here; nobody will call us the "N" word, or put on sheets and come looking for us with torches, but they can smile at us, while not really regarding us as individuals. We feel vaguely diminished as people."

"I think about the story that President Obama related about walking along the street down by the University of Chicago, past a car in which a white man sat at the wheel, only to hear the door lock as he passed." I added. "My feeling is that the white residents of Gethsemane, either have not thought about whether they would be inclined to lock the door, or just do it, as a reflex."

"That is the sort of racism that is largely at the root of the whole Ferguson problem" said Harrison "It can't help but make one angry, because you can't do anything about it."

"That makes me think" said Florence, "have you met LaTasha Cranton, the new chief of police? She has some very constructive ideas about combatting institutional racism, right here in Gethsemane."

"I have in fact met her, and find her a very impressive person" I responded without elaborating on the circumstances of the meeting.

We continued our conversation on a lighter note throughout breakfast leaving us all with a better acquaintance with each other than had been the case at the beginning of the meal.

I returned to my room with an improved feeling about me, and life in general. The phone rang. I answered, hoping it would be Ines.

"Hattie, it's Tasha. I have some questions and information for you. Can you come to my office, say mid-morning tomorrow? Say 9:30 or 10?"

"Sure. Shall I bring refreshments?"

I was happy that she laughed. "No, just bring you."

After some careful consideration the next morning I dressed in my simple black wool suit, white blouse with single strand of pearls, and my thin-brimmed black fedora. The whole look was rather plain, so I searched through my jewelry box to find something to sparkle it up a bit, when my eye fell on the green-eyed scarab, that I hadn't worn for years. Here's to you Milly, I thought to myself.

I called a cab and directed it to the police station which was in a building by itself, close to downtown, but right next to a public park. Just inside the front door was a reception desk that was staffed by a woman in civilian clothes who smiled engagingly as I came to the desk.

In most of my former life, I have made a conscious effort to avoid being in police stations. In the few times in Chicago in which avoidance was impossible, I found that the "reception" area was routinely staffed by some mean-looking, low-pay grade, uniformed cop who would look at visitors in a manner that suggested that he or she was deciding whether just to shoot you or whether you might have legitimate business there. It was my definite sense that the visitor had the burden of proof on the issue. So, I was amazed and somewhat taken aback to hear the pleasant woman say, in an equally pleasant voice: "Welcome to the Gethsemane Police Center. May I help you?"

I told her that I had an appointment with Chief Cranton. She said "Oh yes, you must be Hattie Rosales. Go on up to her office on the second floor. She is expecting you. The elevator is right over there" she pointed to her left" To the right and across the hall when you get off." She smiled again as she answered the phone.

On my way up on the elevator, I realized that the reception area had to be a direct influence of Tasha's and a reflection of her attitude to her job: open, helpful, service oriented, and totally professional. Tasha impressed me more each time that I met her.

At her door, I knocked and, at the invitation, opened the door, pushed the walker into the room. Tasha was seated at her desk which was directly opposite the door, in front of the window looking out over the park.

"Hello, Hattie" she said, standing up and walking over to greet me. "We will be sitting over here at the conference table." She pointed to the table just to my right, in the corner by the sink. "Can I get you coffee, tea?" She asked, after seating me at the table.

"Tea, please. Green, if you have it" I answered.

While Tasha busied herself with tea for me and coffee for her, I had a chance to look around the office. It was impeccably neat, with not a single piece of paper in evidence with the exception of the group of files that sat before the chair in which she obviously intended to sit. Her desk held a pen set and a few mementos. The bookshelves on the same wall as the sink and coffee/tea service were filled with neatly arranged volumes, a few pictures and some small sculptures. The walls had been painted a warm burnt orange color that pulled some of the natural tones of the wood of the bookshelves. It presented an inviting setting, not at all what I would have thought the Chief of any police force would occupy.

"Tea", said Tasha putting down the mug in front of

me, and, returning to the counter to get her mug of coffee, sat down, by the stack of files, picked up her mug, blew on it, set it down, and said, while looking at me, "You look rather serious today, Hattie. Is that a scarab? My undergraduate major was Cultural Anthropology, with an emphasis on the mythology of death."

Note to self. Do not ever, again, underestimate this woman's intelligence or intuitive ability. There was only one other person I had met in whose presence I felt continually behind the curve of intelligence.

Wishing to divert some attention to my mistaken choice of jewelry, I said, as casually as I could, "Do I get a badge?"

"No badge, but let's get started. I have three files, all homicide files, each affecting you differently. The first is the Mortensen file, on which you have more or less by your own steam, become a consultant." She opened the top file on the stack, after having placed it in front of her.

"The autopsy report for J. Hartley Mortensen, shows the time of death to be from 10PM to Midnight. Cause of death was the gunshot to the head. But here's the interesting thing. Decedent's blood shows a large dose of secobarbital, with alcohol, administered such that, at the time of the fatal shot, Mortsensen was essentially comatose. He was out for the count when he was shot."

So, the old Texas two step. I drug the victim and beat it to establish an alibi, and your minion administers the coup de grace. Do si do.

"Any physical evidence? Prints? Glass for the

knock-out drops?" I knew the answer to the question.

"Nothing. Nothing except a very dead body, a bunch of buckshot and some widely distributed biological evidence."

"Tell me about the victim."

Tasha took a breath, looked at the file, returned her gaze to me, and started.

"J. Hartley Mortensen, 'Jack' to his intimates, was a self-made rich guy. From a modest, middle class family in Zanesville Ohio, he worked his way into the Ivy League, Cornell, to be exact. He studied business but was also interested in vinicultural science. The big leap for him was apparently in his junior year, when he had a "Semester Abroad" in the French Bordeaux wine country. He learned wine, and the wine business as an intern. And, oh, did I say, he, by this time, spoke fluent French. He leveraged his experiences, upon graduation, into a wine import business. He learned international trade rules, shipping methods, and the idiosyncratic and irregular American liquor laws. His import business was a huge success."

"That explains the Chateau in the Heartland, I guess" I added, hoping to prompt more.

"It was apparently only the beginning. Jack went back and got a Wharton School MBA, and began to see the advantages of expansion, vertically and horizontally, as the economists say. The result is, to an outside observer, a bewildering array of nested businesses that are all loosely run under the name of KM International. The businesses include foodstuffs, both domestic and imported, clothing, sporting goods, and pharmaceuticals, just to name a few. All of the components are privately held and the accounting information for the whole shebang is complicated and hard to get. We have our accounting types looking into it, but it is slow going."

"How about household staff?"

"Jack employed a full-time, eight-to-five, housekeeper, Edna Hoffman, who lives here in town and who was off at the time of the killing. She had, interestingly enough, no idea of the hidden staircase. Jack also employed a sort of personal chef, Antoine Didion, who commuted from Chicago three days a week and who would prepare meals, not to eat immediately, but to put in the frig, or freeze. Jack, apparently, liked to do meal preparation for himself, whether he ate in his study or in the dining room. He did, frequently host big dinner parties that he always had catered. The outdoor gardening and lawn care was done by a local contractor. So the staff profile outside of eight to five was zero. Jack bounced around in the house like a BB in a boxcar."

"So who are your suspects?"

"Well, from the usual "who possibly benefits?" perspective, there are his business partners in most of the pieces of the enterprise, Stewart Karlin, and his sister, Genevieve Mortensen-Pratt, Jack's ex-wife, Caroline Singleton, and his daughter Britany Mortsensen. I have talked briefly with each of them on the telephone, but have yet to interview them personally.

"Karlin is a tough guy to get to talk to with all of the layers between him and a caller. I. of course, can flash a badge, even on the phone, and finally got to talk to him. He has a pretty good alibi for the night of the murder, having been seen in a bar and a restaurant that night in Minneapolis, where his office is. Karlin is by the way a food wholesale/retail magnate, who was pleased to match up his empire with Mortensen's import/ domestic shipping expertise. He contends that he had no ongoing dispute with Jack, either personally or professionally, and that Jack's death caused him actual financial hardship, in the loss on expertise in a great number of aspects of the business."

"Bottom, line" he said "Nobody can replace Jack's knowledge of the wine business. Viv, I mean Genevieve, is really good, but she is not Jack" Karlin commented when I asked him how the business was damaged by Jack's absence.

"When I asked him, what Jack was like, there was a long pause while he thought about it" Tasha continued, "Then he said 'Jack was extremely good at whatever he did, but he was conscious of the fact and would let you know that he was good. He was never mean, or devious, or dishonest, but he was so taken with his own virtues that it was like being the business partner of god-damned John the Baptist.' "He said that he will make the effort to visit with me in person."

Tasha turned to the next page in the file.

"Genevieve-Mortensen Pratt is one impressive

businessperson" Tasha commented, "She is older than her brother by two-and-a half years, three grades in school, and throughout the K-12 years was the shining star, graduating as the valedictorian of their high school, getting a full ride to Harvard, getting a business degree in three years, moving on to an immediate Harvard MBA. She was pursuing a PhD in economics at the University of Chicago when Jack persuaded her to join his firm as it was just exploding into the conglomerate it is today. She manages the international monetary exchanges, and the division that includes apparel outlets and sporting goods. She goes by 'Viv'"

"When I asked her to consider who would want Jack dead, she responded 'Jack had no enemies to my knowledge. He had a lot of money, of course, which I am sure goes to his kid, as does his interest in the companies. His death means that I have a lot more work to do, without any real compensation for it.'"

"Viv lives in Chicago. She was, at the time of shooting, at dinner at Spiaggia with two of her business school classmates. She claims to know nothing about the configuration of the house, or its staffing. She has been there for business meetings. I have an appointment to meet her in Chicago next week."

Tasha turned another page in the file.

"Caroline Singleton, formerly Caroline Mortensen, was at her home in Oak Park when I called. She was completely direct about how she felt about Jack's death. 'I was getting $15,000 a month in alimony, which terminated at his death. I never disliked Jack; I just got tired of his living smugly in his own world. So not only don't I have a motive to kill him, if you find out who did, let me know, and I will kill the SOB and save you the cost of prosecution.' Britany was on break and staying with Caroline until the semester started, but was not at home on the date of the murder, but was staying for a few days with a friend in Evanston."

Tasha took a breath, and continued.

"Britany Mortensen is nineteen, and a sophmore at Oberlin College, majoring in musical studies and comparative literature. She was staying with her friend, Jillian Zhou, when her dad was shot. I have not yet spoken to Britany, but I have confirmed with the Zhous that Britany was there and that she and Jillian were at a local dance club on the night in question."

"Nothing in any of that to point any fingers. Let me ask you this, Tasha: What's your intuition of what is going on here?"

"I have nothing solid to go on here, but I keep coming back to the fact that there is a whole pile of money running through Jack's enterprises, and that somehow the stream that was, to this point, running to Jack, is now about to be diverted to someone else."

"That sounds perfectly reasonable" I allowed, "but let me repeat a couple of things about this case that are really clear to me. First, and I can not emphasize how evident this is to me, you are dealing with some really dangerous people. Just look at the means they have chosen to accomplish the deed. Do not ever underestimate them, or give them a chance to get you.

"Next, to solve this mess, you are going to have to 'Miss Marple' it; you need to determine the motive behind it. But the motive will not prove the case against the ultimate bad guy. You will never, repeat never, be able to find or convict the trigger-puller. The only way to get to the evil genius is to find the ear."

"I do appreciate your advice, Hattie" Tasha said "but this ain't my first trip to the majors. I intend to keep on top of the evidence and actively get the full story from the suspects."

"Your dollar, Tasha. Let me know what I can do to help. What's next?"


Tasha closed the file in front of her, set it to the side. She took the next on from the stack.

"Janet Jennings. Cause of death: cardiac arrest from a massive overdose of opiods, OxyCodone HCl, to be exact. Autopsy shows that she was a regular user, but ingested the stuff in pill form, not by needle. In her desk, and on her computer were her customer lists for the sales she made of the prescription drugs that she stole from the meds of both the living and deceased Assisted Living residents. The lists include buyers who seem to be junior high and high school students. Our drug officers are beside themselves in getting this break into the underground market for these nasty drugs. They don't think that this is the source of our entire opioid problem, but is an important piece."

She paused, and looked directly at me.

"There are only a couple of loose ends that are not quite consistent with the drug dealer, drug user-dealer overdose scenario, that frankly bother me, and will keep this file open until they get cleared up.

First, is the question of where in the Sam Hill is Janet's coffee cup? The autopsy shows that the fatal drugs were ingested by mouth and with a lot of coffee. There was no soiled cup in her office. Who took it?"

"Next are the three written communications, all printed on the office printer, apparently typed on Darlene's computer, the first the set of directions to Darlene for her tasks on the morning of Janet's demise. Why would Darlene type instructions to herself? The next is the note posted on Janet's door advising that she was in conference. Darlene swears that she didn't type it, and that Janet never typed much of anything herself, and was never, to Darlene's recollection "in conference". The last was in the typed note in the package to the Nursing Home Regulator of the Illinois Department of Public Health. That note, unsigned, on Shady Rest stationery said: "Check the medications of deceased Assisted Living residents at Shady Rest in Gethsemane." Taken all together, don't those notes, suggest that someone wanted Darlene out of the way for long enough to dope Janet off the planet and to have time to get away? If so, who?"

"Hmm" I said, refusing to wilt under Tasha intense gaze, "Curious. I see your point."

She had not moved her eyes from me.

"The file is not closed" she said, at last.

She folded it closed, and put it on top of the Mortensen file.

She pulled in front of her a manila file, a faded orange in color, that had dog-eared corners, and an exterior that showed, in columns, who had checked the file out, and when, with a similar entry about when the file had been checked back into whatever central registry the CPD maintained. In bold, black,

lettering across the front of the file was written "CLOSED".

The folder was sealed, with tape. Tasha walked across the room, pulled a letter opener from her desk, came back to the conference table, slit open the folder, sat back in her chair, spun the file to face me and pushed it across to me.

As I looked at the file, labelled in bold through all of the bureaucratic scribblings, labelings, color codings, and check marks, LUDMILLA NETSUROV, I knew that I now had to confront the unresolved abyss that Milly's death left in my soul.

I looked over at Tasha who was regarding me as if she was the Sphinx, took a deep breath, and opened the file. I had been waiting for years to get to the particulars of Milly's death, but I was not ready for this.

The first item in the file was an 8 by 10 police scene of crime photo, in excrutiating detail. It was Milly's body, face-down. She was wearing, not one of her professional suits or disguises, but one of the floral-patterned, puff-sleeved house dresses, of which she had many, and which she always wore at home. I knew them all. She had been shot, once, in the head.

I completely lost it at this point. My friend, partner, mentor and philosophic compass shot dead, in a heap. The repressed memories of twenty years ago came flooding back.

I opened my mouth to speak, choked on the words, and broke into uncontrollable, unconsolable weeping. I put my head down on my hands and just cried.

Whether it was two minutes, or five, or ten, I finally sat up, looked at Tasha who stoicly took in the scene. I tissued off the tears, cleared my mind, turned the death photo over, and got my brain back into getting some sense out of the police file on Milly's death.

I was now able, with some difficulty, to read the reports of the investigating officers, which included a description of the scene. The victim was found, slumped forward, off a bench in the northwest corner of the park, almost as far as you can get from the bench where we would sit. Milly did not have her purse. Her car was not parked in any of the parking areas either in the park itself or on the adjacent streets. The only forensic evidence was a Nonna Yana box in which was a half-eaten piece of poppy seed cake. No shells, and more significantly, no gun.

Wait a minute. The picture I was getting here was not at all similar to the one I had put together in the immediate aftermath twenty some odd years ago. The police had put it out that it had been a drive by, from which I had concluded that there were multiple gunshot wounds. I tried to remember exactly what Milly had told me that caused me to conclude that she had been involved in a closing that went horribly wrong. It was something along the lines of "I have one more job to do". But that wasn't it, now that I thought about it carefully. It was "I have one more closing I have to work on."

Holy Mother of God. Could it be?

"Tasha, help me out here. Am I reading this file right? The only personal item found at the scene is the Nonna Yana box? And there are no guns or gun-related evidence?" I slid the folder across the table to her. She opened it with the manner of a person who has looked at these files for her whole professional life, had made careful additions to them, relied on them for leads, inspiration, and prompts for courtroom testimony.

"Peters was the on the site investigator. Good cop. This was, what, 1995? He was probably 50 or 55. His strength was the care with which he made minute observations of the scene. His weakness, incidentally, was that he had no idea of what to make of the facts he had collected. He had absolutely no creativity or intuition." She didn't have to say that her particular aptitude was just that.

"No, you are right. No personal items. No weapons on the scene. Only one shot."

So, Milly was on the spot without Life Insurance in complete contradiction of one of her cardinal rules for closings, was not dressed for action, and was sitting down when she was shot. She was not at work.

Tasha was still looking at the file.

"What on earth is "Aguonu Pyragas"? she asked, reading the file entry on what was handwritten on the Nonna Yana box.

It is a Ukranian poppy seed cake, made with honey, hazelnuts and walnuts. Milly loved it."

Tasha looked off into the distance. "It never occurred to me" she said with emphasis.

She was transported into her own thoughts.

So was I.

## 23

# The Djinn Files

It took Lieutenant LaTasha Cranton of the Violent Crimes Section of the South Area of the Chicago Police Department, no small amount of time to find the crime scene of the case to which she had just been assigned, despite the fact that she was a life-long City resident, and an eight-year veteran of the force. All of those years had been spent in the South Area of the enforcement scheme of CPD, the Area which included the truck dispatch center that was the site of her newest murder case. The address showed that Zephyr Trucking was located on Broadway, just east of Old Western Avenue, south of the Calumet Sag Channel, down in Blue Island.

This case was of the type that LaTasha had found herself increasingly involved with. Unlike most homicides, here there was no apparent motive, no obvious suspects, and, most interestingly, no physical evidence left at the scene. In such past cases, LaTasha had distinguished herself by carefully assessing the limited evidence, and drawing intelligent inferences from all of the facts and circumstances of the incident, to derive the connection of crime and perpetrator. In short, where most cops were trained in, and good at, to some degree, the questions of "trees", Lieutenant Cranton was an excellent "forest" person.

After driving her unmarked Department car, slowly east and west along Broadway while looking for the address she had been given, it occurred to her that, since she was looking for a trucking company, that instead of looking for business signs or address markers, she should just look for a place with a bunch of trucks. That worked immediately. She pulled up in front of a locked gate on the north side of Broadway, which gave onto a large compound in which were parked about twenty semi truck trailers. She stopped, got out of the car, and was greeted from the other side of the fence by a familiar face, District 5 Detective Carlton Jablonski, who had hustled out from the building on the southeast corner of the lot. He punched a code into the keypad on the inside of the fence and the gate opened. LaTasha returned to her car, drove through the gate, parked by the nearby building, which appeared to be the dispatch office, and got out to greet her colleague.

"Hi, Carl, How you been?"

"Okay, Tasha. Same old stuff. Too much work, too little pay."

"So what do we have here?"

Latasha had taken the time to note that the entire compound was surrounded by an eight-foot tall, chain link fence, topped by a barbed wire strip, leaning inwards at forty-five degrees, and further topped by a coil of razor wire. There seemed to be no other gates, aside from the keypad activated front gate through which she had entered. Serious security.

"I'm sure you've looked at the file, but let me take you through the particulars, and show you actually where it went down" Carl said, gesturing towards, and leading Lt. Cranton to the dispatch building.

"The victim was Jared Gelbard, night watchman and dispatcher, who was strangled, apparently with some kind of wire at about 3:30 AM on the morning of Thursday, March 18" He stepped into the office, which had a counter to the left of the door, behind which was a desk situated so as to look through the window on the west wall of the office, out to the gate. There was also a desk to the right of the door in front of a row of metal filing cabinets. There were two doors on the wall immediately opposite the entrance door.

"The victim was found, face-down, head towards the door, just past the far end of the counter, by the day shift supervisor as he arrived at about 7AM that morning" Jablonski intoned, looking occasionally at his notes, and pointing at the spot where the victim was found. LaTasha noted that there was no chalk outline or other crime scene marking, and so concluded that the CS unit had been there, and gone, for some time.

"There was no sign of forced entry, either on the door to the building here, or out at the street gate. You saw what that was like. You need an electronic code to get in. The system has not been tampered with or noticeably disabled. Nothing was stolen or tampered with in the office, and all of the keys and computers are accounted for. None of the trailers or the other truck equipment in the maintenance shed had been touched."

"What do we know about the victim?" LaTasha, asked, as she walked over to the two doors at the back of the office, trying each, and discovering that the left door was to a bathroom, with sink and stool, while the right door led to a store room for boxes, and more file cabinets. She confirmed her suspicion that neither room led to a second entrance, such that the front door was the only way into the building.

Jablonski looked at the file again. "He'd worked for Zephyr for just over three years, all on night shift. Good attendance record. Okay performance reviews. He showed up, did his job and did not make waves. He worked alone, and did not have any workplace animosities to deal with."

"Wife?"

"Yes. Mary Ann Gelbard, age thirty. They lived in an apartment in Morgan Park. No kids. She works two jobs: one as a secretary for a Loop insurance company, and as a waitress at an all night diner in Longwood Manor."

"Life insurance on the deceased?"

"None, but Mary Ann discovered, after the death,

that he had deposited $7,500 in their joint bank account, in cash, about three weeks before he was killed."

Lieutenant Cranton stepped to the window, looked out at the yard, and thought a bit.

"What have we got on Zephyr Trucking" she asked Jablonski.

He did not need his notes to answer. "Nothing, except hints, rumors and suspicions. Every once in a while, it is clear that somebody truck-hauls some big-time illegal cargo out of this part of the City, on a no-questions asked, haul it quick, basis. Zephyr always has the right invoices, the right story to show that they are a completely above-board, God-fearing, mayor-kissing, corporate citizen. But we know that huge quantities of contraband come from down here somewhere."

At least that's something, thought Tasha to herself.

"You know what this is, Carl, this is a Djinni file."

"Jeannie who?"

"Not Jeannie, Djinni. D-J-I-N-N-I. A Djinni is a spirit in middle-eastern literature and tradition that is a super-natural being that has random and capricious influence on human life. Djinn are not deities, and have no real agendas, either good or evil. They sometimes take human form, and can be seen by humans, sometimes not. They can be mean, mischievous or benign, all at their own whim. Western depictions of Djinn are cartoonish. Think about the genie (which is just another word for djinni) in Aladdin."

"In my career investigating homicides for CPD, I

have encountered four, now five, cases where there is no motive, no physical evidence, nobody that benefits from the crime, only a dead body in a situation in which there is a mere whiff of the hand of a larger interest. In any of those cases, one has no chance in hell of detecting those critical elements, and therefore no chance of arresting the perpetrators. We might as well just chalk these cases off to a Djinni."

Tasha walked back to the window, crossed her arms and let the facts dance in her head to see if a pattern would emerge.

"What did the neighbors see?" she asked at last.

"Most of the adjacent properties hire night watchmen. We interviewed them all. Not a one saw, or heard, anything out of the ordinary."

So how in the world did the perp get in? Tasha thought to herself, parachute in? Rappell down the fence? Appear, as a Djinni would, out of thin air on the scene of the crime?

As she had trained herself to think in situations of impossible frustration, she quieted her mind, and returned to what she knew, and what must have happened. No neighbor thought they saw or heard anything. But she knew that they must have heard something, but that something was perceived to be nothing out of the ordinary. The perp did get in, and in some insidiously clever way. She cleared her mind and thought about the times, as a patrol officer, she had to perform a stake-out in this grey, smelly, remote, and unappealing neighborhood, sitting in an unmarked car, after dark, in some narrow street, watching for something, for God's sake, not just noises from the Channel or from the highway, but also, in the deep hours of the night the back-up-bells of the garbage trucks.

Stop. Wait. That's it, Lieutenant Cranton's critical brain clicked into locked and loaded mode. The garbage truck.

"Carl, I want to know who does the garbage service on the site. You can call me tomorrow. Anything else I need to know here?"

"I've been saving the report of the State CS people for you. They came up with only two interesting items. There are absolutely no finger prints that don't belong to the scene. There was no blood or bodily fluid, either of the victim, or anybody else. But take a look at the photographs of the footprints pulled from just to the right of the front door."

He pulled from the file a blown up photo, showing two boot or shoe prints of a right foot print, but, as illustrated by the markings on the photograph, of two different sizes.

"Same tread, but two different shoe sizes, about a half-size apart. There were two separate guys here."

So it's Djinn, not a Djinni, LaTasha thought to herself. "What is the other thing?" she asked.

"The CS geeks, probably because we were hounding them for any evidence of anything on Zephyr, fine-tooth-combed the premises. Here is the oddball thing they came up with." Jablonski pulled a photograph that was an extreme enlargement of the shot of a spongy, brownish substance that contained a large number of spherical black dots.

"Okay, Carl, I give up. What in the heck is this?"

"It turns out that this is a cake crumb. The dots are poppy seeds. The remarkable thing to the CS guys was the shear quantity of the seeds, per unit volume. That fact, along with the presence of chopped almonds and hazelnuts, led them to the conclusion that this was a crumb from some kind of Central European poppy seed cake."

"Must have been a slow day at the lab. Great. Wonderful. Enormously helpful. We are looking for a least two guys, who wear almost the same size shoe, who may like poppy seed cake and who strangle people with a wire garotte. I'll just run that through the computer, and we will have an arrest tomorrow. Let me guess, there isn't anything else, is there?"

Jablonski shook his head with an apologetic smile.

"Okay, just get me the name of the garbage service as soon as you can. Thanks for the info, Carl. Keep smiling" LaTasha said as she shook his hand and went out to her car. She waited while Carl punched in the gate code.

"It's not just that we spend all of this time and trouble to investigate these cases that we will never solve" the Lieutenant thought as she waited for the gate to open, "it's that I feel that I have been personally out-thought, out-maneuvered, and out-classed in a chess game where I never see the opponent who has planned all the moves so that I lose before I ever show up on the scene. I hate it."

In his efficient fashion, Jablonski reported that afternoon that Zephyr Trucking used Southside Sanitation for their garbage service.

On the next morning Lt. Cranton was sitting in the dispatch office of Southside at the desk of Billy Ray Dyson, whose desk sign indicated that he was "Chief Dispatcher". Billy Ray was one of the largest human beings that LaTasha had ever met in person, to the point that it seemed that he had attained his current position by literally outgrowing a seat in a garbage truck. She wondered how many digits there were in his pants size.

LaTasha had made a point of wearing her uniform, badge and all, not necessarily because she believed that all garbage haulers were mob-connected, but that enough of them were, and there were enough weird connections within the industry, that it was just as well that these people knew who she was.

Billy Ray leaned forward in his overstressed desk chair to look at his computer screen. "Yeah, Zephyr is one of our customers. Has been for years. We did not pick up as usual after midnight on the 18th, because, it says here, Zephyr's office manager called to cancel the service due to a major vehicle relocation on the site that morning. We were back the next morning."

"So one of your trucks did not stop at Zephyr on the early morning of the 18th?" Tasha asked directly.

"Not as far as this shows."

"Didn't that request strike you as odd?"

"Not really. People jiggle their service schedule all of the time. I did not actually take the call, but we know the Zephyr people well enough to adjust to their plans."

"Anything else oddhappen on the night of the 17th-morning of the 18th?"

"Let me look at the log" Billy Ray moved his mouse and manipulated his keyboard with fingers that appeared to be inflated to three times life size, as his chair screeched in protest.

"I had forgotten about this. At the shift change, that would be about 7PM on the 17th, we lost a truck."

"Whataya mean, you lost a truck?"

"It just disappeared. The crew looked around for it, but it was gone."

"Did you report it as stolen?"

"Nah. We figured it was just a joy rider, although because garbage trucks are big, ugly, slow and smelly that almost never happens. In any event, we found it the next morning, about seven blocks over."

"Was it damaged? Did whoever stole it leave anything in it? Did anyone see who was driving it?"

"It was just fine. Nobody saw anyone in it. There was nothing reported as left behind."

"Well," Tasha told herself "Even if there was an entire poppy seed cake, I still would have no idea who the perps were. I know exactly how these guys did it, have no idea why, and will never know who they are. Checkmate."

Aloud, she said "Thanks for your time, Mr. Dyson. No, don't bother to see me out" not wishing to put his knees and the desk furniture through the ordeal of bearing his weight, "Here's my card, if you think of anything else. Have a nice day."

Back in her office, she labelled the case file "The Poppy Seed Djinn" sealed it, and put it with the four other Djinni folders.

"Maybe, some day" she said, and closed the drawer.

## 24

# Louise and Thelma

Reviewing the details of the police file of Milly's death brought me back to the day in the Spring of 1995 that I think of as the beginning of the end.

In what had become an almost invariable ritual after having visited Sid to pick up the "thank you card" for our last professional efforts, we stopped at Nonna Yana's.

Whether it was because it had just definitely turned to Spring, and there was warmth in the air and green on the trees, or because it was a week before Easter, or just because Irena had put out an extraordinarily good batch of sweets and savories, the place was packed, as we walked in the door at right before noon. As always, Milly visibly lit up, as she viewed the contents of the bakery case, and the happy diners. Irena was taking orders as quickly as she could, while her cashier busily took customer money, making the bell ring each time she punched open the drawer to receive the money and make change.

Because the line to order was three deep, I sat down at a small table for two near the door. I knew that it was not necessary to tell Milly what I wanted to eat, because she and I were going to eat what she decided to get, without my having any real say in the matter.

While I waited, I observed the group of four older gentlemen, who I had come to regard as 'the regulars'. They had, from the first moment I spotted them, whether because of their clothes, their haircuts, mustaches, or general demeanor, reminded me of my uncles, the adults in my neighborhood, and the other males of my parents' age and ethnicities, so that they seemed a living swatch from the fabric of my memory.

They looked a bit different today than they had recently. I realized that the difference was that the ubiquitous, full-length overcoats that they wore in the colder months had been replaced by oddly fitted suits, with ties. All wore their usual fedoras. They sat hunched at the shoulders, leaning on their elbows, clutching coffee cups, occasionally saying a word or two. They no doubt knew what each other were thinking, without having to say it in words, and felt themselves to be engaged in a conversation as garrulous as a late night talk show.

As I watched them, and reflected on my own family experience that any immigrant in the United States at that time had experienced two divergent cultural experiences. On the one hand (current administration excepted), an immigrant found general acceptance by American people, and most probably found a community of people similar in cultural background, so that the process of immigration was not like jumping into ice water. On the other hand, the unremitting effect of the winds of American culture on the basics of an immigrant's past, is like the effect of wind and wave on a building built too close to the ocean's edge: over time, the distinguishing features are eroded, effaced, until what remains is just like the rest of the surroundings.

That, I realized, was the reason I liked Nonna Yana's. It was a place that the customers could remember who they were, where they came from, and not have to chuck it all and just to be "American".

At that point, Milly, having paid, came over to the table.

"Ready, let's go over to the park. I can't wait to show you this stuff." I looked at her a bit apprehensively, as she was carrying, instead of the usual small bag or donut-sized box, a shopping bag full of containers. We lugged the haul across the street to the bench next to the tennis courts.

"Okay, these" said Milly, opening a box containing about ten dumpling-looking dough pockets, "are Pelmeni." With a flourish, she took a bite of one and chewed it appreciatively. "It's the traditional filling of ground pork, beef and lamb. They're good by themselves, but I got two sauces to try" she added pulling two Styrofoam containers from the shopping bag, "horseradish, and a mild flavored vinegar. Try them both."

I think that I had eaten pelmeni at some point, but

never as good as these were. I ate two, one with each kind of sauce until I could not eat another bite. Milly took her time and methodically disposed of the remainder.

"I only bought one garlic pickle, but we can share" Milly said, bringing that package from the bag.

"No, go ahead, Milly. I'm stuffed." The pickle followed the pelmeni.

At about that time, a couple of tennis players occupied the previously empty tennis court. It was a young man and a young woman, each mid-twenty, who one could conclude by their easy manner of conversation with one another, were more than just casual acquaintances. I imagined them as girl friend and boy friend. They changed into court shoes, and replaced their jackets with close-fitting long sleeved shirts, and took their positions on opposite sides of the net. He was tall, probably about six-two, much taller than her five-six or seven. His dark hair tended to drop over his eyes, so that he was constantly brushing it back with his hand. She had banded her light brown hair into a sensible pony tail.

They started to play in earnest. From the beginning, it was clear that his notion of the way to play tennis was to play with power; he hit every shot as hard as he could hit it. He had a mammoth serve, which, unfortunately for him, found its way into the correct court only about forty percent of the time. His partner never chased the balls that were out. For the ones that were in, most of the time she returned the serve to some inconvenient corner of the court, so that, in his surprise at her returning his rocket, he had to race to even put his racket on her shot, most of the time to no good effect. When she served, the ball moved with controlled power, and into tricky places. Her serves were true about ninety-percent of the time.

"Now the cookies" said Milly, pulling from the bag a pie-sized box and lifting the lid. She displayed the contents: rectangular sugar cookies about two by three inches, each frosted with light blue frosting on which identical designs were traced in gold frosting.

"What's the symbol?"

"That's the tryzub, the stylized trident that was the coat of arms of Prince Volodymr of the Ukraine. It has been recently adopted as an official symbol of the country. Have one."

I didn't see how I could refuse, even being full from the pelmeni.

"These are good," I allowed.

"Irena made some with this color combination, and some with the reverse, gold background and light blue frosting. I couldn't make up my mind, so I got a dozen of each."

We munched cookies and watched the tennis players. The controlled competent woman slowly established her superiority in approach, and ultimately the score, as her big-hitting opponent, got increasingly frustrated with his inability to overpower his female opponent, and finally lost his breath, as she ran him from corner to corner, his composure, as he would slam his racket around, and finally the game. He sulked over to his athletic bag, stuffed his racket into it, and stalked off, not waiting for his companion.

"Another cookie?" Milly asked, helping herself to one. I gestured my "no thank you" and said "Now there is a relationship in trouble," nodding towards the court.

"Maybe they'll figure it out." She gave the half smile. "Think about it this way. In any romantic relationship, the fragile, erotic component is really only a small part. If you let some petty distraction get to you, like our friend Boomer here, the relationship doesn't have a chance." She paused and looked off in the distance.

"I miss Vladimir. Every day. He way a good man, in almost all ways. Our intimate life was like a wonderful secret, but, when it comes right down to it, there was almost always something more interesting to do than have sex."

In all the years I had known Milly, this was the first time she had ever said anything about her personal relationship with her husband. I met her after he was gone, so I had no personal experience with her marriage on which to form a personal judgment.

"I do know what you mean. Emilio is a also a good guy, but not a very interesting one. I am not looking forward to next year, when he retires, and he will be around the house all of the time, doing nothing, instead of being at the bank, doing the same."

"Relationships are strange phenomena, like gardens; some flourish, others decay into a bed of weeds. I was just thinking about our tennis player friends. Is it possible that they are not lovers but brother and sister?'

I thought about it. They were close, but there was no kissing or hugging. "I suppose so" I admitted. Why do you ask?"

I was just thinking about my brother Vasyl. Have I ever told you about him? No? Well, he was a year older and was, is and always will be a complete blockhead. He never had an original thought or interesting hobby or engaging friends. He goofed off through school and barely got a diploma, before he went off to work in the mills. He never did a particularly mean thing to me, or talked to me in a rude way, or made fun of me, but he made me, and still makes me mad every time I think about him. Here's why. No matter what, my mother doted on him and frankly favored him over me, while she was alive, without regard to anything either of us said or did. In the competition for parental affection, he won, just by showing up. What should have been a warm, enduring family relationship instead became lifelong antipathy."

"With that all said about relationships, I have to say that the best relationship in my life, is the one with you, Hattie. Together, our Story is larger and more interesting than either of us can claim to be attributable to herself. We are larger than the sum of ourselves."

"So we are kind of like Thelma and Louise?" I kidded gently. "So which one is Thelma, and which one is Louise?"

She looked at me, cracked the half-smile and said

"Think about it this way. In the end did it matter to them? Or to those who knew their story? They could just as well have been Louise and Thelma, because their story is the same, either way."

"Okay, Milly, why don't you tell me what's on your mind. I know you well enough to know that you are thinking deeply about something. We have had about three times the normal quantity of food from Nonna Yana. You have told me about two relationships that you haven't talked about in the thirty-five years since I have known you. And now we are comparing our relationship to that of two women who drove a Cadillac off a cliff. So, what is it?"

She looked at me with some surprise, as if she did not expect me to catch the nuances of her comments. She reached for the box. "I'm having another cookie. Want one?" I declined.

Milly sighed. "You and I share a devil-may-care attitude towards our personal condition outside of our closings in which we more or less feel ourselves to be bullet-proof----- until we aren't. No whining or hypochondria for us. Well, about three weeks ago, I went in for my first physical exam in about five years. I feel great, I get a lot of sleep, I eat well. But I thought I would just get myself checked out. I had all of the routine tests, and was startled when the radiologist who was reading my mammogram called me into her office. She sat me down, and slipped the mammogram onto the viewing apparatus. "This mass here looks bad. You need to get a biopsy right away." I did, and to make a complicated story simple, I have breast cancer. Stage four. That sounds great for a NASA vehicle, but is about as bad as it gets for a woman. The specialist told me "Figure you've got six to nine months".

"Oh, Milly that's awful. But you're a fighter, and I am too. I will do whatever I can to help you beat this thing."

"There are 'interventions' as the doctors call them, like radical surgery, radiation and chemotherapy, all of which cost a lot of money, put you through a lot of agony, and then you die about the same time anyway. This does not sound to me like a good thing."

She paused. " But think about it this way. Everybody dies, but most people have no idea when death will jump out at them, at some unknown moment, from behind a tree, surprise them and take them away to the dark lands. I hope that my knowing the how and when will let me catch Death first, and poke him right in the eyes."

I didn't really know what to say, except " You know I am here for you, whatever happens."

"Thanks, Hattie, that does mean a lot. I had better push off. I have to tell the kids."

As I dropped her off at her house, I watched her let herself into her front door. It felt strange to realize how finite each one of the next days were going to seem.

## 25

# Rematch

Chief Cranton of the Gethsemane Police department was sitting at the conference table in her office in City Hall with Henrietta "Hattie" Rosales, resident of Shady Rest, a local nursing home. The two of them had reviewed, for a variety of reasons three homicide files: the recent shotgun slaying of J. Hartley Mortsensen, international businessman and recent resident of Gethsemane; the apparent drug overdose of Janet Jennings the resident manager of Shady Rest, and finally the 1995 shooting of Hattie's friend and partner, Ludmilla "Milly" Netsurov in a park on the south side of Chicago, which had taken place while LaTasha was a member of the CPD, but in a case not assigned to her.

A detail in the Netsurov file leapt out at her: the victim, at the time of her death, had been eating a Ukranian poppy seed cake.

Why that detail smacked LaTasha in the face was its

coincidental similarity to an odd piece of evidence found at the scene of the last of a series of cases that had been LaTasha's to investigate, which was a small morsel of what the crime lab found to be poppy seed cake. LaTasha had labelled in her mind all of the cases the Djinn files, because all shared the lack of evidence, motive, apparent benefit from the crime, such that these crimes seemed to be committed at random by supernatural beings, like Djinn.

"It never occurred to me" she thought to herself, "that the Djinn could be, as they were often in Islamic tradition, women. Me of all people, who has been looking up at that glass ceiling because none of the morons in charge would recognize my clear capabilities."

"But now that I can imagine it, a lot of the details make sense. The timelines make sense. The opportunities were there." In short, Latasha knew, in the way that all intuitive geniuses know things, that the evidentiary threads that connected the acts in the Djinn files were there, and that she, as an experienced professional could find them and follow them to the solution to these mysteries.

She thought at the time she had closed the Djinn files that they represented a chess match in which she had been checkmated by an unseen opponent. She knew now that, unexpectedly, the board had been replaced and the chess pieces reset on the board, and that it was her first move and advantage.

The question was: Should she pursue the rematch?

A twenty-year younger LaTasha Cranton would not

have spent a minute on the question; She would have jumped at the chance to prove just how good she was, and to vindicate for her fundamental conviction that good cops solve cases, and put perps away, no matter what.

But today, she would think about it.

## 26

# Three point six degrees west

The days, weeks and months after Milly told me about her diagnosis proceeded very differently than the decades of our acquaintance had. At times it seemed that Time was creeping along, clawing each instant forward with its fingernails; at times as if Milly and I were indeed in the back seat of Thelma and Louise's car, as it plunged, grandly but terrifyingly into the canyon below.

I went to visit Milly every day, just to do what I could for her, but really to selfishly maximize my limited time with her, totally for me. At first Milly was taken a bit aback, since our mutual life had settled into a pattern where we more or less left each other alone, pursuing our individual interests in most of our lives, but locking together as a unit for Tupperware events, and for Sid jobs. It had been a very comfortable balance.

But the balance was now disturbed. Milly was dying. And I was not just going to sit idly by while that

238

happened. So I pushed myself into the space that Milly had carved out for herself.

At first, she would look at me quizzically as I showed up, daily at her door.

At first, she would always meet me at the door of her house, and ask some outrageous question or another: "What are you selling? Are you a Jehovah's Witness? There are ordinances against door-to-door solicitations!"

But what had been her "space" was now slowly collapsing, in tune with the inexorable progress of the cancer through her body. She lived alone, meaning that nobody else lived in her house, and she made he own rules. But the downside of that was there was no one there when it hurt, or when Fear of the Unknown drops its calling card on your hall table.

That's where I came in. This was a woman who I had stood shoulder to shoulder with, who served as my mentor, my tutor, and my educational compass. I was going to come to Milly's house every day, whether on a red carpet or with an armed escort.

I stuck with it. Despite her protests, I drove her to her doctor's appointments, the results of which were, invariably, a solemn statement that the "modalities" of chemo and radiation could, underscore could, provide some relief, and some hope of recovery. Ha ha. Milly, after her own researches, had rejected any interventions, and had settled into an acceptance mode.

In that period, I came to know both the desperation, and the resolve that animated Milly forward into a certain outcome.

I came to her house, every day. It was the least I could do, but it did not seem enough.

Milly was physically being eaten alive by the cancer. Her wonderfully exhuberant pounds leaked away, so that I could see the bones of her shoulder, once wrapped in a blanket of solid sinew.

Mostly, our days together were spent at Milly's kitchen table. We would talk, or play cards. Milly wanted to play poker, for money.

"Milly, if there is anything completely certain about the world for me is that I will NEVER play poker for money against you. I watched you over so many years clean out the players at the nickel and dime games after the Tupperware parties. I lost five dollars the first time, but told myself 'never again'. I'm stickin' with that."

But we compromised. At her kitchen table we played uncountable hands of gin rummy, at the stake of a penny a point, while we reminisced about all of our shared experiences.

It wasn't poker, but it was cards, and Milly was way better at cards of any sort than I had ever been. So I lost, probably about two –thirds of the time.

The great thing about gin rummy is that the players have the leisure to talk to one another in those slow intervals between plays.

I was not going to ask direct questions, but I was going to find out some stuff that I never knew.

One day, I was in that position in a gin rummy game

familiar to anyone who has ever played: "the gin hole", that is to say, waiting for one card to be able declare "gin" and win the hand, with the gin points bonus. Specifically, I held three kings (all but the spade), three tens (all but the heart) and a run of six, seven and eight of diamonds. My kicker was the jack of clubs, which I was holding onto, since Milly had picked off the draw pile the jack of spades. I thought that she was saving jacks, and when she would "knock" for some number less than ten, and I would be able to play my jack on her jacks, and "cut" her off, winning the hand, with a penalty of the gin bonus to boot.

"Milly, how did you meet Sid, and get started in the business?"

"Didn't I ever tell you that?" Milly said, drawing and discarding the eight of hearts.

"It was a few years before we met. I don't know exactly when. I had started shooting at Mike's Guns and Ammo after I had responded to a newspaper ad offering shooting lessons for some small amount. I thought 'why not" and went to class, liked it and started going on a regular basis. I joined a league that had both men and women and participated in the events. I found that I had an aptitude for it. Somewhere along the line, Sid showed up on the practice lanes. He was obviously kind of a wreck, being a bit pale and shaky and was working exclusively on shooting with his left hand, at which he was just not very good. He would often watch the rest of us shoot. He spent a lot of time watching me on the range

He watched me win the club championship for ambidextrous rounds at conventional targets."

I drew and discarded the queen of diamonds.

"One day, after a range session, he asked me if I were open to a business proposition. I, of course, needed the money. I did not have a bad feeling about him personally, like that he was going to ask me to do something weird. I said okay, and he gave a piece of paper with the address of E-Z Loans on it, and said 'Be there tomorrow. 10AM.'"

She drew, looked at briefly, and discarded the seven of clubs.

"So that was my first trip to E-Z Loans. It turned out that old Sid had done for a living what we now do for him. About six months before I met him, he took a bullet in his right shoulder during a botched job. It left him with partial use of his gun hand, his right. You may have noticed that he tends to keep his hands out of sight. He wasn't having much success learning to shoot with his left hand."

I took from the draw pile, and discarded with disgust, the worthless three of spades.

"What Sid really wanted was revenge: he asked me to take out the guy that shot him. That was my first job."

She drew a card, put it in her hand, and continued "It was really a piece of cake. I tracked down the guy outside his house, after dark. He had no idea what hit him. I think Sid paid me with his own money. Down for one" she said, discarding, and showing her hand. She had king, queen, jack of spades (not a set of jacks!), three nines, including my nine of diamonds, and three, four and five of clubs. Her kicker was the ace of clubs.

I looked at the card she had discarded. It was the ten of hearts. So of the four cards that would 'gin' me, she had held three. I looked at the next card on the draw pile. It was the five of diamonds. Uncanny. Nine more cents out of my pocket into Milly's.

On other days, we would just talk.

"Milly, have you changed your attitude about religion? I asked one day to see if I could facilitate any spiritual comfort for her.

"No, in a word. If you are asking me whether I believe in an afterlife, I would have to say I don't, at least not in the conventional sense.

Think about it this way. Imagine a person being a radio set, which has the ability to tune in those thoughts, feelings, beliefs, values that make us alive, from some kind of ether in which those radio programs, if you will, reside. The radio set may cease to function at death, but the radio program continues. That part of us lives on, perhaps not identifiable as "us", but continuing nonetheless. It is most closely related to the Buddhist concept of reincarnation."

I just nodded. As always, I have no idea where she gets this stuff, and can barely follow any of it.

"But doesn't religion present answers to tough questions, and give us direction about solving those questions?"

"Sure, religions give answers and directions, but one has to be careful about the assumptions. Think about it this way. Do you know about magnetic declination? (She knew that I had no idea.) The idea there is that if you have a standard magnetic compass and rely on it to do what it purports to do, point to North, you would be wrong. Everywhere on earth, there is a difference between magnetic north and celestial north. That difference is the magnetic declination. In the Chicago area, the difference is 3.6 degrees west. If you start out with a magnetic compass for your directions, you would be off one foot from your intended destination for every 100 feet you travel, or fifty some feet for every mile. Some truth. That is probably way better than the "directions" that religion gives."

"But aren't we entitled to think that our lives have meaning?"

"Of course, but that meaning doesn't come from believing in getting haloes and angel wings after we are dead, or roasting in a barbeque pit. The Meaning of our LIfe comes from what we think, do and say while we are alive, all of which are parts of our Stories. We live on through our Stories. Milly and Hattie's story will live even after Milly dies."

During the late summer of that year, we got Milly admitted to the local Hospice, which provided excellent in-home care, counselling, and most importantly pain management. Milly was a brick in putting up with what must have been episodes of pain that had increasing intensity, and increasing frequency. Milly reluctantly gave in and took the prescribed pain medications. "I've got a few things to finish."

I got an idea of what at least one of the things was when I came by mid-morning the next week and found Milly typing on an electric typewriter that I have never seen before.

"I didn't know you could type."

"It's really not rocket science, Hattie. I am just finishing up the chapter about my take on Nietzsche's theory that the ideal human artistic expression arises from the fusion of the Appollonian and Dionysian impulses."

"I thought that you were skeptical of religious theories."

"I am. Hattie, you need to carefully distinguish between Religion and Philosophy. I reject the former and embrace the latter. Think about it this way. While Religion, confronted with difficult moral and ethical questions, will tell you What to think, Philosophy tells you How to think about those problems. It celebrates the individual without prescribing rigid codes. No Philosopher has ever conducted a Spanish Inquisition."

"Whatever you say. I will make some tea, while you finish up, and then we'll play some cards."

She worked at the typewriter for about a half an hour, then put it away.

"You said 'chapter'; is that part of a book?" I asked, sitting down with two cups of tea.

"It is. You know that I have definite beliefs on life issues. I decided to put them on paper. It's part of my

Story." The shadow of a grimace of pain passed her brow and retreated.

"Before I resume separating you from your spending money, we have some business to go over." She opened a file on the table.

"This is my will, Hattie, along with my lawyer's name. You are my executor, but I don't think the whole thing will be very complicated. I leave my shares in M & H to you. Everything else goes to Hugo and Katarina, in equal shares. Their addresses and phone numbers are in the file. Go ahead and sell the house, neither of them want it. You know that I don't have many tangible things that mean a lot to me. I have made provision for the important items, and given most of the rest away. I suppose that you all will insist on a church service, but you know I will hate it, so keep it simple. I think that's it, except the one additional closing I have to work on."

"You're in no shape to do a closing. Let me take care of whatever you need to have done."

"Believe me, Hattie, you can't do it. Just trust me to take care of it. It will get done tomorrow."

"Okay, but I don't like it."

We sat down and played cards for the next hour or so. Aside from small talk, neither of us had a lot to say. It was almost as if we had said all that we could to each other, and were perfectly happy with each other's company, without needing to talk.

I had to leave late in the afternoon, and stood to go. Milly followed me to the door. As I reached for the knob, she said "Remember. The Story continues. And you owe me $22.05 for gin rummy."

As was the case with so many of the things that Milly brought out of the recesses of her mind, I was taken slightly off base. I recovered and smiled "Well, I'm good for it."

She also smiled. "I know you are." We have never been big huggers, but that moment seemed the time for a hug. It turned out to be totally appropriate, because that was the last time I saw her alive.

Since Milly had indicated that she would be involved in whatever mysterious project, I did not go to her house, but resolved to pry it out of her the next day when I stopped by.

At about 9 PM, that night, Monday the 25, I answered the phone at my house.

It was Milly's son Hugo. Hugo is a great kid, and really part of our family since he is about two years older than Ines. He is a great big, outdoorsy kind of guy. He is a master mason with a local construction company. He was clearly upset. "Aunt Hattie, Mom's dead" he blurted out in one burst, and fell silent, as is trying to compose his next words.

"Oh, Hugo, I am so sorry. Were you and Katarina able to get to the hospital with her?"

You could almost hear him blink. "It wasn't at the hospital. She was shot in some kind of drive-by shooting in a park in town."

What? I bit off the word and kept it to myself. So,

Milly's last job was a dangerous one. It made me mad and guilty that I wasn't there. Nobody would shoot Milly in my presense and live to tell about it.

"Have you talked to the police?"

"Yeah, I just got back from identifying Mom's body. Again, I felt angry and guilty that I was not able to help with that bit of necessary awfulness.

"What did they say about the incident?"

"They told me that the neighbors reported there to be a burst of gunfire, maybe ten or fifteen shots, and when someone called the police, the patrol sergeant, found Mom, dead on the ground."

The police were not very helpful when I called them. I talked to the detective in charge. All he could say was "We've got no real evidence, no eyewitnesses, no suspects only the neighbors who heard the shots. We'll continue to look at it, but for now we're putting it down as a random drive-by, and by a person or persons unknown." I did find out, as I had feared, that the site of the incident was indeed Beverly Park, our old haunt. So, the generally held belief was that Milly, on one of her excursions to Nonna Yana's, had been the victim of some kind of random gang gunfight. As it was, I let Hugo and Katarina believe that, for the little closure it provided them. They had, of course, known about the cancer, and had prepared for an imminent end, but not this one. I let the story stand for our wider set of acquaintances, not all of whom knew of Milly's illness.

For me, the more I thought about what I knew, which

was that Milly had said that she had a closing to deal with, and the fact she refused to involve me, the more I was convinced that Milly had been deliberately blindsided in a well-planned trap, in which she had been invited to the Park on some false pretext. She obliviously suspected the risk, and kept me out. The most likely perpetrators were the employers of the two creeps we eliminated on the golf course. I could see them tracing the cross-bow arrow left in Lex's spine back to Milly, through wherever she bought, or stole it. The icy traces of fear had started in my brain and run to my fingers and toes with the realization that if that were the case, they had made me, as well, and that there was a good chance that somewhere nearby there was an assassin with a couple of clips of 9mm's with my name on them. Time to get out.

We held Milly's funeral at Saint Pancratius, because that was where she had attended, when she did, and that was where most of her family and friends were. The place was as packed, as it used to be when people took Holy Days of Obligation seriously. The sanctuary looked like the Chicago Flower & Garden show with all of the memorial bouquets sent by the staggering number of Milly's circle of friends. One conspicuously large arrangement bore the single name, cryptic to most of the attendees, "Sid". I half expected him to be there but he was not to be found. Neither, to my irritation, was Ines. "I just can't get away, Mom. Give Hugo and Katarina big hugs from me." There was a reception in the parish hall, full of tears, hugs, Tupperware stories, and a small sense of closure. A smaller, but similar memorial was held in Downers Grove.

A couple of days later, I dug through my records, and found the phone number for Sid that he had given us for the golf course affair. I dialed it, waited about twelve rings, before Sid answered, with his typical understated exhuberance,"Yeah?"

"Sid, it's Hattie. I have two things for you. First, somebody took Milly out. You know anything about that?"

"I wondered. No, I haven't heard anything."

"Would the people that employed those low-lifes that we smoked on the golf course be likely to avenge them?"

Sid did not hesitate. "I wouldn't put it past 'em. Those guys are still in business, and are still our bitter rivals. They still are ruthless, mean and dirty people. Yeah, it could be them. Did they get a lead on you two?"

"Maybe, but I'm still going to be careful."

"Sound's smart to me."

"Here's the other thing, Sid. I quit."

There was a bit of a pause this time. "You sure?"

"Real sure."

"We'll miss you, Hattie, and Milly, too. You were the best."

"Thanks, Sid."

He hung up.

During the week following the memorial services, I started in on the details of Milly's estate.

I found the file that Milly entrusted to me with her will and estate details. I made an appointment with her lawyers, Wickham, Barnes & Zelenko at their offices in the Loop. The estates partner who met with me was Rebecca W. Bolton-Kozbur, a cheerful, late-forties, early fifties woman who was wearing a strikingly tailored lilac suit, that would make even Ines look twice. She met me at the door of her office at precisely the scheduled moment, shook my hand and showed me to her client chair, which was a companion chair to hers, across a small conference table away from her desk. The arrangement had the effect of diffusing the usual power and knowledge imbalance between lawyer and client that is ordinarily present when a client sits at a lawyer's desk. I rather regretted having chosen my conservative navy blue suit, with light blue blouse and pocket square. My grey wide-brimmed hat and gloves completed my outfit.

"I'm pleased to meet you, Ms. Rosales, but of course not pleased by the circumstances. Ms. Netsurov has told me a lot about you."

I'll bet. I hope not too much, I thought. "Thank you for seeing me at short notice."

"Not at all a problem," she said opening a file. "This, I hope, will be straightforward. I see you have the original will" she took it from the envelope and quickly reviewed it. "Here are the documents that you need to sign to get the will admitted to probate. Ms. Netsurov and I have worked on it recently, and it is, I am sure quite up to date. I will guide you through the details of the process. I see no reason why you should not go ahead and list the house for sale. I would recommend, unless you feel otherwise, that you use a local Downers Grove Realtor, as they probably know the market best. I will make the inquiries for the values we will need for the inventory. I will do all the necessary tax filings and court reports. I have already made the necessary claim filing for the life insurance."

Life insurance? Milly? After all of the laughs we had on the gun range and elsewhere about the relative uselessness of the financial product life insurance, compared to our Life Insurance, that delivered brief, effective protective messages.

"One other thing, Ms. Rosales. For a couple of reasons relevant to the estate we need you to keep us informed as to any changes in your address."

Rebecca efficiently and clearly estimated the remaining steps of the probate process, the timetable for each step, and her estimated fees. She saw me to the door. "Let us know if you have any questions. We will keep you up to date on estate issues. It has been my pleasure meeting with you."

I left completely impressed with her competence and professionalism.

I did list the house, and didn't think a thing more about the administration until about a month later when I received an official-looking business-sized envelope bearing the logo of Aetna Life Insurance Company. How ironic, I thought, as I recalled Milly's joke as I visited the firing range for the first time. Although Rebecca had told me she had applied, and I was expecting something of the sort, I was totally unprepared for the contents.

The cover letter read:

"We at Aetna Life Insurance extend our profound condolences for the death of your loved one, our insured, Ludmilla Netsurov. We are herewith enclosing the proceeds payments directed by the insured. We note that the coverage amount of $1,000,000 has been doubled by the accidental death clause of the policy to $2,000.000, and has been further increased by post-death interest of $10,015.51." There were six checks enclosed: Three of $100,000 to Ines, Roberto and Javier, one each to Hugo and Katarina in the amount of $730,018.78, and one to me for $249,977.95. To my check was affixed a note: "Originally $250,000, reduced by $22.05 per telephone instructions of the insured". I didn't know whether to laugh or cry. As instructed I forwarded the enclosed form 712 to Rebecca for tax filing. I sent my kids their checks and delivered theirs to Hugo and Katarina.

## 27

My first task as executor of Milly's estate was to go through her personal items carefully, with the nominal purpose of getting the house ready for sale, but with the real purpose of carefully screening for any "tools of the trade" concealed there which would even vaguely suggest our real occupation and might prove difficult to explain to Hugo and Katarina, or anyone one else who happened to come upon them.

I didn't really believe that any part of Milly's armory would be found in the house, since she was the one who prompted me to store my items in a bank safety deposit box. From that fact, I had assumed that Milly personally had followed that practice herself. I intended, therefore, go through the house, room by room, before I turned the contents over to Katarina and Hugo.

As I put the key in the lock and swung the door open, I realized that I had never been in the house without Milly being present. For whatever reason, wishful thinking, or primal intuition, I had the sense that Milly was indeed there, and that, at any moment, I would hear her embracing voice, or her familiar footsteps from the entryway, and then see her stride into the room with yet another of her inscrutable openers.

The feeling of her presence magnified the subtle sounds that the house made: the floorboard creaks, the small pops around the window frames, the coughing and gasping of the heating system; to the point that I had the unshakeable sense that I was not alone.

Deep breath. Step in and begin.

Milly never was conspicuously or obsessively "neat", such that she would not be cleaning, dusting, vacuuming, or polishing in my presence, but the house was spotless, and devoid of clutter. As I moved from room to room, it hit me that Milly lived her day-to-day life exactly like she lived her intellectual life: with well-considered purpose. There was nothing in her house, or her philosophy, that did not, in her way of thinking, belong. I suspected that the only physical items left in the house were those that were no longer of critical importance to her life at the time of her death.

Kitchen first. There were no dirty dishes in the sink, or clean ones in the dishwasher. In the fridge, there were only a few containers (notably pickles of several types), but nothing perishable like milk or cheese, that needed to be discarded. The dishes, tableware, and appliances were neatly stored in the kitchen cabinets. I not only looked into the cupboards, but also carefully reviewed all of the surfaces of the cupboards, the backs of the drawers and the corners of the kitchen cabinets for the presence of an object like, say, a semi-automatic pistol or its ammunition.

The modest living room set and dining room table were just as Milly left them. No hiding places there.

I moved on to Milly's bedroom. I had the notion that this was the most likely spot for dangerous cache. Strangely enough, reflecting on the length of time that Milly and I had been associates, I had never seen this room before. I was struck by, but not surprised by, its austerity. The walls had been painted in a light taupe, and adorned by a few hanging photos of Vladimir, Hugo and Katarina. The closet held neatly hung clothes, including Milly's signature print dresses. One empty hanger shouted its presence among the group.

I spent a considerable amount of time examining the floorboards, the shelf over the hanging clothes and the walls for any concealed doors or seams or hinges, but with no result. The boxes on the shelves held only seasonal clothing items, like sweaters and gloves, but no gun.

I moved over to the bedroom dresser, adorned only by a modest crocheted dresser scarf, and small jewelry box. The dresser drawers were unremarkable, holding only folded underwear, blouses, pajamas and socks.

A look at the contents of Milly's jewelry box seemed to confirm that she had disposed, as she had said she would, by gift or by sale all of the items she cared for. Her wedding rings were gone, as were the items of jewelry that she wore for Tupperware events, leaving in the box only costume jewelry. The red-eyed scarab was not there, I sadly noted.

I next looked under the mattress of the neatly-made bed, and on the floor under it, without result.

By far, the most interesting aspect of the bedroom was the nightstand. Beside the substantial reading lamp there were three books: *The Birth of Tragedy and the Geneology of Morals*, by Frederick Nietzsche; *The Archetypes and the Collective Unconscious* by Karl Jung; and *The Noble Eightfold Path* by Bhikkhu Silacara.

I was sure that I couldn't pronounce the names of any of the authors, let alone derive the slightest meaning from any of the content. Light reading for Milly.

I finished my search of the rest of the house, and of the garage, until I was comfortable in telling Katarina and Hugo that they could come and get such of the remaining items they each wished, without me worrying about some uncomfortable item showing up. After they had finished, I would consign the larger items for sale, and donate the rest to charity.

As I locked the front door, I reflected on what I hadn't found. I hadn't found any weapons, but more strikingly, I had not found a safety deposit box key. I left with the distinct impression that somehow I didn't have the full story of Milly's last days. The last thing I did was to water Milly's beloved perennials in the back yard, not because I know a darn thing about plants, but because I was sure that Milly would want me to do it.

After the house was emptied, it sold quickly, and without any transactional difficulties. I was then able to take a breath, and take stock of my feelings. I had the conviction that Milly had died as the result of an insidious hit, perhaps as revenge for one of our closings, and that it was likely that the hit guys were looking for me too. I was reeling from the sudden loss of my life compass, and the magnetic declination between my personal direction and the turn of events made me think that I had completely lost my life purpose. "I need to get out of here" I thought, aloud, to myself.

So it was some time in October of that year that I brought the matter up with Emilio.

"E, I think that we should move somewhere else."

"What? Where else?" he asked, focusing for a moment on me and the world beyond the Bears game. "The house is paid off, the kids are gone, and we have just the simple life we want" he asserted, glancing back at the television as the Packers kicked off.

You mean, you have the simple life you want, I thought to myself, but said "Look, Emilio, my partner and best friend was just killed. I need to be outta here."

"Hattie, I just can't move now. I reach full retirement with the Bank in February, and need to stay until then to get my full pension. We need that pension to live on." He turned back to the set as the Bears picked up a first down.

I thought "You have no idea how well funded our retirement is, and how that happened" but said "Well, E, I gotta go. I tell you what. Tupperware has been after Milly and me for years to work for them as training consultants. It would involve work at corporate headquarters in Orlando, and at regional seminars across the country. The job would involve a lot of travel, and I'd be gone a lot. I'm gonna do it. You can stay here."

"Okay, babe, sounds like a plan" he said, now completely back in fan mode.

Before I left, I needed to make a trip to Beverly Park to revisit our familiar haunt. I could not bring myself to stop in Nonna Yana's. I had spoken to Irena at the memorial service and could think of nothing else to say. So I parked and sat on our bench overlooking the tennis court. No one was playing, but a high school-aged kid was hitting shots off the rally board. I thought of the poem:

The ballet set remains as first arranged;
Costumes are pressed, the orchestra's in tune.
The cast and patrons note one thing has changed:
The pas de deux is now a pas de une.

The doubles court has seen much better days.
It sadly lacks the "thwock" of tennis ball.
The shot that once inspired partner's praise
Now rattles lonely off the practice wall.

The graceful swan glides slowly on the pond,
Her hearing fixed firmly on the sky
For well-known wing-sound drifting from beyond,
Knowing that her hope is just a lie.

The bitter fact is "one" stands where stood "two";
The balance in the world is now askew.

I sighed, got up and went home.

So began my work for Tupperware's national training office. They paid me to travel to regional host seminars, speaking to large groups of new and prospective
Tupperware saleswomen. In a way, I had circled all the
way back in the Marshall Field's days in the familiar pattern of working in a male-led enterprise where the sales
genius and success came from the hard work of the female sales force. I did enjoy small group sessions in which
I could communicate that success as a Tupperware rep
did not come from thinking primarily of selling stuff, but
from building relationships, through camaraderie, hors
d'oeuvres, and maybe a little alcohol, and then giving the
customers the opportunity to buy a really good product.

The job also gave me a chance to see the kids. I even
got to spend a couple of hours with Ines in New York
every once in a while, when she could fit me in. She was,
at the time the photo editor for a Spanish language wom-
en's magazine slanted towards the high end of fashion,
décor and design. Because of the loss of Milly, the more
or less sudden disconnection from the occupation that I
realized had come to define me as a person, and the interruption in my living situation, I began to feel the urgency
to share with Ines the details of my Story, mostly as a
means of recapturing the losses. The opportunity never

presented itself.

Typical of the problem was the lunch Ines and I had at 21 sometime late in 1996, where I had wrangled from her a promise of her company for the entire week day afternoon. We had one of the corner tables, out of the way of patron traffic and with a waiter who didn't feel obliged to take a reading on our well being every five minutes.

"Ines, I want to tell you about, M & H, Inc. the business that Milly and I ran" I began, "It has an aspect that you did not know about." For a change, Ines was giving me her undivided attention, not looking constantly at her watch, or scanning the newcomers for familiar faces.

"It did start with Tupperware, but Milly had developed a new line of business before I partnered up with her. And that was the real source of the money."

Just at that moment, the waiter came bustling up, carrying an unplugged telephone.

"Ms. Rosales, your office just called and wants you to call right away. Some kind of emergency." He plugged the phone into a jack just past the table. Ines dialed, asked for her personal assistant Arturo, and listened to Arturo's tale of woe.

"Arturo, just tell her that if we don't have those shots by close of business tomorrow, the whole deal is off."

Arturo made some kind of whiny disclaimer of his ability to convey that message, to which Ines said "Okay, I'll be there in twenty minutes. She can't get away with this." She got up, pulled a hundred from her purse, put it on the table and said "That will take care of lunch. I really do have to put this fire out. You know how it is, Mom."

I did indeed. I was getting the impression that not only did Ines not give a damn about my Story, but also that it was destined to wither to dust, untold, and unappreciated.

I had just started to deal with the grief, and ensuing upheaval in my life, when, in the summer of 1997, Emilio had a stroke, one which left him partially paralyzed, speech impaired, and incapable of living at home without skilled nursing care. He had, as he had planned, worked until his full retirement from the Bank, received his commemorative watch, and a going-away party, to which I had been happy to accompany him, but most importantly a very comprehensive health care plan that included long term care. I placed him in an Assisted Living facility in Downers Grover that had very good staff, a few of whom I had known from town life. I went to see him multiple time a week, when I was in town, but noted with sadness, the progressive diminishment of his faculties, to the point that it was a coin toss whether he would recognize me on any given day.

While my the early romantic glow of my relationship with Emilio had not continued into the present , he was an important part of my life, my history, my family, and yes, myself. The loss of him as a companion, even a not very engaged or engaging companion, was just another one of the losses of self that had recently left me with the sense that I was fading away from view, and would in a short time vanish into thin air.

Emilio's condition continued its slow downward spiral, passing through the phase of no longer recognizing me, or anyone else, until his system just gave up in October of 2005. His funeral was a time to relive, in small part, the past, with the gathering of his family, including Is and Es, and their families, as well as my family. Ines, who had by that time moved on to Dallas, made, to my great approval, a special effort to be part of the celebration of life activiites.

At that point, I felt that I had reached the low point of the arc of my Story, and that the rest of my days would be spent quietly in place in Downers Grove.

Boy, was I wrong about that.

In November of that year, after we had buried Emilio, and returned to ordinary daily lives, I received in my mail a typewritten envelope with my name and address professionally enscribed, but bearing no return address.

The envelope contained a single newspaper clipping, neatly cut out as if with a razor blade, dated November 17, 2005.

"Suspected Gang Violence claims victim" shouted the headline.

"Sid Dimucci, manager of E-Z Loans, was gunned down yesterday in the parking lot of that establishment on Western Avenue in what police are describing as a barrage of bullets. The victim, aged 68, had apparently just locked the back door of the building when ambushed by unknown assailants.

The Chicago Police Department have no suspects, or

apparent motive, as nothing was tampered with or removed from the premises, but pointedly do not rule out the possibility that the incident was gang related.

'From the shear number of gunshot wounds suffered by the victim' said Lieutenant Elston Warner of the South District of the Violent Crimes Division, 'We can be pretty sure that this was not a random crime, without a specific objective. The MO is similar to other killings which we know to be gang related. The investigation continues.'

Uh-oh. Maybe the past does not just fade away. Somebody killed Sid, probably as revenge for some prior closing, and maybe even one which Milly and I performed. I kept thinking about the crossbow arrow left on the body on the golf course. Maybe they traced it to Milly, killed her, further traced Milly to Sid. And if so, anyone with an ounce of brains who cared enough to do all of that tracing had me in the crosshairs, too. That realization was enough to wake me out of my complacency, and spur me to get the heck out of town.

I immediately listed my house, sold it, emptied the contents, and stored what I wanted to keep.

I started a search of the communities in the region where I could relocate, more or less anonymously. I seriously considered changing my name, but thought that process would bring more attention to myself than I really wanted.

I decided that I needed to be outside the Chicago metro area, but close enough to be able to easily visit the places I had come to love, like the Art Institute, and rely on, like

Harris Bank. That is how I came across Gethsemane, and came to meet the Hagenbuches at Shady Rest. It seemed the ideal place for my requirements, so I shipped my stuff and moved to Gethsemane in February of 2007. As a precaution, I told my casual acquaintances in Downers Grove that I was moving to Arizona to be close to my son. I had my mail forwarded to a fictitious address in a subdivision in a retirement community in Florida which had several residents named "Rosales". I took care to change the important addresses to my real location.

I reluctantly contacted Tupperware and announced my final retirement, giving them my real address to send my final compensation checks, as well as any newsletters or other communications that they might wish to send me. I realized that I had worked with and for Tupperware more or less continuously since 1961, and the company had become, in part, the professional expression that I had once hoped Marshall Field's would be.

So I became Gethsemane's newest resident, with, I hoped, no ties to my past, and the resolve to forget my E-Z Loans self, and the times with Milly.

But the past cannot be hidden forever, as I discovered.

## 28

# Miss Hinch

*LaTasha Cranton; February 2017*

LaTasha Cranton, Chief of Police in Gethsemane, Illinois, was sitting at her desk in her office on the second floor of City Hall, illuminated by the westering winter sun from the window behind her chair. She did not care for paperwork, preferring to talk directly with her colleagues, the political players of Gethsamane, the officers on her force, suspects in any cases she was working on, and citizens of the town to which she had dedicated her considerable talent. Many years of police experience, mainly through the Chicago Police Department, had taught her that a well-written, carefully preserved record of those interpersonal interactions was invaluable, even to a person like her, who had gifts of intuition far beyond those of her peers.

So every Wednesday, she would review her written notes on all active files, and on the public projects she was pursuing as chief.

The first matter she reviewed was the written evaluation by the Citizens' Police Task Force that she had proposed, populated with well-meaning and intelligent locals, and doggedly pushed to the end of eliminating as much of the institutional racism that sat like a stone on the chest of American, and particularly small-town American, life. It had been just that racism that had blown into tragedy in places like Ferguson, Missouri, and seemingly countless other places. She felt it to be her personal and professional mission to expeditiously institute the programs, policies and procedures in the Gethsemane Police Department that would address any systemic racial issues, and at the same time open clear, comfortable, and regular communications between the police and all demographic components of the once white, but now surprisingly diverse community.

This afternoon, she was reviewing the written recommendations of the CPTF. Their first recommendations:

- Stop immediately Quotas for traffic violations.
- Remove the police from vehicle equipment integrity enforcement, leaving that to the license renewal process.
- Experiment with a program directing random vehicle stops.
- If vehicle stops are appropriate, stop everyone.
- Increase the visibility of cops in schools.
- Expose police to social service training.
- Encourage Black organizations inviting Caucasian

officers to speak, belong.

- Encourage White organizations inviting black officers to speak, belong.

Not a bad first shot, thought Tasha to herself, but only a beginning. She looked at the calendar to fix in her mind the next CPTF meeting, and moved on to the case files on her desk.

Janet Jenkins. The doping nursing home director, who was also a drug thief and drug seller. A pathetic, unympathethic victim, or not? Overdose, or murder? Ya know, I don't really give a damn here, thought Tasha to herself. I'm ready to close this out as an OD. But there is still the coffee cup problem. Unseen hand? Can I waste my time pulling this thread? No, Jenkins file, closed.

Next is the active Harrington file. Tasha felt the familiar homicide discipline click in. This is who she was and where she had thrived in the CPD. She had interviewed Harrington's business partner, Stewart Karlin, at his office in Chicago, after a dizzying blur of exchanged phone messages, voicemail responses, holds, and orbits into cyberspace. When Tasha finally caught up with Karlin, he proved, to Tasha's surprise, not in the slightest evasive, but quietly helpful.

"K & M International is a truly crazy business" he had told her, as he sat down at his desk to talk directly to her. "We have commercial interests all over the world, and in a huge variety of industries. We are not a public company, so are not subject to the kind of accounting rigor that the SEC requires for publicly traded outfits. So it is really hard for any one individual, like Jack or myself, to keep a comprehensive handle on the financial progress of all of the particular divisions. Jack and I both believe in following the numbers, and carefully noting the changes in bottom line results arising from particular new product lines or new approaches to old ones. How we do this is to pick one of our divisions every quarter, carefully review the financials, interview closely the VP in charge of that division, make any adjustments, saving our notes for comparison in the next division review, and move on to the next company segment in the next quarter."

"So what I am hearing you say", said Tasha, "is that the effect of Jack's death on the business itself was negative in that his experience was invaluable to day-to-day operations. What about the effect of his death on the value of the interests of you and the other owners?'

Karlin nodded and began "Jack and I are participants, along with a few of the other principals, in a stock redemption plan. The company is obligated to buy the shares of a deceased owner at a price established by an elaborate formula, based on various financial performance measures. The money to pay the purchase price comes from life insurance policies owned and paid for by the company on the lives of each of us. Nobody in the company either receives or has to pay any cash in reference to his death. So, to answer your question, the effect is that the survivors' proportionate interests in the company are increased. But the appraised value of the company is based on the value with Jack's ongoing contribution, which value now is reduced by the fact that we have to hire and train somebody to do Jack's work. Does that make sense?"

Tasha nodded, even though she wasn't completely sure that she understood.

"Do you have a list of executive compensation that you could share with me?"

"I do." Karlin said, reaching for a binder in his top desk drawer, "I'll make you a copy of this. You will think, when you first look at these that they're pretty high. Well, compared to salaries in similar industries, they are pretty modest, indeed. The difference in this company, as opposed to many others, is that all of the executives are substantial equity owners. Where we all intend to make our money is not in our paycheck, but when some big outfit pays us a lot of money in a corporate buyout. We have ten years as a rough target."

Tasha took a few notes. "Are there any divisions doing very well, or, very badly?", she asked.

"The last internal review showed unusual spikes in sales in the grocery and the sporting goods divisions. As you may know, my business start was with the grocery business, as a stock boy in my family's small store, moving it into a small regional outfit, which grew and grew, until Jack and I combined our efforts with a merger of his retail wine business with my grocery chain. With that background, and with the fact that the grocery division was the subject of Jack and my close review for the last quarter, I can say with a high degree of confidence that the grocery division success has come through remarkably good results of our recent reinvention of our stores. Without boring you with details, we have emphasized cost savings through supply chain management for the grocery part of our stores, while expanding the products available to our customers into a bunch of areas that give us a higher profit margin, and make our customers think of us a one-stop shop. My mom and dad would not recognize what we call a 'grocery store' today."

"I don't know about the reasons for the sudden success of the sporting goods division. It's not my bailiwick, since Viv looks after it. Jack and I were going to tear up the numbers at the next quarterly review."

I don't really want a Business School course here, thought Tasha to herself, but asked "Any planned acquisitions or sales for the company in the near future?"

"Not really. We are digesting our last purchase, the regional trucking company for our refrigerated items. We're always looking for opportunities, but no, nothing is on the agenda."

Tasha had, at that point, closed her notebook and said "I appreciate your time, Mr. Karlin. I just want to tell you that I have the strong sense that the motive for Jack's death is in the operations of the company somewhere. And I firmly intend to keep poking into the facts until I find out what it is."

Back in her office, she reflected on her impression of Karlin. He seemed forthright about the company facts without seeming to want to hide something. He was careful and unemotional in his approach to issues. He made direct eye contact when he spoke. But he just had gone from owning just over a quarter of a very valuable company to owning almost a half.

Chief Cranton turned her attention to her notes about her meeting with Genevieve Mortenson-Pratt that took place a few days after the interview with Karlin. At first, Genevieve had professed to Tasha an "unbelievable backlog" of work which would prevent her from meeting with the Chief any time soon.

Tasha had no interest in playing this game. "I am sure you are busy, Ms. Mortensen-Pratt but I am investigating a murder here, and I think you will find it a large interruption for me to subpoena you to come down here to Gethsemane to talk to me. So let's compromise; you find about two hours to talk to me in the next few days, and I will drive up to your office for our discussion."

So it was that Tasha found herself sitting in the waiting room of an ultra-modern office in the commercial corridor of Oak Brook. "KM International, Inc.- Consumer Recreation Division" read the brass sign over the receptionist's desk. The room was furnished with chrome and leather furniture, with the walls decorated in colorful abstract art.

"Genevieve will see you soon, please have a chair" intoned the receptionist in slow, rounded tones. So, Tasha, who always hated waiting for anything, had no choice but to sit in one of the chrome and leather chairs (which she had to admit were fairly comfortable) and tap her toe for what seemed to her to be a half an hour but which was probably only five minutes.

"Chief Cranton" said Mortensen-Pratt, coming to the doorway from her office to the reception area, "Please follow me."

The two progressed down a carpeted hallway adorned with art similar to the waiting room. At the door of her office, Genevieve Mortensen-Pratt, turned to Tasha, offered her hand, and said "It is a pleasure to meet you, Chief, please come in."

She seated Tasha in the guest chair of her desk, which, Tasha particularly noted, displayed no signs of any work which would explain why it took five minutes to greet a guest with an appointment. In fact there were no papers of any sort visible, but only a large computer screen on the credenza behind the desk.

"How may I help you, Chief?"

"As you know, Ms. Mortensen-Pratt, I am the officer in charge of investigating your brother's murder. I have a few questions for you."

"Make it Viv, if you please Chief, my name is such a mouthful."

"Good. I'm Tasha. For openers, Viv, what all is covered by the 'Consumer Recreation Division?"

"The original company of the division was a three-store traditional sporting goods chain that sold bats and balls, tennis shoes, and basically the stuff that a player uses to play a variety of sports. After we acquired the original units, it became clear to us that, first of all, athletic shoes had become fashion statements, and that a lot of people believed, as a very smart friend of mine had said "Never start a new sport without a new wardrobe." So we moved into apparel, not only sport-specific, but also other fashion clothing, particularly aimed at the people who buy lots of new clothes, that is to say: young people. The business became international, and with the import aspects, we became good at spotting good deals on a whole lot of imported products. Jack started it with the wine business, but we are now a truly international player. We sell not only through our own store fronts, but also sell wholesale to other vendors."

"That all must involve a lot of transactions in foreign currency."

"It surely does. Favorable exchange rates are no small part of the profitability of the business. Because of my education and prior business background, this division does all of the international banking for all of the divisions."

"How does your brother's death affect your role in the division?"

Viv had thought a moment before she answered. "Well not a whole lot on a day-to-day operations basis, because Jack basically left me a lot of freedom to make individual deals, subject only to periodic progress review by Jack and Stewart. The main difference now is that it will be only Stewart to consult with.

"Did you get along with your brother?"

"Of course, there is the sibling history which always has its good and bad memories. But we both knew that this is a business; one that we are in to make money. Personal feelings don't matter."

"How about Stewart Karlin? Do you get along with him?"

"Stew is really good at his area, which does not overlap mine, so I only see him or talk to him at the quarterly divisional reviews."

"I understand that your division is one of the two areas of the firm that is showing a marked increase in profit, and that it is the division for the next quarterly review. So what is going right?"

Viv processed that question for a bit before answering. "Yes, we have had a series of really fortunate deals, where our product has been very well received, and with a very favorable exchange rate. It doesn't happen all of the time, but when it does it looks good on the P&L statement."

Chief Cranton had learned in her long experience of conducting investigations, that in addition to carefully collecting and analyzing physical evidence, and relying on her acute intuition about human motivations, it was often very useful to rattle suspects just a little, about her theory of the case, just to see what they might say or do. As she had with Stewart Karlin, she consciously used this technique on Viv.

"I have to tell you Viv, that it is our current belief that the motive for Jack's murder has to do with some detail of the business operations of KM International. We have our forensic accountants looking through the books. We currently do not have the passwords to the computers in Gethsemane, but we are working on it. In the meantime, I would appreciate your keeping your eye open for any unusual transactions."

"I will. I don't have Jack's passwords, but maybe I can help unlock some of the information. Why don't we schedule a time where we could meet at the house?"

After mutual schedule consultation, it was determined that Viv would meet Tasha at the house at 1PM on the next Thursday.

Back in her office, the Chief closed the file on her desk, and stood with her arms crossed looking out the window at the now darkened landscape. She knew that she had to deal with the problem that was quietly but insistently nagging the edges of her mind. Her eyes came to rest on the CPD citation for exemplary public service as a police officer.

"When it comes down to it" she said to herself, "I am a cop, here to promote public order by seeing that breaches of the law are discovered and punished. I can't turn my back anymore. But I have to tell her."

She oicked up her phone and dialed.

"Hello?"

"Hattie, it's Tasha. I have a couple of things to go over with you. Are you free for lunch tomorrow? Say 12:15 at The Garden Gate?

"Let me check with my appointment secretary. She

says that I'm free, so I will see you there."

"Tomorrow, then" Tasha said, hanging up. In one of those odd bursts of memory, she was suddenly put in mind of the short story that had appeared in her high school English anthology—What was the name of that story?—in any event it was the one where the two disguised women adversaries, one a fleeing murderer, the other a pursuing detective, wound up, not at all by accident, in an all-night café in wintery New York City. The result of the meeting was that the hunted confirmed in her mind the true identity of the pursuer, and being unable to get away, dispatched the pursuer. I will keep that in mind, thought the Chief.

She put away her files, locked her desk, turned out the lights and headed home.

## 29

# The Garden Gate

I was somewhat surprised to get a call from Chief Cranton on the late afternoon, early evening of March 22 inviting me to lunch, mostly because I had gotten the impression that her inquiries involving me had settled into predictable, and from my point of view, safe patterns. I knew that I had not made any mistakes with Dotty, Roy and Janet that would somehow get thrown in my face. At the same time, I had come to know LaTasha Cranton as a person of extraordinary intuitive powers, who could "see" larger contexts of events, and had the tenacity to pursue any line of inquiry to which her intuition led her.

As such, I was on my guard, as I dressed for lunch with careful attention. I picked my hounds tooth suit that I bought in my first year at Marshall Field's, the skirt of which I have personally relined twice. The black and white pattern loves the dead-white blouse I chose, along with a small silver pendant at the buttoned neck. Black gloves, along with the black designer hat that I bought from the French Millinery of Marshall Field's as a starry-eyed twenty something, finished the outfit.

Tasha pulled into the portico of Shady Rest promptly at 12:14. She was driving her City issued, police fitted Ford Crown Victoria. From the outside it looked like any other small-to-mid-size standard American car. But inside, the car was stuffed with high-end cop stuff. It had the police frequency radio, with the hand-held microphone within Tasha's easy reach. There was a holster to the right of the driver's seat that held, to my observation, a Glock semi-automatic. Across the back seat in a discrete rack was a shotgun. The Chief, while appearing to be just an ordinary citizen, could have jumped into any SWAT engagement, maybe with the addition of body armor.

I caned over to the car, and let myself in.

"Hey Tasha, how's the world?" I asked as I got in the car. You could never tell what she was thinking, by any body language or anything else. She said "It's fine. Good to see you, Hattie." I didn't think she meant it, except in a superficial way.

As we drove off downtown, I wanted to set a light mood.

"Do you ever try to call the Space Shuttle with this stuff?" I asked, trying to not sound like a complete smart-alec.

Tasha gave me one of those side-long looks under half closed eyelids, that expressed skepticism, control, and intelligence, all at the same time.

"Hattie, I have no idea where you come up with the stuff you say. "

We chattered about weather and local politics until we eased into a parallel parking spot about a half of a block away from The Garden Gate". A Midwesterner's desired parking spot. But not perfect. The perfect spot would be right in front, fifteen feet away from the destination. I have always been amused about Gethsemane parking preferences, compared to the expensive cut-throat regime of downtown Chicago parking.

In any event, we were now on Main Street Gethsemane within spitting distance of Garden Gate, my favorite, by far, of the restaurants of Gethsemane, which were mostly of the meat and potatoes diner kinds of places where the menus haven't changed in thirty years.

I really don't know whether the proprietors intentionally used the name "Garden" in allusion to the name of the town, Gethsemane, but I did get a flash of premonition of the possible agony lying behind the Gate of the Garden of Gethsemane.

The Garden Gate is run by a couple of domesticated hippees from Champaign who are really good at cooking with fresh local ingredients, in no-nonsense entrees. The décor of the place features earth tones, antique furniture and local art. The overall effect is that of unpretentious comfort.

The waitress seated us at a corner table in the largest dining room. It struck me that, even though she has been here just a short time, it seems that everybody knows

Tasha, and has a word for her. Tasha, while not the back-slapping type, makes a point of giving everybody a cordial response.

We were given menus, and ordered drinks, coffee for Tasha, tea for me, as I did not think I wanted to take the edge off my wits with a glass of wine. I ordered the usual for me, which is the salad with seasonal greens and the vinaigrette de jour. Tasha ordered the tuna salad with fresh-baked sourdough bread.

In an attempt to break up what seemed to me to be an ominous overtone hanging over the table, I ventured "Well, here we are, just two girls from the south side, having a quiet lunch."

Tasha was obviously in a foul mood, because she scowled at me and said "Ya know, Hattie, don't play that "we're just alike because we started out poor" game with me. What that all ignores is that while both of our ancestors came to the US poor, yours came because they wanted to, while mine came, chained together in the hold of the ship of some damn slaver. Then, when they got here, even after the horrors of slavery were over, they were looked down on, not given an even shake on anything and called foul names. And nothing that has happened since, however well-intentioned, has really changed anything. Not the Emancipation Proclamation; not Separate but Equal, not Affirmative Action, not litigation under any of the Federal Civil Rights statutes; not anything. Racism is still here. And it won't stop until white, all white people, acknowledge the past, and the prejudice that thrives within society, and extinguish racism, person by person, day by day, situation by situation. Only then can we call ourselves "The Land of The Free. To make that happen is my job and my mission in life."

"I really stepped on a hot button there, didn't I, Tasha?" but I thought to myself "She's of course right; aside from thinking good thought, I really haven't done a thing to create a racism-free society' and continued "I can't argue with the truth here."

Just then the waitress brought our food, and I couldn't wait to divert the conversation. "Okay, Tasha, what's on your mind?"

She nodded. "I do have a couple of things that I want to talk to you about" she said as she sipped her coffee.

"First, despite having spent a lot of time on the Mortensen case, I am no closer to a solution than I was at the beginning. I have spoken to all of the people of interest to the case, but I don't have any sort of hunch about any of them. That is, frankly, unusual for me at this stage of a case, and it is starting to bug me."

"So who have you talked to?"

"For openers, Jack's daughter, Britany. She is pretty much a self-absorbed college kid who cares about her clothes and her friends to the exclusion of most everything else. She inherits the money that the company will pay Jack's estate to redeem his stock, but it is in trust until she is something like 30, so instead of getting her allowance from Jack, it will come from a bank trust officer. I can't see her having the will or the wit to hire someone to bump her dad off." The waitress refilled Tasha's cup.

"Jack's ex, Caroline Singleton, is so obviously outraged by someone having derailed her alimony gravy train that was, in her mind, a much better situation than being married to Jack, that it is more or less impossible to believe that she would write Jack a cross email, let alone kill him."

"The housekeeper and the chef have more or less unshakeable alibis for both the time of the administration of the knock-out juice, and of the time of the gun shot. Neither is either positively or negatively affected by the death, either financially or any other way, so they don't seem to be very strong suspects"

As I worked on my salad, I changed the subject slightly. "Tasha, you've thought about this. What do you think is the big picture here?"

She finished the bite she was working on. "That's just it. I do not have any sort of feeling from the fact pattern and from the people involved to point me in the right direction. The only vague sense I get is that it has something to do with some operational part of the business."

"I agree with the feeling. It seems to me, without being an accountant and looking at the books, that there is a whole lot of cash running through the company. And when that is the case, someone can get sticky fingers, or hide shady income streams in among the legit ones, or use the cash flow to finance some off-the-sheet scam. Have you gotten into the computers at the house yet?"

"No. We haven't come up with the passwords yet.

But we have a team working on it.

"Judging by the dramatic method of the hit, it has to be something big. Doesn't K&M own a bunch of drugstores? Could they be pushing dope?

"We did think of that. So far, all of our checks of quantities purchased match closely with the quantity of legitimate sales, and inventory. There are no reports of irregularities associated with either their stand-alone pharmacies or their drug stores inside the grocery outlets. But we are still looking."

"Then, I'm guessing that you spent a lot of time interviewing the insiders: Karlin and the sister, what's her name, Genevieve?"

"You're right, and she goes by Viv."

Tasha recounted with particularity the conversations she had with the two K & M International principals. I was impressed by the clarity of her memory and the subtlety of the nuances see derived from her observations of the subjects.

"Apart from any evidence: what did you think of the two of them as people?"

Tasha pondered the question for a minute or so before she answered. "Well, for both being successful contributors to the same company, they are completely different personality types. Karlin is unpretentious and unguarded as to his opinions and beliefs. He doesn't come across as a Type A, but has at his core an unshakeable will to do the business the right way. He liked Jack as a strategic innovator to a degree that he himself was not, but disliked

Jack's hubris."

"Trying to read Viv is like trying to x-ray someone inside a concrete bunker who is wearing a lead suit. Her physical gestures and her words are carefully controlled. It is as if she is the first model of a very intelligent AI project."

"So what I am hearing from you" I said as I folded my napkin and placed it beside my plate, "is that neither of these two are wearing stick-on name badges that say "Hi, my name is ; I doped a man, and then hired a killer to blow his head off."

"Right. But I did do what I have learned in my homicide career was a useful trick when dealing with difficult suspects: I told them both that I thought that the motive for the killing was to be found in the business records of the company, and that we were expending every effort to access those records."

"Stop. Tasha, you told them both that?" I blurted, thinking that more than a few of the closings that Milly and I had administered arose from a situation where a person was about to learn an uncomfortable fact, and had blabbed about it.

"So, what did they say?"

"Well, Stewart Karlin just engaged to help in whatever way he could. But Viv went the extra mile, and suggested that we meet at the house tomorrow and try her passwords on the company computers there.

"Tasha, do I have to remind you that the perp that you are looking for has already callously arranged for the brutal murder of Jack, and would probably go to great, and I mean great, lengths to avoid discovery?"

"I have never in my career been afraid. And I'm not afraid now."

Fine, but failure to fear that which you do not fully understand is folly. I can't say that to Tasha, but I can't sit on it either.

"Tasha, would you like me to go to the house with you? I have not actually met Viv, and maybe a second pair of eyes might be of some advantage."

She looked at me for what seemed a long time.

"Okay, Hattie. I can see that your particular point of view might help us here. I am to meet Viv at the house at 11AM, so I will pick you up at 10:30.

"One more thing, Hattie" Tasha said with a tone that had me sit forward in my chair.

"I told you I told both Viv and Karlin, as suspects, that I was looking into areas that could implicate them. That is a part of the ethos of my life. Because of that same ethos, I have to tell you that not only do I strongly suspect you of being involved in the Shady Rest homicides, but I know in my heart of hearts, what you and your partner Milly were up to, in Chicago, in my District, while I was sworn "To Serve and Protect". I am now and always a cop. So, I will pull the threads on both the Chicago and the Gethsemane sides of the story. If those threads lead to you, so be it."

Great. Again, Tasha has not fully appreciated the effect of her brash declarations.

"You said you were not afraid of Karlin and Viv, even after you told them you were coming for them. Tasha, I'm not afraid of you."

"Duly noted. Ten thirty tomorrow?"

"Fine. Can you drop me off at the Bank? I need to make a deposit. I will grab a cab back to SR."

As she left me off in front of the bank and I watched her drive away, I pondered the question that hung in the air "Do I have one more in me?"

I knew the answer as I entered the bank: "Yes, I do. I certainly do."

## 30

# Shooter down

I got up early that Thursday morning so that I would have enough time to properly prepare for my excursion to the Mansion with Tasha. I noted, with a laugh, that among the medications for the day was, as was inevitable, a Purple Pill. I didn't really need to be told by the Fates or anybody else that something significant was about to happen.

I wanted to avoid the breakfast scene in the dining room, so I stayed in and made myself two pieces of toast to go with the short glass of cranberry juice.

The weather had turned from the grey, miserable winter into that pre-Spring condition where the hints in the air of warmth reduced the need for a winter coat to the option of a light jacket or extra sweater. Since I did not want the complication of an extra outer garment, when I laid out my clothes on Wednesday night, I selected the heavy tweed brown hunting suit with full jacket, and three quarter length skirt. The jacket was belted with deep coat pockets, and loops for shotgun shells. I always thought that the suit gave me that squarish, solid English countrywoman look sported by Margaret Rutherford when she was so badly miscast as Miss Marple. I added a paisley pocket square, an off-white, high necked blouse, a pair of brown lace-up ankle boots, and, of course, my most supple brown gloves. I selected for my hat the asymmetrical small brown fedora with the purple feather. I ordinarily do not like feathers on hats, but somehow it was the right touch for today. I checked my appearance in the mirror and checked my equipment before taking the elevator down to the lobby.

Tasha wheeled her patrol car into the canopy just outside the front door promptly at 10:30. I let myself and my cane into the passenger seat.

"Morning, Hattie."

"Good morning, Tasha. Got a warrant with my name on it?" I noted that she was wearing the uniform today, with black uniform jacket, badge prominently displayed, black skirt and tan blouse.

"Not funny, Hattie. Don't press your luck." I let it drop.

As we left town on the country road that led, via a thirty minute ride, to Jack Harrington's chateau, I asked her "Tasha, just what do you hope to get out of this meeting with Viv?"

"First, I do want to see if she has any passwords or back doors into the computer system that we can use to find out what is happening in the Company that might prompt someone to off Jack." She looked over briefly at me. "I also want to provoke her a little, make her think that I have more information than I really do, to see if she makes some kind of mistake. I have been using the same ploy with Karlin. So far no success on either count."

"And you tell me not to press my luck. May I remind you that you may be provoking a very deadly person?"

"I hear ya, Hattie" was all that she said.

We had travelled about twenty minutes from town when we encountered the portion of road, where, in departure from its Midwestern-straight-as-a-string character, it curved to the right, crossed a small watercourse, then climbed the hill back to the left through a stand of trees. Just before the trees, there was a white sedan, pulled part way off the pavement onto the shoulder, with its hood up. The driver, a tallish woman, was waving her arms to flag us down.

Tasha pulled into a field entrance about fifty feet back of the white car nose pointed toward the gate in the fence.

"Tasha, I don't like this" I said as emphatically as I could. She waved at me dismissively, opened the door, unbuckled the seat belt and started to get out.

"Wait" I said, even louder this time, but Tasha had closed the door and started for the other car. I thought that it was completely ridiculous that Tasha was driving this vehicle with more armament than a light tank, and here she was in an iffy situation without so much as a pocket knife. I had no choice but to get out of the car as quickly as I could, cross behind our car and follow her down the road. I am actually pretty fast with my cane, when I choose to be, but I was about two car lengths behind her when she stopped at the left front quarter panel to talk to the driver, who was leaning over the engine compartment, from the front bumper, about even with the driver's seat.

"…….. and all of a sudden the engine just conked out" she was saying as I drew even with them. They both looked in my direction as I passed them and stood directly behind the driver, about fifteen feet down the road.

I now had a bit of time to assess the situation. The driver, even though she was leaning over the car, appeared to be taller than either Tasha or I. She was in her forties, I thought, and had the athletic build of a long distance runner. She was wearing a black turtleneck, black slacks and black flats. She was wearing aviator glasses and a leather shoulder bag slung diagonally across her chest, with the bag itself on her left side. Her mid-length dark hair was pulled into a short pony tail.

"Let me try the engine" Tasha said "Are the keys in it?" They were but I pretty much knew how that would turn out.

Our friend here had done a pretty good job staging this set-up. But there were three things very wrong with the picture. First, the car, which from its general dinged-up, used-Kleenex look, and Hertz sticker, was obviously a rental, while supposed disabled, showed no symptoms: no smoke, no fluids on the ground, no strange odors. I could almost picture the alternator wire in that shoulder bag.

Second, that wisp of hair that the driver had pulled out was too obviously contrived to make us see a stressed and bedraggled stranded motorist.

Finally, the shoulder bag. You don't drive with the bag across your chest. Why would you, after you have car trouble, put it on that way to look at the engine? Unless the bag has something in it you want at hand.

Tasha had tried unsuccessfully to turn the engine over. She got out and said to the driver "Well, I will go radio in for roadside assistance" as she closed the door and started back down to the patrol car.

The driver quickly turned her aviator glasses on me. I was standing in the same place, leaning on the cane in my left hand, with my right hand in the pocket of my coat.

I knew what the driver's problem was: she was working on Milly's rule about dealing with two adversaries that held that one should eliminate the most dangerous one first, that usually being the one with a gun. The problem with the rule is that you have to correctly assess which one that is.

The driver made her call, stepped to her right so that she had a clear view of Tasha, and pulled from her shoulder bag a nasty little piece of work, a Beretta, I think, with silencer, and started to bring it up to aim at Tasha.

Meanwhile, however I had dropped my cane, assumed a shooter's crouch with left foot forward, pulled the Glock out of my coat pocket, aimed, taking care to make that subtle adjustment in sighting necessary where a target is turned at an angle from you, just as Milly and I had practiced often on the firing range, and fired.

Ms. Would-Be-Killer spun to the pavement, her gun skittering beside her.

Tasha started and ran back towards me, looking down at the body as she passed.

"Hattie, what in the Sam Hill are you doing with a gun?

I pointed the Glock at the sky and said "Life Insurance, Tasha. You should get some." I went over, kicked the Beretta and continued "She was going to kill you, Tasha, and then me."

Tasha was uncharacteristically at a loss for words, blinked a couple of times, and finally said. "Stay here, Hattie, I will radio for the troops".

I felt a variety of sensations, all at once. The adrenalin rush of the moment passed, along with great relief of the anxiety of making good on that one chance to make the shot. At the same time, my chest seemed to suddenly compress so that I had a very hard time breathing. As I struggled to draw breath, I had a sharp pain in my chest that radiated to my right arm. The daylight faded to black as I dropped to the road.

## 31

# But not out

I opened my eyes in an unfamiliar place, at a time to which I had no external reference. I was lying in a bed, the head of which was slightly elevated. The room was basically dark but was illuminated by a series of small fluorescent lights that, on closer examination, proved to be digital read-outs which were accompanied by soft regular noises: beeps, clicks and sounds like respiration. I was covered by a blanket, but the room was noticeably cold.

It dawned on me that I was in a hospital room, as a result of the event out on the county road with Tasha. Whatever it was, I made it.

I was thirsty, and looked around the room to see if there was anyone there from whom I could ask for a drink of water. It was then that I noticed the familiar profile, much in my thoughts, framed by perfectly cut black hair, illuminated by the light of her cell phone screen.

Her designer earrings reflected the lights on the medical displays.

I closed my eyes, moistened my lips, and tried out my voice "It is really a sad note when you have to have a heart attack to get your daughter to visit you."

The cell phone screen light went out.

"Not only a heart attack, but homicide! Geez, Mom."

"You should see what I had planned if that hadn't worked."

"So, how do you feel?"

"Let's see. I'm cold, I'm thirsty, I'm hungry. I have tubes stuck up my nose and other places. I seem to be hooked up to a bunch of machines. But I really feel okay. And, Ines, I am grateful to you for coming. I do know how busy you are."

"It's okay , really. I should have come to see you long before now. I get in my own world too much sometimes. The boys are here too; we're taking turns sitting with you."

"You're all good kids. I have come to realize after hanging around with a bunch of old people that all of us tend to blame our problems on the fact that we don't see our kids enough, where really the problem is that we don't do enough to keep in touch with who we still are; and what our Stories are."

"Speaking of which, do you want to tell me about the gun? I get the idea that you have been trying to do that for a long time."

"Only for just over twenty years. But you know what,

Ines? I don't feel that burning desire anymore. Maybe I will tell you the Story sometime, but the value to me is not in my telling you, but in me recognizing its value and meaning for myself."

"Sounds fair. But I will listen to whatever you have to tell me, whenever you want to tell me. And I will make a point of seeing you more often."

"Thanks, that means a lot to me."

Just then the door to the hall, which was on the opposite side of the bed to Ines' chair was pushed open, admitting Tasha Cranton.

"Hattie, nice to see you back among us" she said stepping over by Ines.

"Ines, do you know Chief Cranton?"

Ines stood and shook Tasha's hand. "I do. She was the one who called and briefed me on your adventure. Nice to see you, Tasha."

"I'm sorry to interrupt you two, but I did want to poke my head in and say hello. I'll sneak right back out."

"No, stay" insisted Ines, "I have to make a couple of calls. I'll sneak out for a bit." She was dialing as she went out the door.

Tasha sat down in the visitor's chair.

"So how are you?"

"I think I'm okay. I don't particularly hurt, I seem to be thinking clearly. I haven't tried to move around, but it all seems to work."

"I'm glad. I've got something for you" she said reaching into her bag and pulling out a flat box, slightly bigger than an index card, and passing it to me. I took the lid off the box. It contained a gold badge, bearing the number 579 and the legend "Gethsemane Police Department. To serve and protect". I teared up, not able to say anything.

"It is the best way I could think of to say thank you. You are now officially a Detective Sergeant on the force, with emeritus status. You don't get paid, but you do get a badge."

"Wouldn't Milly be surprised" I thought to myself "But, as I think about it, I'm pretty sure that she would have done the same thing."

Tasha continued. "I have made a point throughout my personal and professional life to be pointedly not dependent on anyone else. This has been important to me as a woman, as an African-American, as a single mother, and as a cop fighting through a rigid hierarchy. But when I needed someone to literally have my back, even though I didn't know it, you were there. So, thank you, Hattie, plain and simple."

"You are most welcome, Tasha. I'm glad it worked out."

"Let me bring you up on the rest of it. We have no idea of the identity of my assailant. Her prints are not in any of the data bases. The ID's she was carrying, which she used to rent the car, were fake. The phone she had was a burner phone, with no call history or favorite numbers. An invisible woman. Her gun was not registered."

"Not surprising."

"That does remind me, Hattie, your Glock was not

registered either."

"Imagine that."

"I can very well imagine that. Look, Hattie, I'll tell you what. I will run the ballistics on your gun and compare the results with open cases for about fifteen years. If it's clear, I'll give it back to you. But I am begging you not to be shooting it anymore."

"Agreed. Thanks, Tasha. How about the Mortensen case?"

"I found the ear."

"What? How?"

"Well, call me overly sensitive, but it really ticked me off to have someone try to kill me on my way to a meeting with Viv called at Viv's suggestion. So I got search warrants for both her office and her home, both of which we pretty much took apart until we found it, encased in Lucite, in a vault behind a framed picture on the wall of her home office."

"Meanwhile, we finally persuaded Stewart Karlin to come down to Gethsemane to the computer room. I offered to arrest him as a material witness and conduct the interview at the Serious Crimes Division office in downtown Chicago. He graciously consented to the alternative. It turns out that he and Jack shared a password to the detailed accounting system that they used for their quarterly audits. We sat him down and had him look for unusual activity, knowing that the grocery and sporting goods area had shown recent revenue spikes. After about two hours, he spotted an unusually large shipment of running shoes, soccer balls, and team uniforms from a port in Africa to a warehouse the company rents in Mexico. He sent over one of his local guys who found, not only the scheduled item but 5,000 Kalashnikov AK-47's, with ammunition."

"So, K and M International was running guns?"

"At least Viv was, maybe on her own account. We turned her over to the ATF folks and the FBI. They think she was selling to drug cartels. She is lawyered up, isn't saying much, but is not going to be out and about for a good long time. Because, we don't have a line on the shooter, we probably can't nail her for murder."

So, what's the theory of why she pulled all this?"

"The general idea is that she has, for her whole life, been sick of coming out on the short end of comparisons to her brother, even if she is smarter." I thought of Milly's feelings for her brother, Vasyl. Tasha continued "We think she did it basically because she could, and could outsmart him. But he caught her at it, and threatened exposure if it didn't stop. So she had him killed. There is absolutely no evidence of any of that, and we will keep looking, but we view the case as basically closed."

At that point, Ines steamed back into the room. "Since you're okay, Mom, I booked a flight out of O'Hare in about four hours, so I've got to run. I mean what I say about getting together more often. How about it if you come down and see me early in May, if you feel up to it?"

"Let's plan on that. I do appreciate your being here."

"Be well, Mom" she said, kissing me on the cheek,

before making her usual speedy exit. Tasha and I watched her go.

I looked at Tasha. "Maybe you'd like to hear my Story someday."

"Maybe I would."

The nurse came in with medications, procedures and advice.

Tasha got up to leave.

"Thanks again, Sergeant. Keep yourself well. I'll see you soon.

"I'm ready for the next case, Chief. You know where to find me."

## 32

# The Story Continues

I was discharged from the hospital on the day after Ines left into a skilled nursing facility that provided 24 hour supervision until they could send me back to Shady Rest. It was fine, with caring nurse professionals, pretty good food and people who just plain spoiled the socks off you. It was, however, boring as all get out. I was grateful when the medical people, after checking their charts, tests and periodic face-to-face interviews, determined that I was healthy enough to go back to my independent living status, with some adjustments to my medications (I can't wait to see the color palate and size array of my new meds box) and diet.

I did understand that I did, in fact, have a heart attack, probably stress-induced (me, stress? This is my life), but one which, while reacting to a vessel clog, had not closed up completely, but in my naïve kind of understanding, just burped the clot down the road. I'm grateful to be alive, basically because I feel that I have more to add, to record, to amplify into the Story, which I know now is not just about my life.

And so I came back to Shady Rest with a slightly altered point of view. When I moved in, I was frankly on the run. Milly was dead; Sid had been gunned down. I had no idea as to who, what or where would be the circumstances of my violent end. I had chucked me, and my history and abilities into the bottom drawer of importance, and was very reluctant to look at any of it.

But my recent encounters at Shady Rest, and my at the same time collegial and adversarial confrontations and experiences with LaTasha Cranton have helped me touch back to the Hattie who, with Milly, rocked our lives, and laughed at Fate.

When I was finally cabbed back to SR, and pushed my walker to the elevator and then up to my apartment on the third floor. As I keyed my way into my apartment, in the slightly dusty stillness of a place unused for a short, but significant time, I knew where I needed to go. I raced, as fast as my limitations allowed me, to my closets, and threw open the doors to my wardrobe, which was a witness to my clothing life as a helper to Zofie, as an entry-level floor clerk at Marshall Field's, and finally as an almost-stand-just-on-the-edge Personal Shopping Assistant. I touched the individual garments, felt the fabrics and thought back to the beginnings: either their purchase, or their creation on my sewing room table. I'm not just back home, I have returned to the Center.

The next morning, I loaded up my walker, and took the elevator down to the dining room for breakfast, for the first time in what seemed to be weeks, if not years.

I pushed into the dining room and immediately spotted the place I needed to be. I rolled over to the table at which were seated Bella, Betty, with Florence and Harrison Demory .

"Good morning, everyone" I murmured, hoping not to call attention to myself.

Forget that. After the widely publicized (I had not actually read the report of my exploits out in the country) I was regarded, not just as another resident, but as some kind of alien media super-star.

The conversation at the table had stopped, dead, as I sat down, and ordered an egg-white omelet and un-buttered toast.

As you might expect, Bella became the spokesperson for the table, if not the room.

"Hattie, it's so great to see you back, You look great; How are you feeling?"

"I feel wonderful, actually. It is really nice to see you all."

Knowing what was coming, I slowly cut my omelet into small bites, and just waited for how the Question would be posed.

Of course it came from Bella.

"I remember, my boyfriend, Darren Wilberung. This was when were about freshmen or sophomores in college, down at the U. Darren was from downstate, somewhere, such that he had, to my mid-state ear, a charming, southern twang. He was a totally "outdoors" kind of guy who always sought his fun on the trail, in the woods, on the lake. 'Paul Bunyan lives' I always thought. He was a forestry major, at the time that I was studying Elizabethan Poetry. If opposites attract, we connected like yin and yang. We went to movies, we went to dinner, we met on campus between classes. This was serious stuff. The M word was not uncommon in our conversations.

Darren was a serious, and I mean serious, duck hunter. As such, it was more or less inevitable that I, as the love of his life, as repository of his hopes for the future, should be educated in, and exposed to, the niceties of duck hunting. Since I was totally in love with Darren, I was willing to learn about winter shooting garb, to get to know and direct the dogs, and to appreciate the lore of the shotgun. I went to a full course of gun safety classes, learned about the different gauges of shot guns, and acquired a really fetching wardrobe of shooting attire. The matter came to a high point on the Christmas when Darren bought me a custom made sixteen gauge shotgun, with a beautifully carved walnut stock. I felt like I had been given something from the vault holding the royal jewels.

Wedding bells, hearts, flower and happily-ever-after were tripping along in the background.

Until, of course, we went on the first hunting trip. I loved the excitement, wearing my new clothes , the briskness of the weather, and the camaraderie of the group.

The only problem arose whenever I tried to fire that

beautiful shotgun. By the end of the day, I had fired at, and hit, the tailgate of Darren's truck, four of his decoys, one of his dogs and the toe of his hip waders, while he was wearing them. I just couldn't aim and fire the gun with a rational state of mind."

She paused, and waited for the prompt to continue, which did not ensue, and said "That was more or less the end of it. I didn't want to wind up shooting Darren, and he didn't want to lose any more dogs."

To that point, I had been focused on my plate, cutting my eggwhite omelet into minute pieces, looking for a chance to speak to the question hanging over the room.

I put my fork down beside my plate, looked Bella in the eye, and said "Another wonderful story, Bella, I love it when you share your Story, whether embellished or not. This time your story is a question, a question to me. Here's the answer: Someone tried to kill LaTasha Cranton with a gun, but I killed her first."

Bella blinked a couple of times, opened her mouth to speak, but closed it again, speechless for perhaps the first time in her life.

I picked up my fork and finished my egg. To break the silence which was beginning to get oppressive, I asked "So what's new around here? What did I miss?" I was hoping to divert everyone's attention from me back to our ordinary lives.

"Well" started Florence Demory, " the new director starts in this week. We haven't met her yet, but we're looking forward to doing so."

"Maybe we should offer to repaint her office" I suggested, bringing smiles to Betty and Bella's faces. The ice was beginning to break up. More general gossip ensued until all of the tableware was cleared and we went to our separate to do lists.

The big item for me was to go through the mail that I had missed while in the hospital. Darlene, bless her heart, had emptied my mail box each day and put the contents in a large carton stored in Janet's office. The box just fit on the seat of my walker to allow me to roll it all up to the third floor.

I spread the collection out on my kitchen table, put on some water for tea, and began by discarding the obvious stuff: the advertising circulars, charitable solicitations, while keeping anything that looked like a real card, a real bill, or a magazine that I would actually read.

I was about half way through the bulk of the mail, when it jumped out at me. It was an 8 and a half by 11 by 2 USPO box, that had struggled to maintain its original shape, and bore so many stamps re-routing its progress that it looked like the bumper of an RV the goal of whose owner it was to visit every national park and was about half-way there. It took me a little while to decode the notations. The return address was of the law office in the Loop that handled Milly's estate. The original delivery address was my house in Downers Grove and the date of the original dispatch was in January of 2016. From there it was forwarded to the dummy address in the Florida retirement community I had given to the PO in Downers

Grove to throw off any bloodhounds sniffing in my direction. I remembered both that my lawyer had firmly urged me to keep her and her firm apprised of any address change, and that I had completely fluffed that off.

As such, this box, went to Florida from Downers Grove, no doubt bouncing around the nursing homes, retirement villages and apartments in an attempt to find a Rosales whose name was Hattie. When that futile search died out, the box was Returned to Sender, that being the Chicago law firm. Judging from the correctly addressed label, no doubt some associate did an in depth search that found me.

I cut the tape on the seams to reveal, packed in tissue paper, a smaller box about the size of a package of checks. It was marked with my name in that peculiar spiky handwriting that I had not seen in decades; unmistakably Milly's.

Inside was a single safety deposit box key, stamped "HBT" and "754". There was no written explanation, but I didn't need one; I had one almost identical to it. I looked at the clock; it was 10:30. I could easily make it downtown before the Bank closed. I called the limo company, bribed them with a sweet offer, changed into my green 20's movie siren get up complete with green hat and gloves. As almost a reflex action, I pinned to my lapel the green-eyed scarab that I had put away after wearing it to Tasha's office. The limo arrived and was on the Tollway on the way to Chicago in no time. Never had that short trip seemed that long.

When the driver finally deposited me at the Washington St. entrance of GMO Harris Bank, I reminded him that I needed him to wait for me to finish. "This will not take long." I was sure that he was okay with that, since he was scoring a great fare. I wheeled into the lobby and took the elevator down to the safety deposit box area. On the way down, it struck me that the last time I was here was the beginning of my reconnection with myself and my Story, a journey that seemed to have carried me figuratively for decades and for thousands of miles.

I presented the key to the entry clerk, a young woman different than the person who helped me before, but with the same air of an entry level trainee as had the first. She looked up the box records, asked me my name and said "Yes Ms. Rosales, you have entry authority for the box. Just sign here and I will get the attendant to help you." She pressed a button on the desk. The attendant proved to be the same fellow as had helped me before.

"I remember you" he said, smiling "You have one of those hernia boxes."

"I am using a different one this time. I'm guessing that it is not as heavy."

He took my key, and scanned the numbers for 754. It proved to be a different size from my usual box, being wider, but shorter and less deep. My young friend manipulated the locks and slid out the box. "You're right. A whole lot lighter." He took the box to an examination room and shut the door on his way out.

I locked the door and gathered my thoughts before

swinging open the lid. The first item to see was Aetna, Milly's luger. Since Milly had told me that she had made provision for the objects that were meaningful, I would have been very surprised not to come across it. Next was a small velvet jewelry bag that held the red-eyed scarab. "Together again, at last" I thought as I clutched it in my hand.

The rest of the box was filled with papers. On top was a business-sized envelope addressed "Hattie" in Milly's unmistakable handwriting. The envelope flap was not sealed but contained several sheets of Milly's personal stationery. I flattened the sheets out and read:

September 18, 1995

Dear Hattie:

I first have to apologize for the circumstances of the ruse I constructed around my death. I am confident that by now you have figured out that what I wanted to be regarded as an accidental incident was, on the contrary, carefully planned. I have to admit that after all of our years of performing closings, it was strange to be both the planner and the subject. By the time you read this, you will have noted that I had about a million reasons for this bit of subterfuge.

If you think about it, you will see that I could not involve you in the planning in order to avoid any legal unpleasantries for you with the insurance company. I have timed the mailing of the key for twenty years from my death, thinking that any statute of limitations would surely have passed. I certainly wasn't going to ask a lawyer for an opinion on the subject!

I do also want to give you my reasons for choosing the particular means of exit, as opposed to just gutting it out for the three or four months it is going to take. The pain has just gotten so bad, that I cannot keep in touch with my thoughts, feelings and sensibilities. I feel like I am evaporating into a morass of non-entity. It is far better, to my way of thinking, breathe one's last as a result of one's own will.

The manuscript in the bottom of the box is my book: 'Think About It This Way; My Philosophy of Daily Life'. I have done my best to record the application of my reading of Philosophers' works into the elements of my daily existence. Read it, please. If you wish to publish it, I have transferred the copyright to you by document left at my lawyer's office. It is my Story, and, to a large measure, yours too. It is a compelling Story that continues whether I, or you, for that matter, are dead.

For I believe that the true Story of a person's life, and by that I mean the composite of those thoughts, acts, deeds, friendships, beliefs and all other human experience that constitute Meaning, does not start with "Once upon a time" or end with

"She died of cancer" or "She lived happily ever after". No, we all pop, wet, into the middle of an ongoing Story, do what we can to add to it, and leave it still being told and retold, written and re-written. It never ends.

As I close, I want you to pay attention to the tense of the verbs in this paragraph. I love you, Hattie; I thank you for being part of my Story, and thank you for the chance to be part of yours. Together we live on.

With love,
Milly.

If I had encountered this set of expressions, even as recently as the first time I came back to the bank, I would have been debilitated by grief and tears. But now, after my recent escapades, I recognize Milly's views to ring strongly with truth, and in that truth, comfort.

I packed the manuscript, Milly's letter, the scarab and Aetna into the valise I had brought with and rang for the attendant.

"Done?" he asked. I was tempted to answer "No, only beginning" but instead just nodded as he carted the box back to its spot and gave me my key.

At the desk, I asked if I could close the box. "Let me see" she said as she brought up the account. "Sure, there are about four more years pre-paid. We will refund it to you, if you leave your address." "Fine" I said as I wrote my address and turned over the key. "I can't tell you how much I appreciate your help."

The driver was waiting for me outside, and we headed west.

I did not have a lot to say, except to myself: "Think about it this way, You are in the best place you've been in years. You have a Story to read, and, who knows, a few more chapters to write."

CPSIA information can be obtained
at www.ICGtesting.com
Printed in the USA
LVHW080723220719
624774LV00012BA/569/P